Thomas Sturak on
THEY SHOOT HORSES, DON'T THEY?
"Thirty years ago intelligent reviewers on both sides
of the Atlantic hailed THEY SHOOT HORSES,
DON'T THEY? as a 'minor masterpiece' and
'a work of art.' . . . In the years since and
throughout the world, this book has come to be
appreciated as a universally applicable parable of
modern man's existential predicament. . . .

THEY SHOOT HORSES, DON'T THEY? is
bitter, disquieting, and once read not easily
forgotten."

ABC PICTURES CORP. PRESENTS
A PALOMAR PICTURE
A CHARTWINK PRODUCTION

STARRING
JANE FONDA   MICHAEL SARRAZIN   SUSANNAH YORK

THEY SHOOT HORSES, DON'T THEY?

CO-STARRING
GIG YOUNG   BONNIE BEDELIA AND RED BUTTONS

SCREENPLAY BY ROBERT E. THOMPSON   BASED ON THE NOVEL BY HORACE McCOY
ASSOCIATE PRODUCER – MUSIC JOHN GREEN   EXECUTIVE PRODUCER THEODORE B. SILLS
PRODUCED BY IRWIN WINKLER AND ROBERT CHARTOFF   DIRECTED BY SYDNEY POLLACK
PANAVISION   COLOR BY DELUXE   DISTRIBUTED BY CINERAMA RELEASING CORPORATION
A SUBSIDIARY OF THE AMERICAN BROADCASTING COMPANIES, INC.

HORACE McCOY

THEY SHOOT HORSES, DON'T THEY?

A NOVEL

Screenplay by Robert E. Thompson
Foreword to Screenplay by Sydney Pollack

AVON
PUBLISHERS OF
DISCUS • CAMELOT • BARD

AVON BOOKS
A division of
The Hearst Corporation
959 Eighth Avenue
New York, New York 10019

First Avon Printing, February, 1966
Second Printing, December, 1969

Printed in the U.S.A.

TO

MICHAEL FESSIER

AND

HARRY CLAY WITHERS

THEY SHOOT HORSES, DON'T THEY?

THE

PRISONER

WILL

STAND.

1

I STOOD UP. *For a moment I saw Gloria again, sitting on that bench on the pier. The bullet had just struck her in the side of the head; the blood had not even started to flow. The flash from the pistol still lighted her face. Everything was plain as day. She was completely relaxed, was completely comfortable. The impact of the bullet had turned her head a little away from me; I did not have a perfect profile view but I could see enough of her face and her lips to know she was smiling. The Prosecuting Attorney was wrong when he told the jury she died in agony, friendless, alone except for her brutal murderer, out there in that black night on the edge of the Pacific. He was wrong as a man can be. She did not die in agony. She was relaxed and comfortable and she was smiling. It was the first time I had ever seen her smile. How could she have been in agony then? And she wasn't friendless.*

I was her very best friend. I was her only friend. So how could she have been friendless?

IS THERE

ANY LEGAL CAUSE

WHY

SENTENCE

SHOULD NOT NOW

BE PRONOUNCED?

2

WHAT could I say? . . . All those people knew I had killed her; the only other person who could have helped me at all was dead too. So I just stood there, looking at the judge and shaking my head. I didn't have a leg to stand on.

"Ask the mercy of the court," said Epstein, the lawyer they had assigned to defend me.

"What was that?" the judge said.

"Your Honor," Epstein said, "—we throw ourselves on the mercy of the court. This boy admits killing the girl, but he was only doing her a personal favor——"

The judge banged on the desk, looking at me.

THERE BEING
NO LEGAL CAUSE
WHY SENTENCE
SHOULD NOT NOW
BE PRONOUNCED . . .

3

IT WAS funny the way I met Gloria. She was trying to get into pictures too, but I didn't know that until later. I was walking down Melrose one day from the Paramount studios when I heard somebody hollering, "Hey! Hey!" and I turned around and there she was running towards me and waving. I stopped, waving back. When she got up to me she was all out of breath and excited and I saw I didn't know her.

"Damn that bus," she said.

I looked around and there was the bus half a block down the street going towards Western.

"Oh," I said, "I thought you were waving at me. . . ."

"What would I be waving at you for?" she asked.

I laughed. "I don't know," I said. "You going my way?"

"I may as well walk on down to Western," she said; and we began to walk on down towards Western.

That was how it all started and it seems very strange to me now. I don't understand it at all. I've thought and thought and still I don't understand it. This wasn't murder. I try to do somebody a favor and I wind up getting killed myself. *They are going to kill me. I know exactly what the judge is going to say. I can tell by the look of him that he is going to be glad to say it and I can tell by the feel of the people behind me that they are going to be glad to hear him say it.*

Take that morning I met Gloria. I wasn't feeling very good; I was still a little sick, but I went over to Paramount because von Sternberg was making a Russian picture and I thought maybe I could get a job. I

19

used to ask myself what could be nicer than working for von Sternberg, or Mamoulian or Boleslawsky either, getting paid to watch him direct, learning about composition and tempo and angles . . . so I went over to Paramount.

I couldn't get inside, so I hung around the front until noon when one of his assistants came out for lunch. I caught up with him and asked what was the chance to get some atmosphere.

"None," he said, telling me that von Sternberg was very careful about his atmospheric people.

I thought that was a lousy thing to say but I knew what he was thinking, that my clothes didn't look any too good. "Isn't this a costume picture?" I asked.

"All our extras come through Central," he said, leaving me. . . .

I wasn't going anywhere in particular; I was just riding along in my Rolls-Royce, having people point me out as the greatest director in the world, when I heard Gloria hollering. You see how those things happen? . . .

So we walked on down Melrose to Western, getting acquainted all the time; and when we got to Western I knew she was Gloria Beatty, an extra who wasn't doing well either, and she knew a little about me. I liked her very much.

She had a small room with some people over near Beverly and I lived only a few blocks from there, so I saw her again that night. That first night was really what did it but even now I can't honestly say I regret going to see her. I had about seven dollars I had made squirting soda in a drug store (subbing for a friend of mine. He had got a girl in a jam and had to take her to Santa Barbara for the operation) and I asked her if she'd rather go to a movie or sit in the park.

"What park?" she asked.

"It's right over here a little way," I said.

"All right," she said. "I got a bellyful of moving pictures anyway. If I'm not a better actress than most of those dames I'll eat your hat—Let's go sit and hate a bunch of people. . . ."

I was glad she wanted to go to the park. It was always nice there. It was a fine place to sit. It was very small, only one block square, but it was very dark and very quiet and filled with dense shrubbery. All around it palm trees grew up, fifty, sixty feet tall, suddenly tufted at the top. Once you entered the park you had the illusion of security. I often imagined they were sentries wearing grotesque helmets: my own private sentries, standing guard over my own private island. . . .

The park was a fine place to sit. Through the palms you could see many buildings, the thick, square silhouettes of apartment houses, with their red signs on the roofs, reddening the sky above and everything and everybody below. But if you wanted to get rid of these things you had only to sit and stare at them with a fixed gaze . . . and they would begin receding. That way you could drive them as far into the distance as you wanted to. . . .

"I never paid much attention to this place before," Gloria said.

. . . "I like it," I said, taking off my coat and spreading it on the grass for her. "I come here three or four times a week."

"You do like it," she said, sitting down.

"How long you been in Hollywood?" I asked.

"About a year. I been in four pictures already. I'd have been in more," she said, "but I can't get registered by Central."

"Neither can I," I said.

Unless you were registered by Central Casting Bureau you didn't have much chance. The big studios call up Central and say they want four Swedes or six Greeks or two Bohemian peasant types or six Grand Duchesses and Central takes care of it. I could see why Gloria didn't get registered by Central. She was too blonde and too small and looked too old. With a nice wardrobe she might have looked attractive, but even then I wouldn't have called her pretty.

"Have you met anybody who can help you?" I asked.

"In this business how can you tell who'll help you?"

she said. "One day you're an electrician and the next day you're a producer. The only way I could ever get to a big shot would be to jump on the running board of his car as it passed by. Anyway, I don't know whether the men stars can help me as much as the women stars. From what I've seen lately I've about made up my mind that I've been letting the wrong sex try to make me. . . . "

"How'd you happen to come to Hollywood?" I asked.

"Oh, I don't know," she said in a moment—"but anything is an improvement over the life I led back home." I asked her where that was. "Texas," she said. "West Texas. Ever been there?"

"No," I said, "I come from Arkansas."

"Well, West Texas is a hell of a place," she said. "I lived with my aunt and uncle. He was a brakeman on a railroad. I only saw him once or twice a week, thank God. . . ."

She stopped, not saying anything, looking at the red, vaporish glow above the apartment buildings.

"At least," I said, "you had a home——"

"That's what you call it," she said. "Me, I got another name for it. When my uncle was home he was always making passes at me and when he was on the road my aunt and I were always fighting. She was afraid I'd tattle on her——"

"Nice people," I said to myself.

"So I finally ran away," she said, "to Dallas. Ever been there?"

"I've never been in Texas at all," I said.

"You haven't missed anything," she said. "I couldn't get a job, so I decided to steal something in a store and make the cops take care of me."

"That was a good idea," I said.

"It was a swell idea," she said, "only it didn't work. I got arrested all right but the detectives felt sorry for me and turned me loose. To keep from starving to death I moved in with a Syrian who had a hot-dog place around the corner from the City Hall. He chewed tobacco. He chewed tobacco all the time . . . Have

you ever been in bed with a man who chewed tobacco"?

"I don't believe I have," I said.

"I guess I might even have stood that," she said,
"but when he wanted to make me between customers,
on the kitchen table, I gave up. A couple of nights later
I took poison."

"Jesus," I said to myself.

"I didn't take enough," she said. "I only got sick.
Ugh, I can still taste the stuff. I stayed in the hospital
a week. That was where I got the idea of coming to
Hollywood."

"It was?" I said.

"From the movie magazines," she said. "After I got
discharged I started hitch-hiking. Is that a laugh or
not? . . ."

"That's a good laugh," I said, trying to laugh. . . .
"Haven't you got any parents?"

"Not any more," she said. "My old man got killed
in the war in France. I wish I could get killed in a war."

"Why don't you quit the movies?" I asked.

"Why should I?" she said. "I may get to be a star
overnight. Look at Hepburn and Margaret Sullavan
and Josephine Hutchinson . . . but I'll tell you what
I would do if I had the guts: I'd walk out of a window
or throw myself in front of a street car or something."

"I know how you feel," I said; "I know exactly
how you feel."

"It's peculiar to me," she said, "that everybody pays
so much attention to living and so little to dying. Why
are these high-powered scientists always screwing
around trying to prolong life instead of finding pleas-
ant ways to end it? There must be a hell of a lot of
people in the world like me—who want to die but
haven't got the guts——"

"I know what you mean," I said; "I know exactly
what you mean."

Neither of us said anything for a couple of seconds.

"A girl friend of mine has been trying to get me
to enter a marathon dance down at the beach," she

23

said. "Free food and free bed as long as you last and a thousand dollars if you win."

"The free food part of it sounds good," I said.

"That's not the big thing," she said. "A lot of producers and directors go to those marathon dances. There's always the chance they might pick you out and give you a part in a picture. . . . What do you say?"

"Me?" I said . . . "Oh, I don't dance very well. . . ."

"You don't have to. All you have to do is keep moving."

"I don't think I better try it," I said. "I been pretty sick. I just got over the intestinal flu. I almost died. I was so weak I used to have to crawl to the john on my hands and knees. I don't think I better try it," I said, shaking my head.

"When was all this?"

"A week ago," I said.

"You're all right now," she said,

"I don't think so—I better not try it. I'm liable to have a relapse."

"I'll take care of that," she said.

". . . Maybe in a week—" I said.

"It'll be too late then. You're strong enough now," she said. . . .

...IT IS
THE JUDGMENT
AND SENTENCE
OF THIS COURT...

4

THE marathon dance was held on the amusement pier at the beach in an enormous old building that once had been a public dance hall. It was built out over the ocean on pilings, and beneath our feet, beneath the floor, the ocean pounded night and day. I could feel it surging through the balls of my feet, as if they had been stethoscopes.

Inside there was a dance space for the contestants, thirty feet wide and two hundred feet long, and around this on three sides were loge seats, behind these were the circus seats, the general admission. At the end of the dance space was a raised platform for the orchestra. It played only at night and was not a very good orchestra. During the day we had what music we could pick up with the radio, made loud by the amplifiers. Most of the time it was too loud, filling the hall with noise. We had a master of ceremonies, whose duty it was to make the customers feel at home; two floor judges who moved around on the floor all the time with the contestants to see that everything went all right, two male and female nurses, and a house doctor for emergencies. The doctor didn't look like a doctor at all. He was much too young.

One hundred and forty-four couples entered the marathon dance but sixty-one dropped out the first week. The rules were you danced for an hour and fifty minutes, then you had a ten-minute rest period in which you could sleep if you wanted to. But in those ten minutes you also had to shave or bathe or get your feet fixed or whatever was necessary.

The first week was the hardest. Everybody's feet and legs swelled—and down beneath the ocean kept pounding, pounding against the pilings all the time. Before I went into this maraethon dance I used to love the Pacific Ocean: its name, its size, its color, its smell— I used to sit for hours looking at it, wondering about the ships that had sailed it and never returned, about China and the South Seas, wondering all sorts of things . . . But not any more. I've had enough of the Pacific. I don't care whether I ever see it again or not. *I probably won't. The judge is going to take care of that.*

Gloria and I had been tipped off by some old-timers that the way to beat a marathon dance was to perfect a system for those ten-minute rest periods: learning to eat your sandwich while you shaved, learning to eat when you went to the john, when you had your feet fixed, learning to read newspapers while you danced, learning to sleep on your partner's shoulder while you were dancing; but these were all tricks of the trade you had to practice. They were very difficult for Gloria and me at first.

I found out that about half of the people in this contest were professionals. They made a business of going in marathon dances all over the country, some of them even hitch-hiking from town to town. The others were just girls and boys who came in like Gloria and me.

Couple No. 13 were our best friends in the dance. This was James and Ruby Bates, from some little town in northern Pennsylvania. It was their eighth marathon dance; they had won a $1500 prize in Oklahoma, going 1253 hours in continuous motion. There were several other teams in this dance who claimed championships of some kind, but I knew James and Ruby would be right in there for the finish. That is, if Ruby's baby didn't come first. She expected a baby in four months.

"What's the matter with Gloria?" James asked me

28

one day as we came back to the floor from the sleeping quarters.

"Nothing. What do you mean?" I asked. But I knew what he mean. Gloria had been singing the blues again.

"She keeps telling Ruby what a chump she would be to have the baby," he said. "Gloria wants her to have an abortion."

"I can't understand Gloria talking like that," I said, trying to smooth things over.

"You tell her to lay off Ruby," he said.

When the whistle started us off on the 216th hour I told Gloria what James had said.

"Nuts to him," she said. "What does he know about it?"

"I don't see why they can't have a baby if they want to. It's their business," I said. "I don't want to make James sore. He's been through a lot of these dances and he's already given us some good tips. Where would we be if he got sore?"

"It's a shame for that girl to have a baby," Gloria said. "What's the sense of having a baby unless you got dough enough to take care of it?"

"How do you know they haven't?" I asked.

"If they have what're they doing here? . . . That's the trouble now," she said. "Everybody is having babies——"

"Oh, not everybody," I said.

"A hell of a lot you know about it. You'd been better off if you'd never been born——"

"Maybe not," I said. "How do you feel?" I asked, trying to get her mind off her troubles.

"I always feel lousy," she said. "God, the hand on that clock moves slow." There was a big strip of canvas on the master of ceremonies' platform, painted in the shape of a clock, up to 2500 hours. The hand now pointed to 216. Above it was a sign: ELAPSED HOURS—216. COUPLES REMAINING—83.

"How are your legs?"

"Still pretty weak," I said. "That flu is awful stuff. . . ."

"Some of the girls think it'll take 2000 hours to win," Gloria said.

"I hope not," I said. "I don't believe I can hold out that long."

"My shoes are wearing out," Gloria said. "If we don't hurry up and get a sponsor I'll be barefooted." A sponsor was a company or a firm that gave you sweaters and advertised their names of products on the backs. Then they took care of your necessities.

James and Ruby danced over beside us. "Did you tell her?" he asked, looking at me. I nodded.

"Wait a minute," Gloria said, as they started to dance away. "What's the big idea of talking behind my back?"

"Tell that twist to lay off me," James said, still speaking directly to me.

Gloria started to say something else but before she could get it out I danced her away from there. I didn't want any scenes.

"The son of a bitch," she said.

"He's sore," I said. "Now where are we?"

"Come on," she said, "I'll tell him where he gets off——"

"Gloria," I said, "will you please mind your own business?"

"Soft pedal that loud cussing," a voice said. I looked around. It was Rollo Peters, the floor judge.

"Nuts to you," Gloria said. Through my fingers I could feel the muscles twitching in her back, just like I could feel the ocean surging through the balls of my feet.

"Pipe down," Rollo said. "The people in the box can hear you. What do you thing this is—a joint?"

"Joint is right," Gloria said.

"All right, all right," I said.

"I told you once already about that cussing," Rollo said. "I better not have to tell you again. It sounds bad to the customers."

"Customers? Where are they?" Gloria said.

"You let us worry about that," Rollo said, glaring at me.

"All right, all right," I said.

He blew his whistle, stopping everybody from moving. Some of them were barely moving, just enough to keep from being disqualified. "All right, kids," he said, "a little sprint."

"A little sprint, kids," the master of ceremonies, Rocky Gravo, said into the microphone. The noise of his voice in the amplifiers filled the hall, shutting out the pounding of the ocean. "A little sprint—around the track you go—Give," he said to the orchestra, and the orchestra began playing. The contestants started dancing with a little more animation.

The sprint lasted about two minutes and when it was finished Rocky led the applause, and then said into the microphone:

"Look at these kids, ladies and gentlemen—after 216 hours they are as fresh as a daisy in the world's championship marathon dance—a contest of endurance and skill. These kids are fed seven times a day—three big meals and four light lunches. Some of them have even gained weight while in the contest—and we have doctors and nurses constantly in attendance to see that they are in the best of physical condition. Now I'm going to call on Couple No. 4, Mario Petrone and Jackie Miller, for a specialty. Come on, Couple No. 4—there they are, ladies and gentlemen. Isn't that a cute pair? . . ."

Mario Petrone, a husky Italian, and Jackie Miller, a little blonde, went up to the platfrom to some applause. They spoke to Rocky and then began a tap dance that was very bad. Neither Mario nor Jackie seemed conscious that it was bad. When it was over a few people pitched money onto the floor.

"Give, people," Rocky said. "A silver shower. Give."

A few more coins hit the floor. Mario and Jackie picked them up, moving over near us.

"How much?" Gloria asked them.

"Feels like about six-bits," Jackie said.

"Where you from, kid?" Gloria asked.

"Alabama."

"I thought so," Gloria said.

31

"You and I ought to learn a specialty," I said to Gloria. "We could make some extra money."

"You're better off without knowing any," Mario said. "It only means extra work and it don't do your legs any good."

"Did you all hear about the derbies?" Jackie asked.

"What are they?" I asked.

"Some kind of a race," she said. "'I think they're going to explain them at the next rest period."

"The cheese is beginning to bind," Gloria said.

...THAT
FOR THE CRIME
OF MURDER
IN
THE FIRST DEGREE...

5

In the dressing room Rocky Gravo introduced Vincent (Socks) Donald, one of the promoters.

"Lissen, kids," Socks said, "don't none of you be discouraged because people ain't coming to the marathon dance. It takes time to get these things going, so we have decided to start a little novelty guaranteed to pack 'em in. Now here's what we're gonna do. We're going to paint an oval on the floor and every night everybody will race around the track for fifteen minutes and the last couple every night is disqualified. I guarantee that'll bring in the crowds."

"It'll bring in the undertaker too," somebody said.

"We'll move some cots out in the middle of the track," the promoter said, "and have the doctor and nurses on hand during the derby. When a contestant falls out and has to go to the pit, the partner will have to make two laps to make up for it. You kids will get more kick out of it because the crowds will be bigger. Say, when that Hollywood bunch starts coming here, we'll be standing 'em up. . . . Now, how's the food? Anybody got any kicks about anything? All right, kids, that's fine. You play ball with us and we'll play ball with you."

We went out on the floor. None of the contestants had anything to say about the derbies. They seemed to think that anything was a good idea if it would only start the crowds to coming. Rollo came up to me as I sat down on the railing. I had about two minutes more of rest before the next two-hour grind.

"Don't get me wrong about what I said a few minutes ago," he said. "It's not you, it's Gloria."

"I know," I said. "She's all right. She's just sore on the world, that's all."

"Try to keep her piped down," he said.

"That's a hard job, but I'll do the best I can," I said.

In a moment I looked up to the runway from the girls' dressing room and I was surprised to see Gloria and Ruby coming to the floor together. I went over to meet her.

"What do you think about the derbies?" I asked her.

"It's one good way to kill us off," she said.

The whistle started us away again.

"There's not more than a hundred people here tonight," I said. Gloria and I weren't dancing. I had my arm around her shoulder and she had hers around my waist, walking. That was all right. For the first week we had to dance, but after that you didn't. All you had to do was keep moving. I saw James and Ruby coming over to us and I could tell by the expression on his face that something was wrong. I wanted to get away, but there was no place to go.

"I told you to lay off my wife, didn't I?" he said to Gloria.

"You go to hell, you big ape," Gloria said.

"Wait a minute," I said. "What's the matter?"

"She's been after Ruby again," James said. "Every time I turn my back she's after her again."

"Forget it, Jim," Ruby said, trying to steer him away.

"Naw, I won't forget it. I told you to keep your mouth shut, didn't I?" he said to Gloria.

"You take a flying——"

Before Gloria could get the words finished he slapped her hard on the side of the face, knocking her head against my shoulder. It was a hard wallop. I couldn't stand for that. I reached up and hit him in the mouth. He hit me in the jaw with his left hand, knocking me back against some of the dancers. That kept me from falling to the floor. He rushed at me and I grabbed him, wrestling with him, trying to jerk my knee up

36

between his legs to foul him. It was the only chance I had.

A whistle blew in my ear and somebody grabbed us. It was Rollo Peters. He shoved us apart.

"Cut it out," he said. "What's coming off here?"

"Nothing," I said.

"Nothing," Ruby said.

Rollo raised his hand, waving to Rocky on the platform.

"Give," said Rocky, and the orchestra started to play.

"Scatter out," Rollo said to the contestants, who started to move away. "Come on," he said, leading them around the floor.

"Next time I'm going to cut your throat," James said to Gloria.

"F— you," Gloria said.

"Shut up," I said.

I walked away with her, down into a corner, where we slowed up, barely moving along.

"Are you crazy?" I said. "Why don't you let Ruby alone?"

"Don't worry, I'm through wasting my breath on her. If she wants to have a deformed baby, that's okay by me."

"Hello, Gloria," a voice said.

We looked around. It was an old woman in a front row box seat by the railing. I didn't know her name but she was quite a character. She had been there every night, bringing her blanket and her lunch. One night she wrapped up in her blanket and stayed all night. She was about sixty-five years old.

"Hello," Gloria said.

"What was the matter down there?" the old woman asked.

"Nothing," Gloria said. "Just a little argument."

"How do you feel?" the old woman asked.

"All right, I guess," Gloria replied.

"I'm Mrs. Layden," the old woman said. "You're my favorite couple."

"Well, thanks," I said.

"I tried to enter this," Mrs. Layden said, "but they wouldn't let me. They said I was too old. But I'm only sixty."

"Well, that's fine," I said.

Gloria and I had stopped, our arms around each other, swaying our bodies. You had to keep moving all the time. A couple of men moved into the loge behind the old woman. Both of them were chewing unlighted cigars.

"They're dicks," Gloria said under her breath.

". . . How do you like the contest?" I asked Mrs. Layden.

"I enjoy it very much," she said. "Very much. Such nice boys and girls . . ."

"Move along, kids," Rollo said, walking by.

I nodded to Mrs. Layden, moving along. "Can you feature that?" Gloria asked. "She ought to be home putting a diaper on the baby. Christ, I hope I never live to be that old."

"How do you know those fellows are detectives?" I asked.

"I'm psychic," Gloria replied. "My God, can you feature that old lady? She's a nut about these things. They ought to charge her room rent." She shook her head. "I hope I never live to be that old," she said again.

The meeting with the old lady depressed Gloria very much. She said it reminded her of the women in the little town in West Texas where she had lived.

"Alice Faye's just come in," one of the girls said. "See her? Sitting right over there."

It was Alice Faye all right, with a couple of men I didn't recognize.

"See her?" I asked Gloria.

"I don't want to see her," Gloria said.

"Ladies and gentlemen," Rocky said into the microphone, "we are honored tonight to have with us that beautiful moving picture star, Miss Alice Faye. Give Miss Faye a big hand, ladies and gentlemen."

Everybody applauded and Miss Faye nodded her

head, smiling. Socks Donald, sitting in a box seat by the orchestra platform, was smiling too. The Hollywood crowd had started coming.

"Come on," I said to Gloria, "clap your hands."

"Why should I applaud for her?" Gloria said. "What's she got I haven't? . . ."

"You're jealous," I said.

"You're goddam right I'm jealous. As long as I am a failure I'm jealous of anybody who's a success. Aren't you?"

"Certainly not," I said.

"You're a fool," she said.

"Hey, look," I said.

The two detectives had left the box with Mrs. Layden and were sitting with Socks Donald. They had their heads together, looking at a sheet of paper one of them was holding.

"All right, kids," Rocky said into the microphone. "A little sprint before the rest period. . . . Give," he said to the orchestra, clapping his hands together and stamping on the platform, keeping time to the music. In a moment the customers were clapping their hands together and stamping too.

We were all milling around in the middle of the floor, all of us watching the minute hand of the clock, when suddenly Kid Kamm of couple No. 18 began slapping his partner on the cheek. He was holding her up with his left hand, slapping her backwards and forwards with his right hand. But she did not respond. She was dead to the world. She gurgled a couple of times and then slid to the floor, unconscious.

The floor judge blew his whistle and all the customers jumped to their feet, excited. Customers at a marathon dance do not have to be prepared for their excitement. When anything happens they get excited all at once. In that respect a marathon dance is like a bull fight.

The floor judge and a couple of nurses picked up the girl and carried her off, her toes dragging, to the dressing room.

"Mattie Barnes, of Couple No. 18, has fainted," Rocky announced to the crowd. "She has been taken to the dressing room, ladies and gentlemen, where she will have the best of medical attention. Nothing serious, ladies and gentlemen—nothing serious. It just proves that there's always something happening at the world's championship marathon dance."

"She was complaining last rest period," Gloria said.

"What's the matter with her?" I asked.

"It's that time of the month," Gloria said. "And she'll never be able to come back either. She's the type that has to go to bed for three of four days when she gets it."

"Can I pick 'em?" said Kid Kamm. He shook his head, disgusted. "Boy, am I hoodooed! I been in nine of these things and I ain't finished one yet. My partner always caves in on me."

"She'll probably be all right," I said, trying to cheer him up.

"Nope," he said, "she's finished. She can go back to the farm now."

The siren blew, meaning it was the end of another grind. Everybody ran for the dressing rooms. I kicked off my shoes, piling on my cot. I felt the ocean surge once—just once. Then I was asleep.

I woke up, my nose full of ammonia. One of the trainers was moving a bottle across my chin letting me inhale it. (This was the best way to arouse one of us from a deep sleep, the doctor said. If they had tried to wake you up by shaking you, they never would have done it.)

"All right," I said to the trainer. "I'm all right."

I sat up, reaching for my shoes. Then I saw those two detectives and Socks Donald standing near me, by Mario's cot. They were waiting for the other trainer to wake him up. Finally Mario rolled over, looking up at them.

"Hello, buddy," said one of the detectives. "Know who this is?" He handed him a sheet of paper. Now I was close enough to see what it was. It was a page torn out of a detective magazine, containing several pictures.

Mario looked at it, then handed it back. "Yeah, I know who it is," he said, sitting up.

"You ain't changed much," said the other detective.

"You wop son of a bitch," Socks said, doubling his fist. "What're you trying to pull on me?"

"Nix, Socks," the first detective said. Then he spoke to Mario. "Well, Giuseppe, get your things together."

Mario started tying his shoes. "I ain't got nothing but a coat and a toothbrush," he said. "But I would like to say good-bye to my partner."

"You dirty wop son of a bitch," Socks said. "This'll look good in the newspapers, won't it?"

"Never mind your partner, Giuseppe," the second detective said. "Hey son," he said to me, "you tell Giuseppe's partner good-bye for him. Come on, Giuseppe," he said to Mario.

"Take that wop son of a bitch out the back way, boys," said Socks Donald.

"Everybody on the floor," yelled the floor judge. "Everybody on the floor."

"So long, Mario," I said.

Mario did not say anything. It had all been very quiet, very matter-of-fact. These detectives acted as if this kind of thing happened every day.

... OF WHICH
YOU HAVE BEEN
CONVICTED
BY VERDICT
OF THE JURY...

6

So MARIO went to jail and Mattie went back to the farm. *I remember how surprised I was when they arrested Mario for murder. I couldn't believe it. He was one of the nicest boys I'd ever met. But that was then that I couldn't believe it. Now I know you can be nice and be a murderer too. Nobody was ever any nicer to a girl than I was to Gloria, but there came the time when I shot and killed her. So you see being nice doesn't mean a thing. . . .*

Mattie was automatically disqualified when the doctor refused to let her continue in the contest. He said if she did go on with the dance she would injure some of her organs and never be able to have a baby. She raised hell about it, Gloria said, calling the doctors a lot of names and absolutely refusing to quit. But she did quit. She had to. They had the axe over her.

That teamed her partner, Kid Kamm, with Jackie. Under the rules you could do that. You could solo for twenty-fours hours but if you didn't get a partner by then you were disqualified. Both the Kid and Jackie seemed well satisfied with the new arrangement. Jackie had nothing to say about losing Mario. Her attitude was that a partner was a partner. But the Kid was all smiles. He seemed to think that at last he had broken his hoodoo.

"They're liable to win," Gloria said. "They're strong as mules. That Alabama is corn-fed. Look at that beam. I bet she can go six months."

"I'll string along with James and Ruby," I said.

45

"After the way they've treated us?"

"What's that got to do with it? Besides, what's the matter with us? We've got a chance to win, haven't we?"

"Have we?"

"Well, you don't seem to think so," I said.

She shook her head, not saying anything to that. "More and more and more I wish I was dead," she said.

There it was again. No matter what I talked about she always got back to that. "Isn't there something I can talk about that won't remind you that you wish you were dead?" I asked.

"No," she said.

"I give up," I said.

Somebody on the platform turned the radio down. The music sounded like music now. (We used the radio all the time the orchestra wasn't there. This was in the afternoon. The orchestra came only at night.) "Ladies and gentlemen," Rocky said into the microphone, "I have the honor to announce that two sponsors have come forward to sponsor two couples. The Pompadour Beauty Shop, of 415 Avenue B, will sponsor Couple No. 13—James and Ruby Bates. Let's give the Pompadour Beauty Shop, of 415 Avenue B, a big hand for this, ladies and gentlemen—you too, kids. . . ."

Everybody applauded.

"The second couple to be sponsored," Rocky said, "is No. 34, Pedro Ortega and Lillian Bacon. They are sponsored by the Oceanic Garage. All right, now, a big hand for the Oceanic Garage, located at 11,341 Ocean Walkway in Santa Monica."

Everybody applauded again.

"Ladies and gentlemen," Rocky said, "there ought to be more sponsors for these marvelous kids. Tell your friends, ladies and gentlemen, and let's get sponsors for all the kids. Look at them, ladies and gentlemen, after 242 hours of continuous motion they are as fresh as daisies . . . a big hand for these marvelous kids, ladies and gentlemen."

There was some more applause.

"And don't forget, ladies and gentlemen," Rocky said, "there's the Palm Garden right down there at the end of the hall where you can get delicious beverages —all kinds of beer and sandwiches. Visit the Palm Gardens, ladies and gentlemen. . . . Give," he said to the radio, turning the knob and filling the hall with noise again.

Gloria and I walked over to Pedro and Lillian. Pedro limped from a game leg. The story was that he had been gored in a bull ring in Mexico City. Lillian was a brunette. She too had been trying to get in the movies when she heard about the marathon dance.

"Congratulations," I said.

"It proves somebody is for us," Pedro said.

"As long as it couldn't be Metro-Goldwyn-Mayer it might as well be a garage," Lillian said. "Only it seems a litttle queer for a garage to be buying me underclothes."

"Where do you get the underclothes stuff?" Gloria said. "You don't get underclothes. You get a sweatshirt with the garage's name across the back of it."

"I get underclothes, too," Lillian said.

"Hey, Lillian," said Rollo, the floor judge, "the woman from the Oceanic Garage wants to talk to you."

"The what? . . ." asked Lillian.

"Your sponsor, Mrs. Yeargan——"

"For crying out loud," said Lillian. "Pedro, it looks like you get the underclothes."

Gloria and I walked down by the master of ceremonies' platform. It was nice down there about this time of the afternoon. There was a big triangle of sunshine that came through the double window above the bar in the Palm Garden. It only lasted about ten minutes but during those ten minutes I moved slowly about in it (I had to move to keep from being disqualified) letting it cover me completely. It was the first time I had ever appreciated the sun. "When this marathon is over," I told myself, "I'm going to spend the rest of my life in the sun. I can't wait to go to the Sahara desert to make a picture." *Of course, that won't ever happen now.*

47

I watched the triangle on the floor get smaller and smaller. Finally it closed altogether and started up my legs. It crawled up my body like a living thing. When it got to my chin I stood on my toes, to keep my head in as long as possible. I did not close my eyes. I kept them wide open, looking straight into the sun. It did not blind me at all. In a moment it was gone.

I looked around for Gloria. She was standing at the platform, swaying from side to side, talking to Rocky, who was sitting on his haunches. Rocky was swaying too. (All the employes—the doctor, the nurses, the floor judges, the master of ceremonies, even the boys who sold soda pop—had been given orders to keep moving when they talked to one of the contestants. The management was very strict about this.)

"You looked very funny standing out there on your toes," Gloria said. "You looked like a ballet dancer."

"You practice up on that and I'll let you do a solo," Rocky said, laughing.

"Yes," Gloria said. "How was the sun today?"

"Don't let 'em kid you," Mack Aston, of Couple No. 5, said as he passed by.

"Rocky!" a voice called. It was Socks Donald. Rocky got down from the platform and went to him.

"I don't think it's very nice of you to razz me," I said to Gloria. "I don't ever razz you."

"You don't have to," she said. "I get razzed by an expert. God razzes me. . . . You know what Socks Donald wants with Rocky? You want some inside information?"

"What?" I asked.

"You know No. 6—Freddy and that Manski girl. Her mother is going to prefer charges against him and Socks. She ran away from home."

"I don't see what that's got to do with it," I said.

"She's jail bait," Gloria said. "She's only about fifteen. God, with all of it running around loose it does look like a guy would have better sense."

"Why blame Freddy? It may not be his fault."

"According to the law it's his fault," Gloria said. "That's what counts."

I steered Gloria back to where Socks and Rocky were standing, trying to overhear what was being said; but they were talking too low. Rather, Socks was doing all the talking. Rocky was listening, nodding his head.

"Right now," I heard Socks say, and Rocky nodded that he understood and came back on the floor, winking wisely to Gloria as he passed. He went to Rollo Peters and called him aside, whispering earnestly for a few seconds. Then Rollo left, looking around as if he were trying to find somebody, and Rocky went back to the platform.

"The kids only have a few more minutes left before they retire for their well-earned rest period," Rocky announced into the microphone. "And while they are off the floor, ladies and gentlemen, the painters will paint the big oval on the floor for the derby tonight. The derby tonight, ladies and gentlemen: don't forget the derby. Positively the most thrilling thing you ever saw—all right, kids, two minutes to go before you re- tire—a little sprint, kids—show the ladies and gentlemen how fresh you are— You, too, ladies and gentlemen, show these marvelous kids you're behind them with a rally——"

He turned up the radio a little and began clapping his hands and stamping his foot. The audience joined in the rally. All of us stepped a little more lively, but it was not because of the rally. It was because within a minute or two we got a rest period and directly after that we were to be fed.

Gloria nudged me and I looked up to see Rollo Peters walking between Freddy and the Manski girl. I thought the Manski girl was crying, but before Gloria and I could catch up with them the siren blew and everybody made a dash for the dressing rooms.

Freddy was standing over his cot, stuffing an extra pair of shoes into a small zipper bag.

"I heard about it," I said. "I'm very sorry."

"It's all right," he said. "Only she's the one who did the raping. . . . I'll be all right if I can get out of town

49

before the cops pick me up. It's a lucky thing for me that Socks was tipped off."

"Where are you going?" I asked.

"South, I guess. I've always had a yen to see Mexico. So long. . . ."

He was gone before anybody knew it. As he went through the back door I had a glimpse of the sun glinting on the ocean. For a moment I was so astounded I could not move. I do not know whether I was the more surprised at really seeing the sun for the first time in almost three weeks or discovering the door. I went over to it, hoping the sun would not be gone when I got there. *The only other time I ever was this eager was one Christmas when I was a kid, the first year I was big enough to really know what Christmas was, and I went into the front room and saw the tree all lighted up.*

I opened the door. At the end of the world the sun was sinking into the ocean. It was so red and bright and hot I wondered why there was no steam. *I once saw steam come out of the ocean. It was on the highway at the beach and some men were working with gunpowder. Suddenly, it exploded, setting them on fire. They ran and dived into the ocean. That was when I saw the steam.*

The color of the sun had shot up into some thin clouds, reddening them. Out there where the sun was sinking the ocean was very calm, not looking like an ocean at all. It was lovely, lovely, lovely, lovely lovely, lovely. Several people were fishing off the pier, not paying any attention to the sunset. They were fools. "You need that sunset worse than you do fish," I told them in my mind.

The door flew out of my hands, slamming shut with a bang like that of a cannon going off.

"Are you deaf?" a voice yelled in my ear. It was one of the trainers. "Keep that door closed! You wanna be disqualified?"

"I was only watching the sun set," I said.

"Are you nuts? You ought to be asleep. You need your sleep," he said.

"I don't need any sleep," I said. "I feel fine. I feel better than I ever felt in my life."

"You need your rest anyway," he said. "You only got a few minutes left. Get off your feet."

He followed me across the floor to my cot. Now I could notice the dressing room didn't smell so good. I am very susceptible to unpleasant odors and I wondered why I hadn't noticed this smell before, the smell of too many men in a room. I kicked off my shoes and stretched out on my back.

"You want your legs rubbed?" he asked.

"I'm all right," I said. "My legs feel fine."

He said something to himself and went away. I lay there, thinking about the sunset, trying to remember what color it was. I don't mean the red, I mean the other shades. Once or twice I almost remembered; it was like a name you once had known but now had forgotten, whose size and letters and cadence you remembered but could not quite assemble.

Through the legs of my cot I could feel the ocean quivering against the pilings below. It rose and fell, rose and fell, went out and came back, went out and came back. . . .

I was glad when the siren blew, waking us up, calling us back to the floor.

. . . CARRYING
WITH IT
THE EXTREME PENALTY
OF THE LAW. . .

7

THE painters had finished. They had painted a thick white line around the floor in the shape of an oval. This was the track for the derby.

"Freddy's gone," I said to Gloria, as we walked to the table where the sandwiches and coffee had been set up. (This was called a light lunch. We had our big meal at ten o'clock at night.)

"So is the Manski girl," Gloria said. "Two welfare workers came and got her. I bet her old lady burns her cute little bottom."

"I hate to say it," I said, "but Freddy's leaving was the brightest spot of my life."

"What had he ever done to you?" she asked.

"Oh, I don't mean that," I said. "But if he hadn't left I wouldn't have got to see the sunset."

"My God," Gloria said, looking at her sandwich. "Ain't there nothing in the world but ham?"

"To you that's turkey," said Mack Aston, who was in line behind me. He was kidding.

"Here's a beef," said the nurse. "Would you rather have a beef?"

Gloria took the beef sandwich, but kept the ham too. "Put four lumps in mine," she said to Rollo, who was pouring the coffee. "And lots of cream."

"She's got a little horse in her," said Mack Aston.

"Black," I said to Rollo.

Gloria took her food over to the master of ceremonies' platform where the musicians were tuning up their instruments. When Rocky Gravo saw her he jumped down on the floor and began talking to her. There wasn't room there for me, so I went around to the opposite side.

"Hello," said a girl. The shield on her back said: 7. She had black hair and black eyes and was rather pretty. I didn't know her name.

"Hello," I said, looking around, trying to see whose partner she was. He was talking to a couple of women in a front row box.

"How are you making out?" No. 7 asked. Her voice sounded as if she had been well educated.

"What is she doing in this thing?" I asked myself. "I guess I'm doing all right," I replied. "Only I wish it was all over and I was the winner."

"What would you do with the money if you won?" she asked, laughing.

"I'd make a picture," I said.

"You couldn't make much of a picture for a thousand dollars, could you?" she asked, taking a bite of her sandwich.

"Oh, I don't mean a big picture," I explained. "I meant a short. I could make a two-reeler for that, maybe three."

"You interest me," she said. "I've been watching you for two weeks."

"You have?" I said, surprised.

"Yes, I've seen you stand over there in the sun every afternoon and I've seen you with a thousand different expressions on your face. Sometimes I got the idea you were badly frightened."

"You must be wrong," I said. "What's there to be frightened about?"

"I overheard what you said to your partner about seeing the sunset this afternoon," she said, smiling.

"That doesn't prove anything," I said.

"Suppose . . ." she said, glancing around. She looked at the clock, frowning. "We've still got four minutes. Would you like to do something for me?"

"Well . . . sure," I said.

She motioned with her head and I followed her behind the master of ceremonies' platform. This platform was about four feet high, draped with heavy, decorated canvas that fell to the floor. We were standing alone in a sort of cave that was formed by the back of the platform and a lot of signs. Except for the noise she and I might have been the only people left in the world. We were both a little excited.

"Come on," she said. She dropped to the floor and lifted the canvas, crawling under the platform. My heart was beating rapidly and I felt the blood leave my face. Through the balls of my feet, I could feel the ocean surging against the pilings below.

"Come on," she whispered, pulling at my ankle. Suddenly I knew what she meant. *There is no new experience in life. Something may happen to you that you think has never happened before, that you think is brand new, but you are mistaken. You have only to see or smell or hear or feel a certain something and you will discover that this experience you thought was new has happened before. When she pulled at my ankle, trying to get me beneath the platform, I remembered the time when another girl had done exactly the same thing. Only it was a front porch instead of a platform. I was thirteen or fourteen years old then and the girl was about the same age. Her name was Mabel and she lived next door. After school we used to play under the front porch, imagining it was a cove and we were robbers and prisoners. Later on we used it to play papa and mama, imagining it was a house. But on this day I am speaking of I stood by the front porch, not thinking of Mabel or games at all, and I felt something pulling at my ankle. I looked down and there was Mabel. "Come on," she said.*

It was very dark under the platform and while I crouched there on my hands and knees trying to see through the gloom No. 7 suddenly grabbed me around the neck.

"Hurry . . ." she whispered.

"What's coming off here?" growled a man's voice. He was so close I could feel his breath against my hair. "Who is that?"

I recognized the voice now. It was Rocky Gravo's. My stomach turned over. No. 7 let go my neck and slid out from under the platform. I was afraid if I tried to apologize or say anything Rocky would recognize my voice, so I quickly rolled under the curtain. No. 7 was already on her feet moving away, looking back over her shoulder at me. Her face was white as chalk. Neither of us spoke. We strolled onto the dance floor, trying to look very innocent. The nurse was collecting our dirty coffee cups in a basket. Then I discovered my hands and clothes were filthy with dust. I had a couple of minutes before the whistle blew, so I hurried into the dressing room to clean up. When that was done I felt better.

"What a close shave that was," I told myself. "I'll never do anything like that again."

I got back on the floor as the whistle blew and the orchestra began to play. This was not a very good orchestra; but it was better than the radio because you didn't have to listen to a lot of announcers begging and pleading with you to buy something. Since I've been in this marathon I've had enough radio to last me for the rest of my life. *There is a radio going now, in a building across the street from the court room. It is very distinct. "Do you need money? . . . Are you in trouble? . . ."*

"Where've you been?" Gloria asked, taking my arm.

"I haven't been anywhere," I said. "Feel like dancing?"

"All right," she said. We danced once around the floor and then she stopped. "That's too much like work," she said.

As I took my hand from around her waist I noticed my fingers were dirty again. "That's funny," I thought. "I just washed them a minute ago."

"Turn around," I said to Gloria.

"What's the matter?" she asked.

"Turn around," I said.

She hesitated, biting her lip, so I stepped behind her. She was wearing a white woolen skirt and a thin white

58

woolen sweater. Her back was covered with thick dust and I knew where it had come from.

"What's the matter?" she said.

"Stand still," I said. I brushed her off with my hand, knocking most of the dust and lint loose from her sweater and skirt. She did not speak for a moment or two. "I must have got that when I was wrestling in the dressing room with Lillian," she said finally.

"I'm not as big a sap as she thinks I am," I told myself. "I guess you did," I said.

Rollo Peters fell in with us as we walked around the floor.

"Who is that girl?" I asked, pointing to No. 7.

"That's Guy Duke's partner. Her name is Rosemary Loftus."

"All your taste is in your mouth," Gloria said.

"I merely asked who she was," I said. "I haven't got a crush on her."

"You don't need one," Gloria said. "You tell him, Rollo."

"Leave me out of this," Rollo said, shaking his head. "I don't know a thing about her."

"What about her?" I asked Gloria, as Rollo walked away, joining James and Ruby Bates.

"Are you that innocent?" she said. "On the level— are you?" She laughed, shaking her head. "You certainly are a card."

"All right, forget it," I said.

"Why, that dame is the biggest bitch west of the Mississippi River," she said. "She's a bitch with an exclusive education and when you get that kind of bitch you've got the worst bitch of all. Why not even the girls can go to the can when she's around——"

"Hello, there, Gloria," called out Mrs. Layden. She was sitting in her usual seat in the front row box the far end of the hall, away from the master of ceremonies' platform. Gloria and I walked over to the railing. . . .

"How's my favorite couple?" she asked.

"Fine," I said. "How are you, Mrs. Layden?"

"I'm fine too," she said. "I'm going to stay a long time

tonight. See?" She pointed to her blanket and her lunch basket on the chair beside her. "I'll be here to cheer you on."

"We'll need it," Gloria said.

"Why don't you take one of those boxes down there away from the Palm Garden?" I asked. "It gets pretty rowdy at the bar later on when everybody starts drinking——"

"This is fine for me," she said, smiling. "I like to be here for the derby. I want to watch them make the turns. Would you like to see the afternoon paper?" she asked, pulling the paper out from under the blanket.

"Thank you," I said. "I would like to know what's going on in the world. How is the weather outside? Has the world changed much?"

"You're poking fun at me," she said.

"No, I'm not . . . it just seems like I've been in this hall a million years . . . Thanks for the paper, Mrs. Layden. . . ."

As we moved away I unfolded the paper. Big, black headlines hit me in the face.

NAB YOUTHFUL MURDERER
IN MARATHON DANCE

Escaped Criminal Was Taking
Part in Beach Contest

Detectives yesterday picked a murderer from the marathon dance now in progress on the amusement pier at Santa Monica. He was Giuseppe Lodi, 26-year-old Italian, who escaped eight months ago from the Illinois state prison at Joliet after serving four years of a fifty-year sentence for the conviction of the hold-up slaying of an aged druggist in Chicago.

Lodi, entered in the marathon dance under the alias of Mario Petrone, offered no resistance when he was arrested by Detectives Bliss and Voight, of the Robbery Detail. The officers had dropped into the marathon dance seeking diversion from their duties, they said, and recognized Lodi through a picture they had seen in "The Line-Up," a department of a popular detective monthly which contains pictures and measurements of badly wanted criminals . . .

"Can you beat that?" I said. "I was right beside him when all that happened. I certainly feel sorry for Mario now."

"Why?" said Gloria, "what's the difference between us?"

Pedro Ortega, Mack Aston and a few others gathered around us, talking excitedly. I handed the paper to Gloria and walked on alone.

"That's a hell of a thing," I thought. "Fifty years! Poor Mario . . ." *And when Mario hears the news about me, if he ever does, he will think: 'Poor guy! wasting his sympathy on me and him getting the rope. . . .'*

At the next rest period Socks Donald had a surprise for us. He issued the uniforms we were to wear in the derby races; tennis shoes, white shorts, white sweatshirts. All the boys were given thick leather belts to wear around their waists, and on either side of the belt were little handles, like those on luggage. These were for our partners to hold on when we went around the curves. It seemed very silly to me then, but later on I discovered Socks Donald knew what he was doing.

"Lissen, kids," Socks said. "Tonight we start on our first million. There'll be a lot of movie stars here for the derby and wherever they go the crowds will follow. Some team will lose tonight—some team will lose every night. I don't want no squawks about this because it's on the level. Everybody has the same chance. You'll get some extra time to get on your uniforms and some extra time to take them off. And by the way, I talked to Mario Petrone this afternoon. He told me to say good-bye to all his pals. Now, don't forget to give the customers a run for their money in the derby, kids——"

I was surprised to hear him mention Mario's name

because the night before, when Mario was arrested, Socks had wanted to beat him up.

"I thought he was sore at Mario," I said to Rollo.

"Not any more," Rollo said. "That was the best break we ever had. If it hadn't been for that nobody ever would have known there was a marathon dance. That newspaper publicity was just what the doctor ordered. Reservations have been coming in all after-noon."

...YOU,
ROBERT SYVERTEN,
BE DELIVERED...

8

THAT night, for the first time since the contest started, the hall was crowded and practically every seat was taken. The Palm Garden was crowded too and there was a lot of boisterous laughing and talking at the bar. "Rollo was right," I said to myself. "Mario's arrest was the best break Socks ever had." (But not all those people had been attracted by the newspaper publicity. I found out later that Socks was having us advertised over several radio stations.)

We walked around in our track suits while the trainers and nurses set up the floor for the derby.

"I feel naked," I said to Gloria.

"You look naked," she said. "You ought to have on a jock-strap."

"They didn't give me one," I said. "Does it show that much?"

"It's not only that," she said. "You're liable to get ruptured. Get Rollo to buy you one tomorrow. They come in three sizes: small, medium and large. You take a small."

"I'm not by myself," I said, looking around at some of the other boys.

"They're bragging," Gloria said.

Most of the contestants looked very funny in their track suits. I never saw such an odd assortment of arms and legs in my life.

"Look," Gloria said, nodding to James and Ruby Bates. "Ain't that something?"

You could see Ruby was going to have a baby. It

looked as if she had stuffed a pillow under her sweat-shirt.

"It certainly is noticeable," I said. "But remember it's none of your business."

"Ladies and gentlemen," Rocky said into the microphone, "before this sensational derby starts I want to call your attention to the rules and regulations. Because of the number of contestants the derby will be run in two sections—forty couples in the first and forty in the second. The second derby will be run a few minutes after the first one and the entries in each one will be decided by drawing the numbers out of a hat.

We'll run these derbies in two sections for a week, the couple in each one making the least number of laps to be eliminated. After the first week there will be only one derby. The kids will race around the track for fifteen minutes, the boys heeling and toeing, the girls trotting or running as they see fit. There is no prize for the winner, but if some of you ladies and gentlemen want to send up some prize money to encourage the kids, I know they will appreciate it.

"You will notice the cots in the middle of the floor, the nurses and trainers standing by with sliced oranges, wet towels, smelling salts—and the doctor in charge to see that none of these kids carry on unless they're in good physical condition."

The young doctor was standing in the middle of the floor, his stethoscope hanging from his neck, looking very important.

"Just a minute, ladies and gentlemen—just a minute," Rocky said. "I have in my hand a ten-dollar bill for the winner of tonight's derby, contributed by that marvelous little screen star, none other than Miss Ruby Keeler. A hand for Miss Keeler, ladies and gentlemen——"

Ruby Keeler stood up, bowing to the applause.

"That's the spirit, ladies and gentlemen," Rocky said. "And now we need some judges, ladies and gentlemen, to check the laps each couple makes." He stopped to wipe the perspiration off his face. "All right now, ladies

and gentlemen, I want these judges out of the audience
—forty of them. Step right up here—don't be afraid——"

Nobody in the audience moved for a moment, and
then Mrs. Layden crawled under the railing and
started across the floor. As she passed Gloria and me
she smiled and winked.

"Maybe she'll turn out to be useful after all," Gloria
said.

Soon others followed Mrs. Layden until all the
judges had been selected. Rollo gave each of them a
card and a pencil and seated them on the floor around
the platform.

"All right, ladies and gentlemen," Rocky said.
"We've got enough judges. Now we'll have the drawing for the first derby. There are eighty numbers in
this hat and we'll draw forty of them. The other
couples will be in the second derby. Now we need
somebody to draw the numbers. How about you,
lady?" he asked Mrs. Layden, holding out the hat. Mrs.
Layden smiled and nodded her head.

"This is a big moment in her life," Gloria said sarcastically.

"I think she is a very sweet old lady," I said.

"Nuts," Gloria said.

Mrs. Layden began drawing out the numbers, passing them to Rocky who announced them into the microphone.

"The first one," he said, "is couple No. 105. Right
over here, kids—all you couples who are drawn stand
over here on this side of the platform."

As fast as Mrs. Layden would draw the numbers
Rocky would announce them, then pass them to one
of the judges. That was the couple he checked, counting the number of laps they made.

". . . Couple No. 22," Rocky said, handing the number to a young man who wore spectacles.

"Come on," I said to Gloria. That was our number.

"I'd like that one," I heard Mrs. Layden say to
Rocky. "That's my favorite couple."

"Sorry, lady," Rocky said. "You have to take them
in order."

When the drawing was finished and we were all together near the starting line, Rocky said, "All right, ladies and gentlemen, we're almost ready. Now, kids, all you boys remember heel and toe. If one of you has to go to the pit for any reason whatsoever, your partner has to make two laps of the track to count for one. Will you start 'em off, Miss Keeler?"

She nodded and Rocky handed Rollo the pistol. He took it to Miss Keeler, who was sitting in a front-row box with another girl I didn't recognize. Jolson was not there.

"All right, ladies and gentlemen, hold your hats," Rocky said. "All right, Miss Keeler. . . ." He signaled to her with his hand.

Gloria and I had edged along the side of the platform towards the starting line and when Miss Keeler pulled the trigger we jumped away, pushing and shoving to get in front. Gloria had me by the arm.

"Hold on to the belt," I yelled, struggling to get through the crowd. Everybody was stumbling over everybody else, trying to get in front . . . but in a minute we spread out and began pounding around the track. I was taking such long steps Gloria had to trot to keep up with me.

"Heel and toe there," Rollo said. "You're running."

"I'm doing the best I can," I said.

"Heel and toe," he said. "Like this——"

He stepped in front of me, illustrating what he meant. I had no trouble at all in learning. The trick was to keep your shoulders and arms properly timed. I had no trouble at all in figuring that. It seemed to come to me naturally. It was so simple I thought for a moment I must have done some heel-and-toe walking before. I couldn't remember it, so evidently I hadn't. I've got a marvelous memory.

We had been going about five minutes and were well up towards the front when I felt Gloria stop propelling herself; that is, she stopped traveling under her own power. I was dragging her. I felt as if she were trying to pull the belt through my stomach.

"Too fast?" I asked, slowing down.

"Yes," she replied, almost out of breath.

One of the nurses slammed a wet bath towel around my neck, almost knocking me off balance. "Rub your face with it," I said to Gloria. . . . Just then couple No. 35 cut in front of us, trying to get into the turn first. The spurt was too much for the girl. She began to stagger, loosening her hold on his belt.

"Stand by No. 35," yelled Rocky Gravo, but before a nurse or trainer could reach her she had fallen on her face, sliding a couple of feet across the floor. If I had been alone I could have side-stepped the body, but with Gloria hanging on me I was afraid if I dodged I would sling her off. (Making these turns with a girl hanging on you was like playing pop-the-whip.)

"Look out!" I yelled, but the warning was too late to do any good. Gloria stumbled over the body pulling me down with her, and the next thing I knew four or five couples were piled together on the floor, struggling to get up. Rocky said something into the microphone and the crowd gasped.

I picked myself up. I wasn't hurt, only I knew from the way my knees were burning that all the skin was rubbed off. The nurses and trainers rushed over and began tugging at the girls, carrying Gloria and Ruby to the cots in the pit.

"Nothing serious, ladies and gentlemen," Rocky said. "Just a little spill . . . something happens every minute in the derbies . . . while the girls are in the pit the boys have to make two laps to count as one full lap for the team. All right, kids, give those solos the inside track."

I began walking very fast so as not to lose our position in the race. Now that Gloria wasn't hanging on to the strap any more I felt light as a feather. A nurse and a trainer began working over her while the doctor listened to her heart with his stethoscope. The nurse was holding smelling salts at her nose and the trainer was massaging her legs. Another trainer and nurse were doing the same thing to Ruby. I made four laps before Gloria came back to the floor. She was very pale.

"Can you hold out?" I asked, slowing down. She said yes with her head. The people were applauding and stamping their feet and Rocky was speaking words into the microphone. Ruby came back into the race, looking all in too.

"Take it easy," Rollo said, moving beside me. "You're in no danger——"

Then I felt a sharp pain in my left leg that shot up through my body and almost blew off the top of my head. "My God," I told myself; "I'm paralyzed!"

"Kick it out, kick it out," Rollo said.

I couldn't bend my leg. It simply wouldn't work. It was stiff as a board. Every time I took a step the pain went through the top of my head.

"There's a charley horse on Couple 22," Rocky said into the microphone. "Stand by there, trainers ——"

"Kick it out, kick it out," Rollo said.

I kicked my leg against the floor but that was more painful than ever.

"Kick it out, kick it out——"

"You son-of-a bitch," I said; "my leg hurts——"

Two of the trainers grabbed me by the arms and helped me to the pit.

"There goes the brave little girl of No. 22," Rocky announced, "little Gloria Beatty. What a brave kid she is! She's soloing while her partner is in the pit with a charley horse—look at her burn up that track! Give her the inside, kids——"

One of the trainers held my shoulders down while the other one worked my leg up and down, beating the muscles with the heels of his fists.

"That hurts," I said.

"Take it easy," said the trainer who was holding my shoulders. "Didn't you ever have one of those things before?"

Then I felt something snap in my leg and the pain was suddenly gone.

"Okay," the trainer said.

70

I got up, feeling fine, and went back on the track, standing there waiting for Gloria. She was on the opposite side from me, trotting, her head bobbing up and down every time she took a step. I had to wait for her to come around. (The rules were you had to come out of the pit at the point where you went in.) As Gloria neared me I started walking and in a moment she had coupled on to the belt.

"Two minutes to go," Rocky announced. "A little rally, ladies and gentlemen—" They began clapping their hands and stamping their feet, much louder than before.

Other couples began to sprint past us and I put on a little more steam. I was pretty sure Gloria and I weren't in last place, but we had both been in the pit and I didn't want to take a chance on being eliminated. When the pistol sounded for the finish half the teams collapsed on the floor. I turned around to Gloria and saw her eyes were glassy. I knew she was going to faint.

"Hey . . ." I yelled to one of the nurses, but just then Gloria sagged and I had to catch her myself. It was all I could do to carry her to the pit. "Hey!" I yelled to one of the trainers. "Doctor."

Nobody paid any attention to me. They were too busy picking up the bodies. The customers were standing on their seats, screaming in excitement.

I began rubbing Gloria's face with a wet towel. Mrs. Layden suddenly appeared beside me and took a bottle of smelling salts off the table by the cot.

"You go on to your dressing room," she said. "Gloria'll be all right in a minute. She's not used to the strain."

I was on a boat going to Port Said. I was on my way to the Sahara Desert to make that picture. I was famous and I had plenty of money. I was the most important motion picture director in the world. I was more important than Sergei Eisenstein. The critics of *Vanity Fair* and *Esquire* had agreed that I was a genius. I was walking around the deck, thinking of that marathon dance I once had been in, wondering what had become of all those girls and boys, when something hit me a terrific blow in the back of the head, knocking me unconscious. I had a feeling I was falling.

When I struck the water I began lashing out with my arms and legs because I was afraid of sharks. Something brushed my body and I screamed in fright.

I woke up swimming in water that was freezing cold. Instantly I knew where I was. "I've had a nightmare," I told myself. The thing that had brushed my body was a hundred-pound block of ice. I was in a small tank of water in the dressing room. I was still wearing my track suit. I climbed out, shivering, and one of the trainers handed me a towel.

The other trainers came in, carrying one of the contestants who was unconscious. It was Pedro Ortega. They carried him to the tank and dumped him in.

"Is that what happened to me?" I asked.

"That's right," the trainer said. "You passed out just as you left the dance floor—" Pedro whimpered something in Spanish and splashed the water, fighting to get out. The trainer laughed. "I'll say Socks knew what he was doing when he brought that tank in here," he said. "That ice water fixes 'em right up. Get off those wet pants and shoes."

...BY THE
SHERIFF OF
LOS ANGELES
COUNTY
TO THE
WARDEN OF
STATE PRISON...

9

HOURS ELAPSED 752
Couples Remaining 26

THE derby races were killing them off. Fifty-odd couples had been eliminated in two weeks. Gloria and I had come close to the finish once or twice, but by the skin of our teeth we managed to hang on. After we changed our technique we had no more trouble: we had stopped trying to win, not caring where we finished so long as it wasn't last.

We had got a sponsor too: Jonathan Beer, Non-Fattening. This came just in time. Our shoes were worn out and our clothes were ragged. Mrs. Layden sold Jonathan Beer on the idea of sponsoring us. *Sell St. Peter on the idea of letting me in, Mrs. Layden. I think I'm on my way.* They gave Gloria and me three pairs of shoes, three pairs of gray flannel trousers and three sweaters each with their product advertised on the backs of them.

I had gained five pounds since the contest started and was beginning to think that maybe we had some chance to win that thousand dollar first prize after all. But Gloria was very pessimistic.

"What are you going to do after this thing is over?" she asked.

"Why worry about that?" I said. "It's not over yet. I don't see what you're kicking about," I told her.

"We're better off than we've ever been—at least we know where our next meal is coming from."

"I wish I was dead," she said. "I wish God would strike me dead."

She kept saying that over and over again. It was beginning to get on my nerves.

"Some day God is going to do that little thing," I said.

"I wish He would . . . I wish I had the guts to do it for Him."

"If we win this thing you can take your five-hundred dollars and go away somewhere," I said. "You can get married. There are always plenty of guys willing to get married. Haven't you ever thought about that?"

"I've thought about it plenty," she said. "But I couldn't ever marry the kind of man I want. The only kind that would marry me would be the kind I wouldn't have. A thief or a pimp or something."

"I know why you're so morbid," I said. "You'll be all right in a couple of days. You'll feel better about it then."

"That hasn't got anything to do with it," she said. "I don't even get a backache from that. That's not it. This whole business is a merry-go-round. When we get out of here we're right back where we started."

"We've been eating and sleeping," I said.

"Well, what's the good of that when you're just postponing something that's bound to happen?"

"Hey, Jonathan Beer," Rocky Gravo called out. "Come over here——"

He was standing by the platform with Socks Donald. Gloria and I went over.

"How'd you kids like to pick up a hundred bucks?" Rocky asked.

"Doing what?" Gloria asked.

"Well, kids," Socks Donald said, "I've got a swell idea only I need a bit of some help——"

"That's the Ben Bernie influence," Gloria said to me.

"What?" Socks said.

"Nothing," Gloria said. "Go on—you need a bit of some help——"

"Yeah," Socks said. "I want you two kids to get married. A public wedding."

"Married?" I said.

"Now, wait a minute," Socks said. "It's not that bad. I'll give you fifty dollars apiece and after the marathon is over you can get divorced if you want to. It don't have to be permanent. It's just a showmanship angle. What do you say?"

"I say you're nuts," Gloria said.

"She doesn't mean that, Mr. Donald—" I said.

"The hell I don't," she said. "I've got no objections to getting married," she said to Socks, "but why don't you pick out Gary Cooper or some big-shot producer or director? I don't want to marry this guy. I got enough trouble looking out for myself——"

"It don't have to be permanent," Rocky said. "It's just showmanship."

"That's right," Socks said. "Of course, the cere-mony'll have to be on the square—we'll have to do that to get the crowd. But——"

"You don't need a wedding to get a crowd," Gloria said. "You're hanging 'em off the rafters now. Ain't it enough of a show to see these poor bastards falling all over the floor every night?"

"You don't get the angle," Socks said, frowning.

"The hell I don't," Gloria said. "I'm way ahead of you."

"You want to get in pictures and here's your chance," Socks said. "I already got some stores lined up to give you your wedding dress and your shoes and a beauty shop that'll fix you up—there'll be a lot of directors and supervisors here and they'll all be look-ing at nobody but you. It's the chance of a lifetime. What do you say, kid?" he asked me.

"I don't know—" I said, not wanting to make him sore. After all, he was the promoter. I knew if he got sore at us we were as good as disqualified.

"He says no," Gloria said.

77

"She does his thinking for him," Rocky said sarcastically.

"Okay," Socks said, shrugging his shoulders. "If you can't use a hundred dollars maybe some of these other kids can. At least," he said to me, "you know who wears the drawers in your family." He and Rocky both laughed.

"You just can't be polite to anybody, can you?" I said to Gloria when we had walked away. "We'll be out in the street any minute now."

"Might as well be now as tomorrow," she said.

"You're the gloomiest person I ever met," I said. "Sometimes I think you would be better off dead."

"I know it," she said.

When we came around by the platform again I saw Socks and Rocky talking earnestly to Vee Lovell and Mary Hawley, Couple No. 71.

"Looks like Socks is selling her a bill of goods," Gloria said. "That Hawley horse couldn't get in out of the rain."

James and Ruby Bates joined up and we walked four abreast. We were on friendly terms again since Gloria had stopped trying to talk Ruby into having an abortion performed. "Did Socks proposition you to get married?" Ruby asked.

"Yes," I said. "How did you know?"

"He's propositioned everybody," she said.

"We turned him down cold," Gloria said.

"A public wedding isn't so bad," Ruby said. "We had one——"

"You did?" I said, surprised. James and Ruby were so dignified and quiet and so much in love with each other I couldn't imagine them being married in a public ceremony.

"We were married in a marathon dance in Oklahoma," she said. "We got about three hundred dollars worth of stuff too. . . ."

"Her old man gave us the shotgun for a wedding present—" James said, laughing.

Suddenly a girl screamed behind us. We turned around. It was Lillian Bacon, Pedro Ortega's partner.

78

She was walking backwards, trying to get away from him. Pedro caught up with her, slamming her in the face with his fist. She sat down on the floor, screaming again. Pedro grabbed her by the throat with both hands, choking her and trying to lift her up. His face was the face of a maniac. There was no doubt he was trying to kill her.

Everybody started running for him at the same time. There was a lot of confusion.

James and I reached him first, grabbing him and breaking his hold on Lillian's neck. She was sitting on the floor, her body rigid, her arms behind her, her head thrown back, her mouth open—like a patient in a dentist's chair.

Pedro was muttering to himself and did not seem to recognize any of us. James shoved him and he staggered backward. I put my hands under Lillian's armpits, helping her to her feet. She was shaking like a muscle dancer.

Socks and Rocky rushed up and took Pedro by either arm.

"What's the big idea?" Socks roared.

Pedro looked at Socks, moving his lips but not saying anything. Then he saw Rocky and the expression on his face changed, becoming one of ferocious resentment. He suddenly twisted his arms free, stepping backward and reaching into his pocket.

"Look out—" somebody cried.

Pedro lunged forward, a knife in his hand. Rocky tried to dodge, but it all happened so quickly he never had a chance. The knife caught him across the left arm two inches below the shoulder. He yelled and started running. Pedro turned around to follow but before he could take a step Socks hit him in the back of the head with a leather blackjack. You could hear the plunk above the music of the radio. It sounded exactly like somebody thumping their finger against a watermellon. Pedro stood there, an idiotic grin on his face and Socks hit him again with the blackjack.

Pedro's arms fell and the knife dropped to the floor. He wobbled on his legs and then he went down.

"Get him out of here," Socks said, picking up the knife.

James Bates, Mack Aston and Vee Lovell lifted Pedro, carrying him off to the dressing room.

"Keep your seats, ladies and gentlemen—" Socks said to the audience. "Please——"

I was bracing Lillian from behind. She was still shaking.

"What happened?" Socks asked her

"He accused me of cheating—" she said. "Then he hit me and started choking me——"

"Go on, kids," Socks said. "Act like nothing has happened. Hey, nurse—help this girl to the dressing room—" Socks signaled to Rollo on the platform and the siren blew for a rest period. It was a few minutes early. The nurse took Lillian out of my arms and all the girls gathered around them, going into the dressing room.

As I went off I could hear Rollo making some kind of casual announcement over the loud speakers.

Rocky was standing at the wash basin, his coat and shirt off, dabbing at his shoulder with a handful of paper towels. The blood was streaming down his arm, running off his fingers.

"You better get the doctor on that," Socks said. "Where the hell is that doctor?" he bellowed.

"Here—" the doctor said, coming out of the lavatory.

"The only time we need you you're sitting on your ass," Socks said. "See what's the matter with Rocky."

Pedro was lying on the floor with Mack Aston straddling him, working on his stomach like a life guard with a man who has been drowning.

"Watch it—" Vee Lovell said, coming up with a bucket of water. Mack stepped back and Vee dumped the water in Pedro's face. It had no effect on him. He lay there like a log.

James Bates brought another bucket of water and doused him with that. Now Pedro began to show signs of life. He stirred, opening his eyes.

"He's coming to," Vee Lovell said.

"I better get Rocky to the hospital in my car," the doctor said, taking off his linen coat. "He's got a deep cut—almost to the bone. It'll have to be sutured. Who did it?"

"That bastard—" Socks said, pointing to Pedro with his leg.

"He must have used a razor," the doctor said.

"Here—" Socks said, handing him the knife. Socks had the leather blackjack in his other hand, the thong still around his wrist.

"Same thing," the doctor said, handing back the knife.

Pedro sat up, rubbing his jaw, a dazed look on his face.

"It wasn't your jaw," I said to him in my mind, "it was the back of your head."

"For Christ's sake, let's get going," Rocky said to the doctor. "I'm bleeding like a stuck pig. And you, you son of a bitch," he said to Pedro; "I'm going to prefer charges against you——"

Pedro looked at him fiercely, saying nothing.

"There won't be any charges filed," Socks said. "I'm having enough trouble keeping open now. Next time be careful who you cheat with."

"I wasn't cheating with anybody," Rocky said.

"Balls—" Socks said. "Take him out the back way, Doc."

"All right, Rocky," the doctor said. Rocky started out. The temporary gauze bandage on his arm was soaked already. The doctor draped a coat around Rocky's shoulders and they went out.

"Are you trying to bust up this contest?" Socks asked, turning his full attention to Pedro. "Whyn't you wait till this was over to get him?"

"I tried to cut his throat," Pedro stated calmly, in precise English. "He seduced my fiancée——"

"If he seduced your fiancée around here he's a magician," Socks said. "There's no place to seduce anybody."

"I know a place," I said in my mind.

Rollo Peters came in to the dressing room. "You

guys ought to be getting your sleep," he said. "Where's Rocky?" he asked, looking around.

"The doc took him to the hospital," Socks told him. "How are they out there?"

"They're calmed down," Rollo said. "I told 'em we were rehearsing a novelty act. What was the matter with Rocky?"

"Nothing much," Socks said. "He just damn near had his arm cut off by this greaseball, that's all." He handed him Pedro's knife. "Here, take this thing and get rid of it. You do the announcing till we find out about Rocky."

Pedro got up off the floor. "I am very sorry this happened before the audience," he said. "I am very sorry I have a very quick temper——"

"I guess it could have been worse," Socks said. "It could have happened at night when we had a full house. How's your head?"

"It is sore," Pedro said. "I am very sorry this happened. I wanted to win the thousand dollars——"

"You still got a chance," Socks said.

"You mean I am not disqualified? You mean you forgive me?"

"I forgive you—" Socks said, dropping the black-jack into his pocket.

...TO BE
BY SAID
WARDEN...

10

"Ladies and gentlemen," Rocky announced, "before the derby starts the management has asked me to tell you that there will be a public wedding here one week from tonight—a real, bona-fide wedding right here on the floor between Couple No. 71, Vee Lovell and Mary Hawley. Step out there, Vee and Mary, and let the ladies and gentlemen see what a cute couple you are——"

"—That is," Rocky said, "if they are not eliminated in the derby by then. We hope not, anyway. This public wedding is in line with the management's policy to give you nothing but high-class amusement——"

Mrs. Layden tugged at the back of my sweatshirt.

"What's the matter with Rocky's arm?" she asked in a whisper. You could see Rocky had had some kind of an accident. His right arm was through his coat sleeve in the usual way, but his left arm was in a sling and on that side he wore his coat like a cape.

"He sprained it," I said.

"They only took nine stitches in it," Gloria said, under her breath.

"That's why he wasn't here last night," Mrs. Layden said. "He had an accident——"

"Yes'm——"

85

"Did he fall?"

"Yes'm, I think so——"

"—introducing that beautiful screen star Miss Mary Brian. Will you take a bow, Miss Brian?"

Miss Brian took a bow. The audience applauded.

"—and that master comedian, Mr. Charley Chase——"

There was more applause as Charley Chase stood up in a box seat and took a bow.

"I hate these introductions," Gloria said.

"It would be all right if you were being introduced though, wouldn't it?" I said.

"Good luck—" Mrs. Layden said as we moved towards the platform.

"I'm sick of this," Gloria said. "I'm sick of looking at celebrities and I'm sick of doing the same thing over and over again——"

"Sometimes I'm sorry I ever met you," I said. "I don't like to say a thing like that, but it's the truth. Before I met you I didn't know what it was to be around gloomy people. . . ."

We crowded behind the starting line with the other couples.

"I'm tired of living and I'm afraid of dying," Gloria said.

"Say, that's a swell idea for a song," said James Bates, who had overheard her. "You could write a song about an old nigger down on the levee who was tired of living and afraid of dying. He could be heaving cotton and singing a song to the Mississippi River. Say, that's a good title—you could call it Old Man River——"

Gloria looked daggers at him, thumbing her nose.

"Hello, there—" Rocky called out to Mrs. Layden, who had arrived at the platform. "Ladies and gentlemen—" he said into the microphone, "I want to introduce to you the champion marathon dance fan of the world—a woman who hasn't missed a single night since this contest started. This is Mrs. Layden, and the management has issued a season pass to her—good any time, good all the time. A big hand for Mrs. Layden, ladies

and gentlemen.—Will you take a bow, Mrs. Layden
——"

Mrs. Layden hesitated a moment, badly rattled,
not knowing exactly what she should do or say. But
as the audience applauded she took a couple of steps
forward, bowing awkwardly. You could see this was
one of the biggest surprises of her life.

"You people who are dance fans have seen her here
before," Rocky said. "She is a judge in the derby every
night—we couldn't have a derby unless she was here.
How do you like the marathon dance, Mrs. Layden?"
he asked, stooping down on his haunches and moving
the microphone so she could talk into it.

"She hates it," Gloria said under her breath. "She
wouldn't come to one on a bet, you dumb bastard——"

"I like it," Mrs. Layden said. She was so nervous she
could hardly speak.

"Who's your favourite couple, Mrs. Layden?"

"My favorite couple is No. 22—Robert Syverten and
Gloria Beatty."

"Her favorite couple is No. 22, ladies and gentlemen,
sponsored by Jonathan Non-Fattening Beer—You're
pulling for them to win, are you Mrs. Layden?"

"Yes, I am and if I were younger, I'd be in this contest myself."

"That's fine. Thank you very much, Mrs. Layden.
All right—and now it gives me pleasure to present you
with a season pass, Mrs. Layden—the gift of the management. You can come in any time without paying——"

Mrs. Layden took the pass. She was so overwhelmed
with gratitude and emotion that she was smiling and
crying and nodding her head at the same time.

"That's another big moment," Gloria said.

"Shut up!" I said.

"All right—are the judges ready?" Rocky asked
straightening up.

"All ready," said Rollo, helping Mrs. Layden to a
chair in the judges' row.

"Ladies and gentlemen," Rocky announced, "most
of you are familiar with the rules and regulations of the

derby—but for the benefit of those who are seeing their first contest of this kind, I will explain so they will know what is going on. The kids race around the track for fifteen minutes, the boys heeling-and-toeing, the girls running or trotting as they so desire. If for any reason whatsoever one of them goes in the pit—the pit is in the center of the floor where the iron cots are—if for any reason one of them goes in the pit, the partner has to make two laps of the track to count for one. Is that clear?"

"Get going," somebody in the audience yelled.

"Are the nurses and trainers ready? Is the doctor standing by? All right—" He handed the starter's pistol down to Rollo. "Will you start the kids off, Miss Delmar?" Rocky asked into the microphone. "Ladies and gentlemen, Miss Delmar is a famous Hollywood author and novelist——"

Rollo took the pistol to Miss Delmar.

"Hold your hats, ladies and gentlemen," Rocky sang out. "Orchestra, get ready to give. All right, Miss Delmar——"

She shot the pistol and we were off.

Gloria and I let the racehorses set the pace. We made no effort to get up in front. Our system was to set a steady clip and hold it. There was no special prize money tonight. Even if there had been it would have made no difference to us.

The audience applauded and stamped their feet, begging for thrills, but this was one night they didn't get them. Only one girl, Ruby Bates, went into the pit and that was only for two laps. And for the first time in weeks nobody collapsed on the floor when the race was over.

But something had happened that frightened me. Gloria had pulled on my belt harder and longer than she ever had before. For the last five minutes of the derby it seemed she had no power of her own. I had practically dragged her around the track. I had a feeling we had just missed being eliminated ourselves. *We had just missed. Later that night Mrs. Layden told me she had spoken to the man who had checked us. We*

*had made only two more laps than the losers. That
chilled me. I made up my mind then that from now on
I had better forget my system and open up.*

The losers were Basil Gerard and Geneva Tomblin,
Couple No. 16. They were automatically disqualified.
I knew Geneva was glad it was over. Now she could
get married to the Captain of that live bait boat she had
met during the first week of the contest.

Geneva came back on the floor while we were
eating. She was dressed for the street and carried a
small grip.

"Ladies and gentlemen—" Rocky said into the microphone "—there's that marvelous kid who was eliminated
tonight. Doesn't she look pretty? A big hand, ladies
and gentlemen——"

The audience applauded and Geneva bowed from
side to side as she walked towards the platform.

"That's sportsmanship, ladies and gentlemen—she and
her partner lost a hard-fought derby, but she is smiling
—I'll let you in on a little secret, ladies and gentlemen—" he moved his face closer to the microphone and
whispered loudly: "She's in love—she's going to get
married. Yes, sir, ladies and gentlemen, the old marathon dance is the original home of romance, because
Geneva is marrying a man she met right here in this
hall. Is he in the house, Geneva? Is he here?"

Geneva nodded, smiling.

"Where is the lucky man?" Rocky asked. "Where
is he? Stand up, skipper, and take a bow——"

Everybody in the audience craned their necks, looking around.

"There he is—" Rocky shouted, pointing to the opposite end of the hall. A man had stepped over the railing from the box and was walking down the floor towards Geneva. He had the peculiar walk of a sailor.

"Say a word, skipper—" Rocky said, tilting the microphone stand over.

"I fell in love with Geneva the first time I saw her,"
the skipper said to the audience, "and a couple of days
later I asked her to quit the marathon dance and marry

me. But she said no, she didn't want to let her partner down; and there wasn't nothing for me to do but stick around. Now I'm glad she's disqualified and I can hardly wait for the honeymoon——"

The audience rocked with laughter. Rocky pulled the microphone stand upright again. "A silver shower for the new bride, ladies and gentlemen——"

The skipper grabbed the stand, yanked the microphone down to his mouth. "Never mind any contributions, folks," he said. "I guess I'm plenty able to take care of her——"

"The original Popeye," Gloria said.

There was no silver shower. Not a single coin hit the floor.

"You see how modest he is," Rocky said. "But I guess it's all right for me to tell you he is the captain of the Pacific Queen, an old four-master that's now a live-bait barge anchored three miles off the pier. There are water taxies every hour during the day—and if any of you folks want some good deep-sea fishing go out with the skipper——"

"Kiss her, you chump," somebody in the audience yelled.

The skipper kissed Geneva, then steered her off the floor while the audience howled and applauded.

"That's the second wedding the marathon dance has arranged, ladies and gentlemen," Rocky announced. "Don't forget our big public ceremony here next week when Couple No. 71, Vee Lovell and Mary Hawley, will get married right before your very eyes. Give——" he said to the orchestra.

Basil Gerard came out of the dressing room in his street clothes and went to the table to get his last meal on the house.

Rocky sat down on the platform, swinging his legs off.

"Look out for my coffee—" Gloria said.

"Okay, okay," Rocky said, moving the cup a little. "How's the food?"

"All right," I said.

Two middle-aged women came up to us. I had seen

90

them several times before, sitting in box seats. "Are you the manager?" one of them asked Rocky.

"Not exactly," Rocky said. "I'm the assistant manager. What was it you wanted?"

"I'm Mrs. Higby," the woman said. "This is Mrs. Witcher. Could we talk to you in private?"

"This is private as any place I got," Rocky said. "What was it you wanted?"

"We are the president and the vice-president——"

"What's the matter?" asked Socks Donald, coming around behind me.

"This is the manager," Rocky said, looking relieved.

The two women looked at Socks. "We are Mrs. Higby and Mrs. Witcher," Mrs. Higby said. "We are the president and the vice-president of the Mothers' League for Good Morals——"

"Aw-aw," Gloria said, under her breath.

"Yes?"

"We have a resolution for you," Mrs. Higby said, thrusting a folded paper into his hand.

"What's this all about?" Socks asked.

"Simply this," Mrs. Higby said. "Our Good Morals League has condemned your contest——"

"Wait a minute," Socks said. "Let's go to my office and talk this thing over——"

Mrs. Higby looked at Mrs. Witcher, who nodded. "Very well," she said.

"You kids come along—you too, Rocky. Hey nurse—take these cups and plates away—" He smiled at the two women. "You see," he said, "we don't let the kids do anything that would waste their energy. This way, ladies——"

He led the way off the floor behind the platform to his office, in a corner of the building. As we walked along Gloria pretended to stumble, falling heavily against Mrs. Higby, grabbing her around the head with her arms.

"Oh, I beg your pardon—I'm sorry—" Gloria said, looking on the floor to see what she had stumbled over.

Mrs. Higby said nothing, looking fiercely at Gloria,

straightening her hat. Gloria nudged me, winking behind Mrs. Higby's back.

"Remember, you kids are witnesses—" Socks whispered as we went into his office. This office had formerly been a lounge and was very small. I noticed there had been very little change in it since the day Gloria and I had come here to make entries for the marathon. The only change was two more pictures of nude women Socks had tacked on the wall. Mrs. Higby and Mrs. Witcher spotted these instantly, exchanging significant looks.

"Sit down, ladies," Socks said. "What is it, now?"

"The Mothers' League for Good Morals has condemned your contest," Mrs. Higby said. "We have decided it is low and degrading and a pernicious influence in the community. We have decided you must close it——"

"Close it?"

"At once. If you refuse we shall go to the City Council. This contest is low and degrading——"

"You got me all wrong, ladies," Socks said. "There's nothing degrading about this contest. Why, these kids love it. Every one of them has gained weight since it started——"

"You have a girl in this contest who is about to become a mother," Mrs. Higby said, "one Ruby Bates. It is criminal to have that girl running and walking all day when her baby is about to be born. Moreover, it is shocking to see her exhibiting herself to the world in that half-dressed condition. I should think she at least would have the decency to wear a coat——"

"Well, ladies," Socks said, "I never looked at that angle before. Ruby always seemed to know what she was doing—and I never paid no attention to her stomach. But I can see your point. You want me to put her out of the contest?"

"Most certainly," Mrs. Higby said. Mrs. Witcher nodded her head.

"All right, ladies," Socks said, "anything you say. I'm not hard to do business with. I'll even pay her hospital bills. . . . Thanks for telling me about it. I'll take care of that right away——"

"That isn't all," Mrs. Higby said. "Do you plan to have a public wedding next week or was that merely an announcement to draw a crowd of morons?"

"I never pulled anything phony in my life," Socks said. "That wedding is on the level. I wouldn't double-cross my customers like that. You can ask anybody I do business with what kind of a guy I am——"

"We are familiar with your reputation," Mrs. Higby said. "But even at that I can hardly believe you intend to sponsor a sacrilege like that——"

"The kids who are going to get married are very much in love with each other," Rocky said.

"We won't permit such mockery," Mrs. Higby said. "We demand that you close this contest immediately!"

"What'll happen to these kids if he does?" Gloria asked. "They'll go right back on the streets——"

"Don't try to justify this thing, young woman," Mrs. Higby said. "This contest is vicious. It attracts the bad element. One of your participants was an escaped murderer—that Chicago Italian——"

"Well, ladies, you surely don't blame me for that," Socks said.

"We certainly do. We are here because it is our duty to keep our city clean and free from all such influences——"

"Do you mind if me and my assistant go outside to talk this over?" Socks asked. "Maybe we can figure this out——"

". . . Very well," Mrs. Higby said.

Socks motioned to Rocky and they went outside.

"Do you ladies have children of your own?" Gloria asked, when the door had closed.

"We both have grown daughters," Mrs. Higby said.

"Do you know where they are tonight and what they're doing?"

Neither woman said anything.

"Maybe I can give you a rough idea," Gloria said. "While you two noble characters are here doing your

93

duty by some people you don't know, your daughters are probably in some guy's apartment, their clothes off, getting drunk."

Mrs. Higby and Mrs. Witcher gasped in unison.

"That's generally what happens to the daughters of reformers," Gloria said. "Sooner or later they all get laid and most of 'em don't know enough to keep from getting knocked up. You drive 'em away from home with your goddam lectures on purity and decency, and you're too busy meddling around to teach 'em the facts of life——"

"Why—" said Mrs. Higby, getting red in the face.

"I—" Mrs. Witcher said.

"Gloria—" I said.

"It's time somebody got women like you told," Gloria said, moving over and standing with her back to the door, as if to keep them in, "and I'm just the baby to do it. You're the kind of bitches who sneak in the toilet to read dirty books and tell filthy stories and then go out and try to spoil somebody else's fun——"

"You move away from that door, young woman, and let us out of here!" Mrs. Higby shrieked. "I refuse to listen to you. I'm a respectable woman. I'm a Sunday School teacher——"

"I don't move a f — — inch until I finish," Gloria said.

"Gloria——"

"Your Morals League and your goddam women's clubs," she said, ignoring me completely, "—filled with meddlesome old bitches who haven't had a lay in twenty years. Why don't you old dames go out and buy a lay once in a while? That's all that's wrong with you. . . ."

Mrs. Higby advanced on Gloria, her arm raised as if to strike her.

"Go on—hit me," Gloria said, not moving. "Hit me! —You even touch me and I'll kick your f — — head off!"

"You—goddam—whore!" Mrs. Higby said, furious with passion.

The door opened, bumping Gloria away from it. Socks and Rocky came in.

"This—this—" Mrs. Higby said, shaking her finger at Gloria.

"Don't stutter," Gloria said, "—say it. You know how to say the word. Whore. W-h-o——"

"Pipe down!" Socks said. "Ladies, me and my assistant have decided to take any suggestions you have to offer——"

"Our suggestion is you close this place at once!" Mrs. Higby said. "Else we shall go to the City Council in the morning——"

She started out, followed by Mrs. Witcher.

"Young woman," Mrs. Higby said to Gloria, "you ought to be in a reform school!"

"I was in one once," Gloria said. "There was a dame just like you in charge. She was a lesbian. . . ."

Mrs. Higby gasped again and went out, followed by Mrs. Witcher.

Gloria slammed the door behind them, then sat down in a chair and began sobbing. She covered her face with her hands and tried to fight it off, but it was no use. She slowly leaned forward in the chair, bending double, shaking and twitching with emotion, as if she had completely lost control of the upper half of her body. For a full moment the only sounds in the room were her sobs and the rise and fall of the ocean which came through the half-raised window.

Then Socks went over and laid his hand tenderly on Gloria's head. "Nix, kid, nix—" he said.

"Keep all this under your hat," Rocky said to me. "Don't say anything to the others——"

"I won't," I said. "Does this mean we'll have to close up?"

"I don't think so," Socks said. "It just means we'll have to try to grease somebody. I'll talk to my lawyer in the morning. In the meantime, Rocky—break the news to Ruby. She's got to quit. A lot of women have been squawking about her—" He looked at the door. "I should have stuck to my own racket," he said. "God-dam bastard women . . ."

...EXECUTED
AND PUT
TO DEATH...

11

MARATHON DANCE WAR STILL RAGES

Mothers' League Threatens

Mass Meeting Unless City

Council Will Close Contest

IS THIRD DAY OF CONTROVERSY

THE Mothers' League for Good Morals continued their war on the marathon dance today, threatening to take the issue directly to the citizens themselves unless the City Council closes the contest. The marathon dance has been in progress at a beach resort for the past 36 days.

Mrs. J. Franklin Higby and Mrs. William Wallace Witcher, president and first vice-president of the Morals League, appeared before the City Council again this afternoon, protesting the continuance of the dance. They were told by the Council that the City Attorney was making a thorough study of the law to determine what legal steps could be taken.

"We can't take any action until we know how the law reads," Tom Hinsdell, Council chief, said. "So far we have failed to find any specific statute that covers this case, but the City Attorney is examining all the codes."

"Would the City Council hesitate if a plague threatened our city?" Mrs. Higby said. "Certainly it wouldn't. If there are no specific laws to fit this situation let them pass emergency laws. The marathon dance is a plague—it is low and degrading and in the same hall there is a public bar that is a rendezvous for gangsters, racketeers and notorious criminals. Surely this is not the proper atmosphere for children . . ."

I HANDED the newspaper back to Mrs. Layden. "Mr. Donald told us his lawyer said the city couldn't do anything," I said.

"That doesn't make much difference," Mrs. Layden said. "Those women are out to close it and law or no law, they'll do it."

"I don't see any harm in the marathon," I said, "but they're right about the bar. I've seen a lot of tough characters in the Palm Garden. . . . How long do you think it'll take them to close us up?"

"I don't know," she said. "But they'll close it. What are you going to do then?"

"The first thing I'm going to do is get a lot of sun," I said. "I used to love the rain and hate the sun, but now it's the other way around. You don't get much sun in here——"

"After that what are you going to do?"

"I haven't made any plans," I said.

"I see. Where's Gloria?"

"She's putting on her track suit. She'll be out in a minute."

"She's beginning to weaken, isn't she? The doctor said he had to look at her heart several times a day."

"That doesn't mean anything," I said. "He looks at all of them. Gloria's all right."

Gloria wasn't all right and I knew it. We were having a lot of trouble with the derbies. I never will know

100

how we got by the last two nights. Gloria was in and out of the pit a dozen times in the two races. But I didn't jump at conclusions simply because the doctor examined her heart six or seven times a day. I knew he could never locate her trouble with a stethoscope.

"Lean over here, Robert," Mrs. Layden said. It was the first time she had ever used my given name and I was a little embarrassed. I leaned over the railing, swaying my body so nobody could say I was violating the rules of the contest by not being in motion. The hall was packed and jammed. "You know I'm your friend, don't you?" Mrs. Layden said.

"Yes'm, I know that."

"You know I got you your sponsor, don't you?"

"Yes'm, I know that."

"You trust me, don't you?"

"Yes'm, I trust you."

"Robert—Gloria's not the right kind of girl for you."

I didn't say anything, wondering what was coming next. I had never been able to understand why Mrs. Layden had taken such an interest in me unless . . . But it couldn't be that. She was old enough to be my grandmother.

"She'll never be any good," Mrs. Layden said. "She's an evil person and she'll wreck your life. You don't want your life wrecked, do you?"

"She's not going to wreck my life," I said.

"Promise me when you get out of this you'll never see her again."

"Oh, I'm not going to marry her or anything like that," I said. "I'm not in love with her. She's all right. She just gets a little depressed sometimes."

"She's not depressed," Mrs. Layden said. "She's bitter. She hates everything and everybody. She's cruel and she's dangerous."

"I didn't know you felt that way about her, Mrs. Layden."

"I'm an old woman," she said. "I'm a very, very—old, old woman. I know what I'm talking about. When this thing is over—Robert," she said suddenly, "I'm not as poor as you think I am. I look poor but I'm not poor at all. I'm rich. I'm very rich. I'm very eccentric. When you get out of here——"

"Hello—" Gloria said, coming from nowhere.

"——Hello," Mrs. Layden said.

"What's the matter?" Gloria asked quickly. "Am I interrupting something?"

"You're not interrupting anything," I told her.

Mrs. Layden opened the newspaper and started reading it. Gloria and I walked towards the platform.

"What was she saying about me?" Gloria asked.

"Nothing," I said. "We were just talking about the marathon closing——"

"You were talking about something else too. Why did she shut up like a clam when I got there?"

"You're imagining things—" I said.

"Ladies and gentlemen—" Rocky said into the microphone, "—or maybe after reading the newspapers," he went on when the crowd had quieted down, "I should say—Fellow Morons." There was a big laugh at this; the crowd knew what he meant. "You can see we're still going in the world's champion marathon dance," he said, "and we'll keep on going until only one contestant is left—the final winner. I want to thank you very much for coming out tonight and I'd like to remind you that tomorrow night is the night you can't afford to miss—our big public wedding, when Couple No. 71—Vee Lovell and Mary Hawley—will be married right here before your very eyes by a well-known minister of the city. If you haven't made your reservations you better do so at once——

"And now, before the derby starts, I'd like to introduce a few of our celebrities—" He looked at a piece of paper. "Ladies and gentlemen, one of our honor guests is none other than that handsome screen star, Bill Boyd. Will you take a bow, Mr. Boyd?——"

Bill (Screen) Boyd stood up, taking a bow, while the audience applauded.

"Next, another screen and stage star—Ken Murray. Mr. Murray has a party of distinguished guests with him. I wonder if he'd come up to the platform and introduce them himself?——"

The audience applauded loudly. Murray hesitated, but finally stepped over the railing and went to the platform.

"All right, folks—" he said, taking the microphone. "First a young featured player, Miss Anita Louise——"

Miss Louise stood.

"——and now Miss June Clyde——"

Miss Clyde stood.

"——Miss Sue Carol——"

Miss Carol stood.

"——Tom Brown——"

Tom Brown stood.

"——Thornton Freeland——"

Thornton Freeland stood.

"——and that's all, folks——"

Murray shook hands with Rocky and went back to his party.

"Ladies and gentlemen—" Rocky said.

"There's a big director over there he didn't introduce," I said to Gloria. "There's Frank Borzage. Let's go speak to him——"

"For what?" Gloria said.

"He's a director, isn't he? He might help you get in pictures——"

"The hell with pictures," Gloria said. "I wish I was dead——"

"I'm going," I said.

I strolled down the floor in front of the boxes, feeling very self-conscious. Two or three times I almost lost my nerve and turned back.

"It's worth it," I told myself. "He's one of the finest directors in the world. Some day I'll be as famous as he is and then I'll remind him of this——"

"Hello, Mr. Borzage," I said.

"Hello, son," he said. "Are you going to win to-night?"

"I hope so . . . I saw 'No Greater Glory.' I thought it was swell," I said.

"I'm glad you liked it——"

"That's what I want to be some day," I said. "A director like you——"

"I hope you are," he said.

"Well—" I said, "good-bye——"

I went back to the platform.

"That was Frank Borzage," I said to Kid Kamm.

"Yeah?——"

"He's a big director," I explained.

"Oh—," the Kid said.

"All right—" Rocky said. "Are the judges ready? Have they got their score sheets, Rollo?—All right, kids——"

We moved out to the starting line.

"Let's not take any chances tonight," I whispered to Gloria. "We can't fool around——"

"On your marks, there, kids," Rocky said. "Stand by nurses and trainers—Hold your hats, ladies and gentlemen—Orchestra, get ready to give——"

He shot the pistol himself.

Gloria and I jumped away, pushing through into second place, directly behind Kid Kamm and Jackie Miller. They were in front, the position usually held by James and Ruby Bates. As I went into the first turn I thought about James and Ruby, wondering where they were. It didn't seem like a derby without them.

At the finish of the first lap Mack Aston and Bess Cartwright sprinted in front of us and went into second place. I began to heel-and-toe faster than I ever had before. I knew I had to. All the weaklings had been eliminated. All these couples were fast.

I stayed in third place for six or seven laps and the audience began howling and yelling for us to move up. I was afraid to try that. You can pass a fast team only on the turn and that takes a lot of energy. So far Gloria was holding up fine and I didn't want to put too much pressure on her. I wasn't worried as long as she could keep propelling herself.

After eight minutes I commenced to get hot. I yanked off my sweatshirt and tossed it to a trainer. Gloria did likewise. Most of the girls were out of their sweatshirts now and the audience was howling. When the girls removed their sweatshirts they wore only small brassieres, and as they trotted around the track their breasts bounced up and down.

"Everything is fine now unless somebody challenges us," I told myself.

Just then we were challenged. Pedro Ortega and Lillian Bacon sped up alongside, trying to get inside at the turn. This was about the only way to pass a couple but it was not as easy as it sounds. You had to get at least two paces ahead on the straightaway and then swing sharply over at the turn. This was what Pedro had in the back of his mind. They collided with us at the turn, but Gloria managed to keep her feet and I dragged her through, holding our place.

I heard the audience gasp and I knew that meant somebody was staggering. In a moment more I heard a body hit the floor. I didn't look around! I kept poundin. This was old stuff to me now. When I got on the straightaway and could look without breaking my stride, I saw it was Mary Hawley, Vee Lovell's partner, who was in the pit. The nurses and trainers were working on her and the doctor was using his stethoscope——

"Give the solo the inside, kids—" Rocky yelled.

I moved over and Vee passed me. Now he had to make two laps to our one. He glanced in the pit as he passed, a look of agony on his face. I knew he was not in pain; he was only wondering when his partner would be out. . . . On his fourth solo lap she got up, coupling on again.

I signaled to the nurse for a wet towel and on the next lap she slammed it around my neck. I stuck the end of it between my teeth.

"Four minutes to go—" Rocky yelled.

This was one of the closest derbies we'd ever had. The Kid and Jackie were setting a terrific pace. I knew Gloria and I were in no danger as long as we held our own, but you never could tell when your partner would collapse. Past a certain point you kept moving automatically, without actually being conscious of moving. One moment you would be traveling at top speed and the next moment you started falling. This

105

was what I was afraid of with Gloria—collapsing. She was beginning to drag on my belt a little.

"Keep going!" I shouted to her in my mind, slowing down a fraction, hoping to relieve the strain on her. Pedro and Lillian evidently had been waiting for this. They shot by us on the turn, taking third place. Directly behind me I could hear the pounding of the others and I realized the entire field was bunched at Gloria's heels. I had absolutely no margin now.

I hitched my hip up high. That was a signal for Gloria to shift her hold on the belt. She did, changing to the right hand.

"Thank God," I said to myself. That was a good sign. That proved she was thinking all right.

"One minute to go—" Rocky announced.

I put on the steam now. Kid Kamm and Jackie had slowed the pace somewhat, thus slowing Mack and Bess and Pedro and Lillian. Gloria and I were between them and the others. It was a bad position. I prayed that nobody behind us had the energy for a spurt because I realized that the slightest bump would break Gloria's stride and put her on the floor. And if anybody hit the floor now . . .

I used every ounce of my strength to move up, to get just one step ahead, to remove that threat from behind. . . . When the gun sounded for the finish I turned around to catch Gloria. But she didn't faint. She staggered into my arms, shiny with perspiration, fighting to get air.

"Want a nurse?" Rocky yelled from the platform.

"She's all right," I said. "Let her rest a minute——"

Most of the girls were being helped into the dressing room, but the boys crowded around the platform to see who had been disqualified. The judges had handed their tally sheets to Rollo and Rocky, who were checking them.

"Ladies and gentlemen—" Rocky announced in a minute or two. "Here are the results of the most sensational derby you have ever seen. First place—Couple No. 18, Kid Kamm and Jackie Miller. Second place—Mack Aston and Bess Cartwright. Third place—Pedro

Ortega and Lillian Bacon. Fourth place—Robert Syverten and Gloria Beatty. Those were the winners—and now, the losers—the last team to finish—the couple that, under the rules and regulations, is disqualified and out of the marathon dance. That is Couple No. 11—Jere Flint and Vera Rosenfield——"

"You're crazy!" Jere Flint shouted, loud enough for everybody in the hall to hear. "That's wrong—" he said, moving closer to the platform.

"Look at 'em yourself," Rocky said, handing him the tally sheets.

"I wish it had been us," Gloria said, lifting her head. "I wish I had thrown the race——"

"Sh-h-h—" I said.

"I don't give a damn what these score cards say; they're wrong," Jere Flint said, handing them back to Rocky. "I know they're wrong. How the hell could we get eliminated when we weren't last?"

"Are you able to keep track of the laps while you're racing?" Rocky asked. He was trying to show Jere up. He knew it wasn't possible for anybody to do that,

"I can't do that," Jere said. "But I know we didn't go into the pit and Mary did. We started ahead of Vee and Mary and we finished ahead of 'em——"

"How about that, mister?" Rocky said to a man standing near-by. "You checked Couple No. 11——"

"You're mistaken, fellow," the man said to Jere. "I checked you carefully——"

"It's too bad, son," Socks Donald said, coming through the crowd of judges. "You had tough luck ——"

"It wasn't tough luck; it was a goddam frame-up," Jere said. "You ain't kidding anybody. If Vee and Mary had been eliminated you wouldn't have a wedding tomorrow——"

"Now—now—" Socks said. "You run on to the dressing room——"

"Okay," Jere said. He walked over to the man who had kept check on him and Vera. "How much is Socks giving you for this?" he asked.

"I don't know what you're talking about——"

Jere turned sidewise, slamming the man in the mouth with his fist, knocking him down.

Socks ran over to Jere, squaring off, glaring at him his hand in his hip pocket.

"If you pull that blackjack on me I'll make you eat it," Jere told him. Then he walked away, going across the floor towards the dressing room.

The audience was standing, jabbering, trying to see what was going on.

"Let's get dressed," I said to Gloria.

... UPON
THE 19TH DAY
OF THE MONTH
OF SEPTEMBER,
IN THE YEAR
OF OUR LORD,
1935 ...

12

ALL day Gloria had been very morbid. I asked her a hundred times what she was thinking about. "Nothing," she would reply. *I realize now how stupid I was. I should have known what she was thinking. Now that I look back on that last night I don't see how I possibly could have been so stupid. But in those days I was dumb about a lot of things . . . The judge is sitting up there, making his speech, looking through his glasses at me, but his words are doing the same thing to my body that his eyesight is doing to his glasses—going right through without stopping, rushing out of the way of each succeeding look and each succeeding word. I am not hearing the judge with my ears and my brain any more than the lenses of his glasses are catching and imprisoning each look that comes through them. I hear him with my feet and my legs and torso and arms, with everything but my ears and brain. With my ears and brain I hear a newsboy in the street shouting something about King Alexander, I hear the rolling of the street cars, I hear automobiles, I hear the warning bells of the traffic semaphores; in the courtroom I hear people breathing and moving their feet, I hear the wood*

speaking in a bench, I hear the light splash as some-
one spits in the cuspidor. All these things I hear with
my ears and my brain, but I hear the judge with my
body only. If you ever hear a judge say to you what
this one is saying to me, you will know what I mean.

This was one day Gloria had no reason to be morbid. The crowds had been coming and going all day,
since noon the place had been packed, and now, just
before the wedding, there were very few vacant seats
left and most of them had been reserved. The entire
hall had been decorated with so many flags and so
much red, white and blue bunting that you expected
any moment to hear firecrackers go off and the band
play the national anthem. The whole day had been
full of excitement: the workmen decorating the in-
terior, the big crowds, the rehearsals for the wedding,
the rumors that the Morals League women were coming down to set fire to the hall—and the two complete
new outfits the Jonathan Beer people had sent Gloria
and me.

This was one day Gloria had no reason to be morbid,
but she was more morbid than ever.

"Son—" a man called from a box. I had never seen
him before. He was motioning for me to come over.

"You won't be in that seat long," I told him in my
mind. "That's Mrs. Layden's regular seat. When she
comes you'll have to move."

"Aren't you the boy of Couple 22?" he asked.

"Yessir," I said.

"Where's your partner?"

"She's down there—" I replied, pointing towards
the platform where Gloria stood with the other girls.

"Get her," the man said. "I want to meet her."

"All right," I said, going to get Gloria. "Now who
can that be?" I asked myself.

"There's a man down here who wants to meet you,"
I said to Gloria.

"I don't want to meet anybody."

"This man's no bum," I said. "He's well-dressed. He
looks like somebody."

"I don't care what he looks like," she said.

112

"He may be a producer," I said. "Maybe you've made a hit with him. Maybe this is your break."

"The hell with my break," she said.

"Come on," I said. "The man's waiting."

She finally came with me.

"This motion picture business is a lousy business," she said. "You have to meet people you don't want to meet and you have to be nice to people whose guts you hate. I'm glad I'm through with it."

"You're just starting with it," I said, trying to cheer her up. *I never paid any attention to her remark then, but now I realize it was the most significant thing she had ever said.*

"Here she is—" I said to the man.

"You don't know who I am, do you?" the man asked.

"No, sir——"

"My name is Maxwell," he said. "I'm the advertising manager for Jonathan Beer."

"How do you do, Mr. Maxwell," I said, reaching over to shake hands with him. "This is my partner, Gloria Beatty. I want to thank you for sponsoring us."

"Don't thank me," he said. "Thank Mrs. Layden. She brought you to my attention. Did you get your packages today?"

"Yessir," I said, "and they came just in time. We certainly needed clothes. These marathon dances are pretty hard on your clothes—Have you ever been here before?"

"No, and I wouldn't be here now if Mrs. Layden hadn't insisted. She's been telling me about the derbies. Are you having one tonight?"

"A little thing like a wedding couldn't stop the derby," I said. "It goes on right after the ceremony——"

"So long—" Gloria said, walking off.

"Did I say something wrong?" Mr. Maxwell asked.

"No, sir—she's got to go down there and get her final instructions. The wedding starts pretty soon."

He frowned and I could tell he knew I was merely lying to cover Gloria's bad manners. He watched Gloria walking down the floor a minute and then looked back at me. "What chance do you have to win the derby tonight?" he asked.

"We've got a good chance," I said. "Of course, the big thing is not so much to win as it is to keep from losing. If you finish last you're disqualified."

"Suppose Jonathan Beer offered twenty-five dollars to the winner," he said. "You think you'd have a chance to get it?"

"We'll certainly try like the devil," I told him.

"In that case—all right," he said, looking me up and down. "Mrs. Layden tells me you're ambitious to get in the movies?"

"I am," I said. "Not as an actor though. I want to be a director."

"You wouldn't like a job in the brewery business, eh?"

"I don't believe I would——"

"Have you ever directed a picture?"

"No, sir, but I'm not afraid to try it. I know I could make good," I said. "Oh, I don't mean a big feature like Boleslawsky or Mamoulian or King Vidor would make—I mean something else at first——"

"For instance——"

"Well, like a two- or three-reel short. What a junk-man does all day, or the life of an ordinary man—you know, who makes thirty dollars a week and has to raise kids and buy a home and a car and a radio—the kind of a guy bill collectors are always after. Something different, with camera angles to help tell the story——"

"I see—" he said.

"I didn't mean to bore you," I said, "but it's so seldom I can find anybody who'll listen to me that when I do I never know when to stop talking."

"I'm not bored. As a matter of fact, I'm very much interested," he said. "But maybe I've said too much myself——"

"Good evening—" Mrs. Layden said, entering the box. Mr. Maxwell stood up. "That's my seat, John," Mrs. Layden said. "You sit over here." Mr. Maxwell laughed and took another chair. "My, my, don't you look handsome," Mrs. Layden said to me.

114

"This is the first time in my life I ever had on a tuxedo," I said blushing. "Mr. Donald rented tuxedoes for all the boys and dresses for the girls. We're all in the wedding march."

"What do you think of him, John?" Mrs. Layden asked Mr. Maxwell.

"He's all right," Mr. Maxwell said.

"I trust John's judgement implicitly," Mrs. Layden said to me. I began to understand now why Mr. Maxwell had asked me all those questions.

"——Down this way, you kids—" Rocky said into the microphone. "Down this way— Ladies and gentlemen. We are about to have the public wedding between Couple No. 71—Vee Lovell and Mary Hawley—and please remember, the entertainment for the night is not over when the marriage is finished. That's only the beginnin'—" he said; "—only the beginnin'. After the wedding we have the derby——"

He leaned over while Socks Donald whispered something to him.

"Ladies and gentlemen," Rocky announced, "I take great pleasure in introducing the minister who will perform the service—a minister you all know, Rev. Oscar Gilder. Will you come up, Mr. Gilder?"

The minister came out on the floor and walked towards the platform while the audience applauded.

"Get your places," Socks said to us. We went to our assigned positions, the girls on one side of the platform and the boys on the other.

"Before the grand march starts," Rocky said, "I want to thank those who have made this feature possible." He looked at a sheet of paper. "The bride's wedding gown," he said, "was donated by Mr. Samuels of the Bon-Ton Shop. Will you stand, Mr. Samuels?"

Mr. Samuels stood, bowing to the applause.

"Her shoes were donated by the Main Street Slipper Shop—Is Mr. Davis here? Stand up, Mr. Davis."

Mr. Davis stood.

"——Her stockings and silken—er—you-know-whats were donated by the Polly-Darling Girls' Bazaar. Mr. Lightfoot, where are you?——"

Mr. Lightfoot stood as the audience howled.

"——and her hair was marcelled by the Pompadour Beauty Shop. Is Miss Smith here?"

Miss Smith stood.

"——And the groom's outfit, from head to foot, was donated by the Tower Outfitting Company. Mr. Tower——"

Mr. Tower stood.

"——All the flowers in the hall and that the girls are wearing are the gift of the Sycamore Ridge Nursery. Mr. Dupré——"

Mr. Dupré stood.

"——And now, ladies and gentlemen, I turn the microphone over to the Rev. Oscar Gilder, who will perform the ceremony for these marvelous kids——"

He handed the microphone stand to Rollo, who stood it on the floor in front of the platform. Rev. Gilder moved behind it, nodding to the orchestra, and the wedding march began.

The procession started, the boys on one side and the girls on the other, going down to the end of the hall and then back to the minister. It was the first time I had seen some of the girls when they weren't in slacks or track suits.

We had rehearsed the march twice that afternoon, being taught to come to a full stop after each step before taking another. When the bride and groom came into view from behind the platform, the audience cheered and applauded.

Mrs. Layden nodded to me as I passed.

At the platform we took our places while Vee and Mary, and Kid Kamm and Jackie Miller, the best man and the maid-of-honor continued to where the minister was standing. He motioned for the orchestra to stop and began the ceremony. All during the ceremony I kept looking at Gloria. I hadn't had a chance to tell her how rude she had been to Mr. Maxwell, so I tried to catch her eye to let her know I had plenty to tell her when we got together.

"——And I now pronounce you man and wife—" Dr. Gilder said. He bowed his head and began to pray:

The Lord is my shepherd; I shall not want. He maketh me to lie down in green pastures: he leadeth me beside the still waters. He restoreth my soul: he leadeth me in the paths of righteousness for his name's sake. Yea, though I walk through the valley of the shadow of death, I will fear no evil: for thou art with me; thy rod and thy staff they comfort me. Thou preparest a table before me in the presence of mine enemies: thou anointest my head with oil; my cup runneth over. Surely goodness and mercy shall follow me all the days of my life; and I will dwell in the house of the Lord for ever.

. . . When the minister had finished Vee kissed Mary timidly on the cheek and we swarmed around. The hall rocked with applause and shouts.

"Just a minute—just a minute—" Rocky yelled into the microphone. "Just a minute, ladies and gentlemen——"

The confusion died down and at that moment, at the opposite end of the hall, in the Palm Garden, there was the clear, distinct sound of glass shattering.

"Don't—" a man screamed. Five shots followed this, so close together they sounded like one solid strip of noise.

Instantly the audience roared.

"Keep your seats—keep your seats—" Rocky yelled. . . .

The other boys and girls were running towards the Palm Garden to see what had happened, and I joined them. Socks Donald passed me, reaching into his hip pocket.

I jumped over the railing into an empty box and followed Socks into the Palm Garden. A crowd of people were standing in a circle, looking down and jabbering to each other. Socks pushed through and I followed him.

A man was dead on the floor.

"Who did it?" Socks asked.

"A guy over there—" somebody said.

Socks pushed out with me behind him. I was a little surprised to discover Gloria was directly behind me.

The man who had done the shooting was standing at the bar, leaning on his elbow. Blood was streaming down his face. Socks went up to him.

"He started it, Socks," the man said. "—He was trying to kill me with a beer bottle——"

"Monk, you son of a bitch—" Socks said, hitting him in the face with the blackjack. Monk sagged against the bar but did not fall. Socks continued to hit him in the face with the blackjack, again and again and again, splattering blood all over everything and everybody nearby. He literally beat the man to the floor.

"Hey, Socks—" somebody called.

Thirty feet away there was another group of people standing in a circle, looking down and jabbering to each other. We pushed our way through—and there she lay.

"Goddam—" Socks Donald said.

It was Mrs. Layden, a single hole in the front of her forehead. John Maxwell was kneeling beside her, holding her head . . . then he placed the head gently on the floor, and stood up. Mrs. Layden's head slowly turned sidewise and a little poof of blood that had collected in the crater of her eye spilled out on the floor.

John Maxwell saw Gloria and me.

"She was coming around to be a judge in the derby," he said. "She was hit by a stray bullet——"

"I wish it was me—" Gloria said under her breath.

"Goddam—" Socks Donald said.

We were all assembled in the girls' dressing room. There were very few people outside in the hall, only the police and several reporters.

"I guess you kids know why I got you in here," Socks said slowly, "and I guess you know what I'm going to say. There ain't no use for anybody to feel bad about what's happened—it's just one of those things. It's tough on you kids and it's tough on me. We had just got the marathon started good——

"Rocky and I have been talking it over and we've decided to take the thousand-dollar prize and split it up between all of you—and I'm going to throw in another grand myself. That'll give everybody fifty bucks a piece. Is that fair?"

"Yes—" we said.

"Don't you think there's any chance to keep going?" Kid Kamm asked.

"Not a chance," Socks said, shaking his head. "Not with that Purity League after us——"

"Kids," Rocky said, "we've had a lot of fun and I've enjoyed working with you. Maybe some time we can have another marathon dance——"

"When do we get this dough?" Vee Lovell asked.

"In the morning," Socks said. "Any of you kids that want to can stay here tonight, just like you been doing. But if you want to leave, there's nothing to stop you. I'll have the dough for you in the morning any time after ten. Now, I'll say so-long— I got to go to police headquarters."

...IN
THE MANNER
PROVIDED BY
THE LAWS
OF
THE STATE
OF
CALIFORNIA
AND...

13

GLORIA and I walked across the dance floor, my heels making so much noise I couldn't be sure they belonged to me. Rocky was standing at the front door with a policeman.

"Where you kids going?" Rocky asked.

"To get some air," Gloria said.

"Coming back?"

"We'll be back," I told him. "We're just going to get a little air. It's been a long time since we been outside——"

"Don't be long," Rocky said, looking at Gloria and wetting his lips significantly.

"F—— you," Gloria said, going outside.

It was after two o'clock in the morning. The air was damp and thick and clean. It was so thick and so clean I could feel my lungs biting it off in huge chunks.

"I bet you are glad to get that kind of air," I said to my lungs.

I turned around and looked at the building.

"So that's where we've been all the time," I said. "Now I know how Jonah felt when he looked at the whale."

"Come on," Gloria said.

We walked around the side of the building onto the pier. It stretched out over the ocean as far as I could see, rising and falling and groaning and creaking with the movements of the water.

"It's a wonder the waves don't wash this pier away," I said.

"You're hipped on the subject of waves," Gloria said.

"No, I'm not," I said.

"That's all you've been talking about for a month——"

"All right, stand still a minute and you'll see what I mean. You can feel it rising and falling——"

"I can feel it without standing still," she said, "but that's no reason to get yourself in a sweat. It's been going on for a million years."

"Don't think I'm crazy about this ocean," I said. "It'll be all right with me if I never see it again. I've had enough ocean to last me the rest of my life."

We sat down on a bench that was wet with spray. Up towards the end of the pier several men were fishing over the railing. The night was black; there was no moon, no stars. An irregular line of white foam marked the shore.

"This air is fine," I said.

Gloria said nothing, staring into the distance. Far down the shore on a point there were lights.

"That's Malibu," I said. "Where all the movie stars live."

"What are you going to do now?" she finally said.

"I don't know exactly. I thought I'd go see Mr. Maxwell tomorrow. Maybe I could get him to do something. He certainly seemed interested."

"Always tomorrow," she said. "The big break is always coming tomorrow."

Two men passed, carrying deep-sea fishing poles. One of them was dragging a four-foot hammerhead shark behind him.

"This baby'll never do any more damage," he said to the other man. . . .

"What are you going to do?" I asked Gloria.

"I'm going to get off this merry-go-round," she said. "I'm through with the whole stinking thing."

"What thing?"

"Life," she said.

"Why don't you try to help yourself?" I said. "You got the wrong attitude about everything."

"Don't lecture to me," she said.

"I'm not lecturing," I said, "but you ought to change your attitude. On the level. It affects everybody you come in contact with. Take me, for example. Before I met you I didn't see how I could miss succeeding. I never even thought of failing. And now——"

"Who taught you that speech?" she asked. "You never thought that up by yourself."

"Yes, I did," I said.

She looked down the ocean towards Malibu. "Oh, what's the use in me kidding myself—" she said in a moment. "I know where I stand . . ."

I did not say anything, looking at the ocean and thinking about Hollywood, wondering if I'd ever been there or was I going to wake up in a minute back in Arkansas and have to hurry down and get my newspapers before it got daylight.

"—Sonofabitch," Gloria was saying to herself. "You needn't look at me that way," she said. "I know I'm no good——"

"She's right," I said to myself; "she's exactly right. She's no good——"

"I wish I'd died that time in Dallas," she said. "I always will think that doctor saved my life just for one reason——"

I did not say anything to that, still looking at the ocean and thinking how exactly right she was about being no good and that it was too bad she didn't die that time in Dallas. She certainly would have been better off dead.

"I'm just a misfit. I haven't got anything to give anybody," she was saying. "Stop looking at me that way," she said.

"I'm not looking at you any way," I said. "You can't see my face——"

"Yes, I can," she said.

She was lying. She couldn't see my face. It was too dark.

"Don't you think we ought to go inside?" I said. "Rocky wanted to see you——"

"That p——k," she said. "I know what he wants, but he'll never get it again. Nobody else will, either."

"What?" I said.

"Don't you know?"

"Don't I know what," I said.

"What Rocky wants."

"Oh—" I said. "Sure. It just dawned on me."

"That's all any man wants," she said, "but that's all right. Oh, I didn't mind giving it to Rocky; he was doing me as much of a favor as I did him—but suppose I get caught?"

"You're not just thinking of that, are you?" I asked.

"Yes, I am. Always before this time I was able to take care of myself. Suppose I do have a kid?" she said. "You know what it'll grow up to be, don't you. Just like us."

"She's right," I said to myself; "she's exactly right. It'll grow up to be just like us——"

"I don't want that," she said. "Anyway, I'm finished. I think it's a lousy world and I'm finished. I'd be better off dead and so would everybody else. I ruin everything I get around. You said so yourself."

"When did I say anything like that?"

"A few minutes ago. You said before you met me you never even thought of failing. . . . Well, it isn't my fault. I can't help it. I tried to kill myself once, but I didn't and I've never had the nerve to try again. . . . You want to do the world a favor? . . ." she asked.

I did not say anything, listening to the ocean sloshle against the pilings, feeling the pier rise and fall, and thinking that she was right about everything she had said.

Gloria was fumbling in her purse. When her hand came out it was holding a small pistol. I had never seen the pistol before, but I was not surprised. I was not in the least surprised.

"Here—" she said, offering it to me.

"I don't want it. Put it away," I said. "Come on, let's go back inside. I'm cold——"

"Take it and pinch-hit for God," she said, pressing it into my hand. "Shoot me. It's the only way to get me out of my misery."

"She's right," I said to myself. "It's the only way to get her out of her misery." *When I was a little kid I used to spend the summers on my grandfather's farm in Arkansas. One day I was standing by the smokehouse watching my grandmother making lye soap in a big iron kettle when my grandfather came across the yard, very excited. "Nellie broke her leg," my grandfather said. My grandmother and I went over the stile into the garden where my grandfather had been plowing. Old Nellie was on the ground whimpering, still hitched to the plow. We stood there looking at her, just looking at her. My grandfather came back with the gun he had carried at Chickamauga Ridge. "She stepped in a hole," he said, patting Nellie's head. My grandmother turned me around, facing the other way. I started crying. I heard a shot. I still hear that shot. I ran over and fell down on the ground, hugging her neck. I loved that horse. I hated my grandfather. I got up and went to him, beating his legs with my fists. . . . Later that day he explained that he loved Nellie too, but that he had to shoot her. "It was the kindest thing to do," he said. "She was no more good. It was the only way to get her out of her misery. . . ."*

I had the pistol in my hand.

"All right," I said to Gloria. "Say when."

"I'm ready."

"Where?——"

"Right here. In the side of my head."

The pier jumped as a big wave broke.

"Now?——"

"Now."

I shot her.

The pier moved again, and the water made a sucking noise as it slipped back into the ocean.

I threw the pistol over the railing.

127

One policeman sat in the rear with me while the other one drove. We were traveling very fast and the siren was blowing. It was the same kind of a siren they had used at the marathon dance when they wanted to wake us up.

"Why did you kill her?" the policeman in the rear seat asked.

"She asked me to," I said.

"You hear that, Ben?"

"Ain't he an obliging bastard?" Ben said, over his shoulder.

"Is that the only reason you got?" the policeman in the rear seat asked.

"They shoot horses, don't they?" I said.

...MAY GOD HAVE MERCY ON YOUR SOUL...

THEY SHOOT HORSES, DON'T THEY?

Screenplay by Robert E. Thompson

FOREWORD TO THE SCREENPLAY
by
SYDNEY POLLACK

FOR YEARS people in Hollywood have been talking
about making a film from Horace McCoy's brilliant
novel—it's said that one of the first to express interest
was Charlie Chaplin—but it has taken nearly thirty-
five years for the film finally to be made. Some of the
reasons for the delay can be guessed at. It has surely
been thought by many people in the film industry to
be too "down beat" to have wide audience appeal;
and then possibly there hasn't before been sufficient
distance in time from the painful events that provide
the background for the novel, for the period and the
book to be seen clearly. Happily the time is past when
it was necessary for all stories to be romanticized or
to be given happy endings in order to be made into
films. And I don't know how many years must pass
for an event or a period to be considered "history,"
but certainly the '30s and dance marathons meet the
requirements now: indeed, a tendency seems to be
abroad to romanticize, to glamorize the '30s. In any
event, we have finally gotten around to making a film
of *They Shoot Horses, Don't They?*

The cases are not rare where very bad books have
made very good films. A novel can provide an in-
triguing basis on which the process of adaptation becomes one of creation—of new character complica-
tions and depths, and often of entirely new events and
environments. But *They Shoot Horses, Don't They?*
is a splendid novel to begin with, and in essential form
and content a very "cinematic" one; it demanded to
be treated with great care and attention to Horace
McCoy's intents and methods. Which is not to say
that a literal, line-by-line *transcription* was called for
—a novel is not a film script and will not serve as one.
So, for the delicate job of *translating*—rather than

133

transcribing—from the one medium to the other, I went to Robert E. Thompson, a man who both loved and understood the novel. He wrote the final screenplay in about six weeks. A couple of the specific problems which we hope we've solved in effecting this translation may be worth brief discussion.

For one example, the stark simplicity of the book is essential to its power. But where Horace McCoy can give an extremely lean character line, relying on the reader to fill in the "backs" and "sides" of a character from his own imagination, a film director's problem is rather different. When a film maker stands a person on the screen, that character has breadth and depth simply by virtue of being seen, and those dimensions must be filled in with action and dialogue in order for the character not to seem hollow. So some invention was needed to make the characters fully three-dimensional without violating the spare, simple flavor which McCoy intended and which does contribute so much to the work's success.

Then, the structure of the novel, although it *almost* anticipates the much later cinematic device of the flash-forward, in fact tells its story in flash-backs. Time present is established in the brief opening section as Robert Syverton's trial for the shooting of Gloria. But since it seemed very important to the film to create a sense of immediacy in the marathon itself, and thanks to the acceptance into the syntax of film of the flash-forward, we chose to reverse McCoy's structure. The marathon is established as time present and glimpses of Robert's trial are interspersed throughout the film as flash-forwards. The reversal may be considered only a technical change: the "facts" of the story are delivered to the film's viewers in substantially the same order as they were to the readers of the novel; but it is by just such nearly undetectable devices—when they're properly chosen and well executed—that all narrative art is made to realize its fullest potential.

McCoy was writing about people who go 'round and 'round, putting one foot in front of the other, waiting for a pot of gold at the end of a rainbow; they continue because the prospects of reality in the outside world are just too tough. I think that's the reason he didn't have a winner in the marathon: that would have been antithetical to his concept, which was what we have since learned to call existential and absurdist. He solved this problem by having the marathon aborted, the police forcing it to close because of a shooting that takes place in the dance hall. It seemed to me that to present-day film audiences that device would seem arbitrary, particularly in the context of the already melodramatic circumstances of the marathon itself. And then, there is the inevitability, even relentlessness, of Gloria's movement toward death. We wanted to retain that inevitability. It seemed that the shooting and the ending of the marathon left questions open as to what might have become of Gloria if the dance had played itself out. Would she still have committed suicide? Even if she had won? And so, retaining McCoy's concept of "no winners," we tried to bring the characters to his conclusion without using the shooting.

I have a personal aversion to ending a film at its precise high point. (At the ending of "A Streetcar Named Desire," when Blanche is led out she says, "I've always relied on the kindness of strangers." Most people, thinking about the play, remember that as its last line. But there is a moment's pause after Blanche leaves, and back at the poker table one of the characters says, "The name of this game is 'Seven Card Stud.'") The last shot in our film, which happens the moment after Robert delivers the climactic line, "They shoot horses, don't they?" is a long view of the dancers filing back onto the floor and beginning their excruciating parade all over again, apparently in the blind hope that this dance of life—or dance of death—will go on and on and on. As the sign on top of the clock says, "How long can they last?"

The shooting went smoothly. Because it was necessary to capture the gradual deterioration of each of the contestants, we shot in continuity: we began on page one and continued in sequence right to the end. This is almost never done in making films, for economic reasons too complicated to get into here. But the luxury of shooting in this way contributed greatly to everybody's sense of involvement. As we worked on, you could see the fatigue come over the actors as they entered the set. For sixty-three days we worked in the same surroundings, indoors, on the dance floor, with the same band. The dancers began to meld into each other, each learning the most comfortable position to assume in relation to his partner. After the first few weeks you could feel the depression and it became impossible for me to tell sometimes whether it was makeup or real exhaustion. The work was certainly very far from glamorous.

The novel is often called a "minor masterpiece." It was well reviewed on its publication in 1935, but has never achieved the celebrity in this country that it did abroad, especially among the French existentialists. It is a perfect allegory, a perfect microcosm of existence as seen through McCoy's eyes, and although a film, once begun, takes on its own life and dictates its own path and movement, our hope here was to remain as true as possible to McCoy's intentions and the existential world about which he wrote.

FADE IN:

1. EXT PASTURE DAY (PAST) ANGLE ON STALLION

loping free and unhindered . . . turning, stopping, racing.

2. TRAVELING

with the stallion. Its long mane now a lacy filigree printed against the sky, now a swirl of matted hues. Soft diffused sunlight singes the grass and sky. The pasture is set high so that there is no sense of constriction. The last fringe of grass seems merely to bend into an infinity of limitless time and space.

3. CAMERA LOPING RAPIDLY

through the tall grass towards the sun. The SOUND of waves lapping a distant shore.

4. EXT BEACH DAY (PRESENT) EXTREME LONG SHOT

of ROBERT walking TOWARDS CAMERA. Behind him the grey, desolate, gull-flecked beach stretches on until sand and water seem to become one. We HEAR very faintly in the distance:

ROCKY'S VOICE

Okay! Now all you kids got a release form. You fill it out, you sign it . . . then you hand it over when you get your official entry numbers.

5. CLOSE TRAVELING

with Robert as he walks along the edge of the beach, inadverently crossing and recrossing the constantly shifting boundary between sand and water. His trousers are rolled. A pair of scuffed and weathered cowboy boots are laced about his neck. In the further distance we HEAR band sidemen TUNING their instruments, RIFFING through a few practice bars of some period standard . . . and always in the foreground . . . the rhythmic systole and diastole of WAVES.

6. EXT PASTURE DAY (PAST) LOW ANGLE

on the stallion rearing into a sudden glare of sunlight, its muscles rippling in long waves.

7. MOVE IN TO CLOSE ANGLE

of young boy. He watches the stallion with the kind of raptness peculiarly granted to the still innocent. He wears knickers and a cap. His features are obscured by the thrust of sunlight, but we sense that he is perhaps eight or nine years old. This is ROBERT AS A CHILD.

ROCKY'S VOICE

Only READ it first. You break a leg, we fix it. You catch a cold, there's free aspirin. But acts of God, the management is strictly not to be held to account.

8. FULL SHOT OF GRANDFATHER

Gnarled hands . . . slightly and very reluctantly stooped. Wearing overalls and a kerchief, he carries a canvas game bag and a shotgun crooked down through one arm. Like the boy, whom he stands beside now, his features are obscured, but we realize that he is far too old to be the boy's father. He touches the boy's shoulder to urge him along.

ROCKY'S VOICE

Fire, flood and double pneumonia, that's between you and Him. So read it, and then sign. But no release . . . no number. Understood? Okay. Now I know a lotta you been the circuit. Well, there's nothing that different here. Better maybe. But the same setup, the same kind of rules. For the benefit of first-timers: We go round the clock.

9. EXT BEACH DAY (PRESENT) MEDIUM SHOT OVER ROBERT

in f.g. toward BALLROOM. It is set at the end of a pier. In front of the entrance are several huge klieg lights and a trailered mule dynamo. The lights are aimed toward the sky but they are untended and unlighted. Strung across the entrance is a mammoth banner:

1932   MARATHON DANCE   1932
Grand Prize
$1,500
Admission: 25c
GALA OPENING TONIGHT!

10. REVERSE ANGLE ON ROBERT

He stares off towards the ballroom as the fringe of a spent wave scuds across his feet.

ROCKY'S VOICE

And around, and around. Ten-minute break every two hours. Rollo!

We HEAR an UNDULATING SIREN BLAST. Its tone is sharp, piercing, urgent.

11. EXT PASTURE DAY (PAST) PANNING SHOT ON STALLION

circling the unbounded pasture . . . loping . . . then cantering. Faster. Faster.

ROCKY'S VOICE

That's it! You hear that, it's break time. You hear it again, back on the floor. You dance an hour fifty minutes, then you're off ten. Then ditto, ditto, ditto

. . . straight on till there's one and JUST ONE couple left. You keep moving no matter what. All the time. Anybody stops: Rollo!

We HEAR the loud CLACK, CLACK of a hand CRICKET.

12. CLOSE ON BOY

moving off, but still watching the stallion over his shoulder. (ROCKY'S VOICE IS CONTINUOUS THROUGHOUT THE FOLLOWING.)

> ROCKY'S VOICE
> That's the warning signal. If it's YOUR PARTNER, you got exactly thirty seconds to get him moving again.

13. PANNING WITH THE STALLION

still circling. Tighter. Faster.

14. CLOSER ON BOY

Watching . . . breathless.

15. PANNING WITH STALLION

still faster. Wilder. Background beginning to blur now.

> ROCKY'S VOICE
> No excuses! No explanations! *Thirty seconds.*

16. EXTREME CLOSEUP ON BOY

Watching even more raptly.

17. FLYING WITH THE STALLION

Still faster . . . faster . . . with a kind of abandoned

freedom, legs kicking high, mane swirling to the wind, almost free of the ground itself, almost flying . . .

18. LOW AND FAST MOVING

with the legs of the stallion. A design of blurred and abstract motion until suddenly one of its hooves catches and its whole body wrenches, twists in a convulsion of knotted muscles.

> ROCKY'S VOICE
> If it's two knees: Rollo!

19. EXTREME CLOSE BOY

crying out (silent). We HEAR the SHARP SCREECH of a POLICE WHISTLE.

20. LOW ANGLE UP TO STALLION (SLOW MOTION)

falling. Falling again. Again.

> ROCKY'S VOICE
> That's it, out! Ohh . . . you . . . Tee! We're going to run it as fair as human nature allows, so when one of the judges rules, that's it. No appeals.

21. EXT BEACH DAY (PRESENT) ACROSS ROBERT

out to the ocean. His boots are on now and we PAN with him as he brushes sand from his trousers and moves slowly towards the distant ballroom.

> ROCKY'S VOICE
> (getting louder now)
> When your partner's ruled out, you can solo for twenty-four hours. If you match up with another solo . . . fair enough. Otherwise . . . that's it.

22. EXT PASTURE DAY (PAST) HIGH ANGLE

DOWN TOWARDS fallen stallion. Boy and Grandfather. The boy tries to thrust his way past the Grand-father and toward the stallion but is stopped. He refuses to hear what his Grandfather is telling him. He shakes his head back and forth violently and shouts (silent) "No! No! No!"

ROCKY'S VOICE

There'll always be a trainer or nurse on duty. And a doctor out here twenty-four hours a day. Okay; food: Four regular meals and three small ones each day.

23. MED   ON BOY AND GRANDFATHER

as he holds the boy aside with one hand. With the other he levels the shotgun toward the stallion.

ROCKY'S VOICE

Now . . . the audience. *Respect*. That's what I expect and that's what they'll expect. They're paying: You're performing. You strike up a friendly back and forth; okay. But coo-coo birds and smut artists; out!

24. TIGHT ON BOY

raging helplessly against this sudden and first knowledge of death, fate . . . chance.

ROCKY'S VOICE

Sponsors: first come, first served. After that you luck it or hustle one on your own. Naturally after we get rolling we'll throw in some wrinkles to hypo up the crowds. But I'll explain those when it's time.

25. TIGHT ON STALLION

feebly, impotently struggling to raise its head.

26. EXTREME CLOSEUP   SHOTGUN

(shouting)

Hey! What the hell's going on over there?! Shut that door!!

The gun FIRES. It is the FIRST ON-SCREEN SOUND from the PAST. As the SHOT begins to reverberate:

27. INT   BALLROOM   DAY   MED. ANGLE ON ROBERT

slamming the door behind him. The light burns through the frosted glass, blurring his face.

28. ROBERT'S POV

A group of a hundred-odd couples, dwarfed by the arching vastness of the empty, dimly-lit, cavernous ballroom. Final preparations for the Marathon going on in b.g.

(NOTE: Contestants all dressed in style of the period and nearly all carrying satchels or cardboard suitcases.)

29. CLOSE ON ROCKY GRAVO

standing on a low platform facing the would-be CONTESTANTS. He is in his early forties. A little liverish, a little pouchy, but withal, still handsome. He wears faded "Balboa blue denims," a suede and wool cardigan and soft kid leather arch support cushioned shoes. He holds a paper cup. Several other cups are scattered at his feet. He stares across the heads of the contestants in the direction of Robert's interruption.

30. TRAVELING WITH ROLLO PETERS

the head floor judge. A man in his mid-thirties. Short, slightly bandy-legged but moving gracefully, lightly

—like a dancer . . . or a fighter. He might have been either. He skirts the edge of a knot of contestants and flashes Robert a warning gesture for silence, then impatiently waves him over toward the others.

31. MOVING WITH ROBERT

as he hesitates for an instant, unhappy at being the center of attention, then nods and starts forward. He tries to move soundlessly but his boots GRATE against the polished wood floor.

32. CLOSE ROCKY

looking toward Robert. The quality of his annoyance is patent. Perhaps because if he feels contempt or bitterness (or for that matter desire or hope) it is always a generalized feeling, always one held with a little detachment. Rocky is someone who came to some early and unpleasant truths about human nature. Nothing has caused him to reassess that early evaluation.

33. SHOOTING THROUGH THE CONTESTANTS

as Robert melds himself to the outer edge. It has been a small, momentary ordeal for him . . . but he has accomplished the action and survived it.

34. ON ROCKY

who continues to stare for a LONG BEAT toward where Robert *had* been. A practiced smile:

ROCKY
Okay, kids. Couple of hours we fling open the magic doors to fame and fortune, so line up and get your numbers.

CUT TO:

35. CLOSE ON A STACK OF CARDBOARD PLAQUES

each with a number and a twine halter rope. PULL
BACK TO REVEAL a long table at other side of
platform. The contestants are filing by in front of
the other FLOOR JUDGES, a NURSE, and a bored-
looking DOCTOR. (Doctor is fifty-odd, slightly
gaunt.) Fingers and teeth somewhat nicotine-stained.
A week or two past a haircut or has trimmed it himself. Though he probably has a license, it's been some
years since he had an office wall to hang it on.

36. STARTING ON ROCKY

behind the table overseeing the check-through of
contestants by Rollo and other judges. MOVE
ACROSS TABLE TO SEE couples hand in the release, open their suitcase, and submit to a cursory
look-over by nurse or Doctor. (NOTE: This is 1932;
bottom of the American depression.) As this business
goes on, CAMERA restlessly roams the crowd and
introduces:

37. SAILOR

A garrulous, easygoing, essentially likable guy. In
bell-bottom whites. The jacket is old and frayed but
freshly bleached, clean and pressed. The chevrons
have long since disappeared but their outlines are still
visible. Despite the fact that he dyes his hair, he is
noticeably older than the others. He pinches out the
loose coal of a brown paper cigarette and tucks the
stub into his blouse pocket.

> SAILOR
> Some system. Just like the Fleet . . . line up and wait.
> Only longer.

38. SHIRL

Sailor's partner. A cheaply peroxided blonde of twenty-odd. Her print dress is a size too small on her. She smiles often, quickly . . . and, as she does now, without any particular reason.

39. BACK TO SAILOR

> SAILOR
> (craning his neck toward desk)
How about goosin' it a little?!

40. ON ROLLO

at desk snapping his head up.

> ROLLO
You'll get your turn. Just take it easy, hunh?

He goes back to rummaging through the tin suitcase of a thin, slightly pock-marked young man. He pauses suspiciously over a couple of pharmacy bottles rolled up in an undershirt.

> ROLLO
> (indicating bottles)
What's this stuff . . . hootch?

> POCK-MARKED YOUNG MAN
No. It's for my stomach. I got a bad stomach.

41. ANOTHER ANGLE   TO INCLUDE ROCKY

Rollo gestures to him and hands over one of the bottles. Rocky holds it to the light, shakes it, then hands it to the Doc.

> DOCTOR
> (uncorks, sniffs)
Paregoric.
> (at Rocky's look)
Opium base.

ROCKY
(to Rollo)

No number.

POCK-MARKED YOUNG MAN

It's medicine. I got to take it for my stomach.

ROCKY

So take it somewhere else. I got enough trouble without a hophead.

Rollo shuts the tin suitcase with a SNAP!

ROLLO

You heard 'im, school's over. Blow!

POCK-MARKED YOUNG MAN

You can't do that, it ain't fair.

ROLLO

Hire a lawyer. Next! Come on, move it up.

42. ANOTHER SECTION OF THE LINE

Just in front of Sailor is ALICE LeBLANC, immediately distinctive in a silver-sequined, full-length sheath which clings to her body. Extremely and naturally beautiful, with an attitude and manner curiously remote . . . she never quite looks at anyone, never quite listens. English.

SAILOR
(to Alice, looking over her tightly
rounded backside)

One more to go.

He smiles through her blank look, then gestures to her dress.

SAILOR

You gonna dance in that? I mean if we ever get aboard?

147

Alice smiles vacantly.

43. ANOTHER ANGLE

to include Alice's partner, JOEL. Too handsome, so
that his features edge toward prettiness. That's his
own private curse, because he's an actor and it's the
wrong year for prettiness. The wrong decade. Still
he's done bits. And while he's long between now, he
knows another will turn up. That, and only that,
makes the present bearable.

> JOEL
> (answering Sailor sardonically)
> I can't see why not. It's quite comfortable, you know.

Sailor laughs, looks to Shirl, then back to Alice:

> SAILOR
> Wait, move up, wait! Once between hitches I worked
> a cattle boat out'a Galveston. Same thing. Know what
> I mean?

> ALICE
> I . . . No, I don't think so actually.

> SAILOR
> I mean, if you think about it, cattle ain't got it much
> worse than us.

> GLORIA'S VOICE
> They got it better. There's always somebody to feed
> 'em.

Sailor turns to see:

44. MED. CLOSE ON GLORIA BEATTY

Pretty, young, hungry and essentially an outsider.
She seems hard and hostile . . . compulsive. But we
will discover that she is quite unpredictable, complex

and strangely vulnerable . . . perhaps frightened. Her partner STANLEY ANTRIM is, like her, a cardless atmosphere extra in the movies. There is a slightly watery look to his eyes, and he tries desperately to hide the fact that he has a cold.

45. WIDER ANGLE

to include Sailor. Delighted to have a new audience.

> SAILOR
> Yeah, sure . . . stuffin' 'em up good for the slaughter pen. Right down a chute, and some big, dumb bo-hunk's standin' there with a sledge hammer.
> (imitates hammer)
> Voomp!!

> GLORIA
> They don't know it's gonna happen. That makes 'em one up on us, don't it?

> SAILOR
> (he never saw it that way)
> Yeah, I guess . . . if you look at it that way.

46. MED. ANGLE ON ROBERT

watching all this in fascination and trying to remain inconspicuous.

47. BACK TO THE CONTESTANTS

filing by. As they shuffle forward, Stanley muffles a cough in his hand.

> SAILOR
> What's wrong with him?

> GLORIA
> (quickly)
> Nothing.

48. AT TABLE

as Alice and Joel arrive and Rocky is sizing up Alice. He glances at her bag, which contains another gown identical to the one she is wearing except that the color is gold.

ROCKY

You got a specialty?

ALICE

I'm Alice LeBlanc. I'm an actress—from London.

ROCKY

What've you got? Like an act, or a bit maybe? Let's see a little.

JOEL

Aah—if you give us a few minutes we could work something up.

49. CLOSEUP   ALICE

A beat, then she closes her eyes. She opens her mouth slightly . . . but she says nothing. Silence.

50. CLOSEUP   ROCKY

Puzzled.

51. CLOSEUP   ALICE

Still a beat longer. Then:

ALICE
(stilted, yet passionate)

"Yes, they told me you were fools, and that I was not to listen to your fine words nor trust to your charity."

52. FEATURING ROCKY

but including others. All surprised at hearing these words. It's not quite what Rocky bargained for.

53. TIGHT CLOSEUP ON ALICE

She falters slightly. Then continues.

> ALICE
> "If only I could still hear the wind in the trees, the larks in the sunshine, the young lambs . . ."

54. CLOSE ON JOEL

> JOEL
> Ahhh . . . a . . . Alice.

55. FULL SHOT

to include Rocky, Alice, Joel, Rollo and a group at table.

> ROCKY
> . . . Heyy, that's great! I really mean it. Shakespeare, hunh?

> ALICE
> It's from "St. Joan."

> ROCKY
> Yeah, that's what I figured. Ahh . . . the only thing is . . . maybe it's a little highbrow.
> (pats her arm)
> You leave it to me. I'll work out something just right for you.

Joel and Alice move o.s. with their things.

56. OVER ROLLO

as Sailor and Shirl step INTO SCENE.

ROLLO

Okay, next.

Sailor watches Rollo sort through his things, then start to scan his filled-out questionnaire. Sailor betrays a slight apprehensiveness, but covers it quickly.

SAILOR
(pointing to numbered cards)
Hey, what've you got left? How about seven? That's my lucky number. Not that we're . . .

He stops as he sees Rollo react to something on the questionnaire. Rollo turns and hands it to Rocky, pointing to an item. Rocky stares at it, then to Sailor, then back to questionnaire.

ROCKY

Thirty-one . . . ?

SAILOR

Yeah, thirty-one. What do I need, a note from my mother?

ROCKY
(shrugs)
It's your feet, Sailor.

57. RAKING THE CONTESTANTS

as Sailor and Shirl move on and Gloria and Stanley move in front of the table. As they do, Stanley tries to swallow down another cough. His very attempt to hide it makes it more evident.

58. TWO SHOT   ROCKY AND ROLLO

ROCKY

You sick or something?

GLORIA

He's all right.

ROCKY

Yeah . . . ? Doc!!

He gestures for the old Doctor, who sticks a swab
down Stanley's throat. Gloria is worried.

DOCTOR
(mumbling, to Stanley)
Open up . . . wider . . . wider.
(shrugs)
Bronchitis . . . maybe.

ROCKY
Yeah, or maybe the Mongolian crud.
(to Stanley)
No dice, kid. You infect the whole place, then I got
the health department setting up a squawk. That's the
way it is.

Rollo hands Stanley his satchel, then motions for the
next couple to move up. CAMERA DOLLIES into
TIGHT TWO SHOT OF GLORIA AND STAN-
LEY.

STANLEY
I'm sorry, Gloria.

GLORIA
That's a big help. You're the one talked me into this
thing!

STANLEY
I'm sorry . . . Gloria.

59. ACROSS ROCKY AND ROLLO

to the next couple: RUBY and JAMES BATES. A
country couple. He's a good deal older than his years,
has knocked about for a long time and survived. She
defers to him in a natural and simple way, depends
upon him . . . looks up to him. And not merely be-

cause she is pregnant . . . though she is that, and
noticeably. Rollo begins to sort through their things
when Gloria pushes past them to the TABLE.

GLORIA
(to Rocky)
What about me?

ROCKY
I'm sorry.

GLORIA
That's what *he* said. I can't buy coffee and sinkers
with it.

ROCKY
Look, if I start making exceptions—

GLORIA
(pointing to Ruby)
What about her? If she's not pregnant, then I'm Nel-
son Eddy.

ROCKY
What's healthier than havin' a kid? And it gives the
audience somethin' to root for.

GLORIA
So what'm I supposed to do—run out quick and get
knocked up?

60. CLOSEUP   ROCKY

ROCKY
We could discuss it . . . later.

61. CLOSEUP   GLORIA

This is an old story.

GLORIA
That soap's a little hard. What else you got to suggest?

154 -

62. GROUP SHOT AT TABLE ROCKY, ROLLO, JAMES, RUBY
    AND GLORIA

ROCKY

Get another partner.

GLORIA

Yeah, where?

Rocky waves off vaguely . . . then stops as he sees:

63. MED. ANGLE ON ROBERT

standing quietly aside.

ROCKY'S VOICE

Hey, cowboy.

Robert looks around . . . then points to himself.

ROCKY'S VOICE

Yeah, you, come 'ere.

CAMERA DOLLIES WITH ROBERT as he crosses
over to table. Checking in continues in b.g.

ROBERT
(apologetically)

Look . . . I was just out walking . . . I didn't come
here to . . .

ROCKY

That a fact. What's your name?

ROBERT

Robert. Robert Syverton. Back home they . . .

ROCKY
(while examining other entry forms)

Yeah. You got a partner, Richard?

155

ROBERT

No, I just . . . It's Robert!

ROCKY
(looking up, gesturing)
There you are, miss.

GLORIA

How's he gonna dance in those things?

ROBERT

You mean the boots? They're not mine. I roomed with another guy, but he went away and left them behind. They fitted me, so . . .

GLORIA
(to Rocky)
He'll break an arch.

ROCKY

So dig him up a pair of shoes.
(as she considers)
Or maybe you'd rather wait for the Prince of Wales?

GLORIA

Have I got a choice?

ROCKY
(smiles pleasantly)
Sure . . . take it or leave it.

64. CLOSEUP GLORIA

weighing it. Over shot we HEAR, distantly at first, but then louder, a DRUM ROLL. As it grows in intensity:

CUT TO:

65. INT BALLROOM NIGHT TIGHT ON HANDS OF DRUMMER

continuing the roll. CAMERA PULLS BACK AND UP and we *BEGIN CREDITS.* THE BAND (all Negro) segues into "Sweet Sue."

ROCKY'S VOICE
Yowza, yowza, yowza . . . Welcome to the Dance of Destiny, ladies and gentlemen.

CAMERA CONTINUES PULLBACK and we see Rocky in a white double-breasted tuxedo jacket on the bunting-decorated platform. He stands in front of a table with a mike on it. There is a bar stool behind. He sways just slightly in time to the music. On the platform with him is TURKEY. He wears wire-rimmed glasses and has two expressions: blank and dour. He seldom reacts or speaks.

ROCKY'S VOICE
Around and around and around, AND we're only beginning, folks, only beginning.

66. CLOSE ON A GIANT CLOCK

A pastel light floods it. It shows:

HOURS ELAPSED 0000
COUPLES REMAINING 102
HOW LONG CAN THEY LAST?

ROCKY'S VOICE
The clock of fate!

67.-72. ANGLES ON THE AUDIENCE

In the vast reaches of the ballroom they seem only a handful. Mostly middle-class and middle-aged. Some are simply curious, but most know what they seek in this place: spectacle, pain and superiority. They eat: popcorn and hot dogs, fried chicken, etc. (NOTE: This is the time of Prohibition and if there is any drinking it is done surreptitiously.)

On and on and on. And when will it end, when will the clock stop . . .?

73.-78. MOVING THROUGH THE DANCERS

They dance easily. Still fresh and neat-looking. Some are professional marathon dancers, easily spotted because they don't waste energy dancing, but sway from foot to foot. A handful of desperate farmers in bib-overalls lurch awkwardly with their women. MARIO PETRONE and JACKIE MILLER, a young powerfully built couple with a professional look. CECIL and AGNES. She is huge, about forty-fiveish and wheezing already. He is terribly neat, balding, about sixty and wears a flower in his lapel.

ROCKY'S VOICE

When . . . ?! Only when the last two of these wonderful, starry-eyed kids are left. Only when the last two of these dancers stagger and sway, stumble and swoon across a sea of defeat and despair . . . to victory.

79. MED. ANGLE ON BLEACHERS

To feature MRS. LAYDON. She is about sixty-five, smiling, has a picnic basket and a pillow. Over her arm is a wool folded blanket. She is carefully examining a sheet with the names of all the contestants.

ROCKY'S VOICE

One couple, and only one, will waltz out of here over broken bodies and broken dreams carrying the Grand Prize of *One Thousand Five Hundred Silver Dollars!*

80. TRAVELING WITH ROLLO

and another tuxedoed FLOOR JUDGE as they swoop and glide on roller skates, whistles in mouths. Rollo holds his ever-present HAND CRICKET.

I said *the* prize. Only two of these crazy, wonderful, aspiring kids will dance on to fame and fortune.

81. MED. ON ROCKY

The band in b.g.

ROCKY

Those who give up . . . those who give out . . . those who give in—OUT. Tough rules, but these are tough times. In the words of our great leader, Herbert Hoover—
                  (waits for the boos)
Whatta we say about the Depression?
                  (gives razzberry)
That's what we say about it.
                        (waving)
Come on! Let's hear it!

82. ON AUDIENCE

The response is mild. END CREDITS.

83. TWO SHOT   ROCKY AND TURKEY

Rocky, still smiling, covers the mike with his hand and glances aside toward Turkey.

ROCKY

It's walking-dead night. Pour me a shot of water, Turkey.

Turkey hands him a paper cup. Rocky turns to face the audience.

ROCKY

So pick *your* couple, folks. Struggle with them! Hope with them! Cry with them! See if *you* can pick out that one lucky pair . . . and then cheer them on! Let 'em hear you care!
                  (claps hands)
Let 'em know you're with 'em all the way!

84. FULL ON AUDIENCE   FEATURE MRS. LAYDON

The APPLAUSE is scattered and halfhearted.

85. CLOSE ON ROCKY

managing to beam.

> ROCKY
> (to dancers)
> You hear that, kids? You hear those wonderful peo-
> ple rooting for you?

86. MED. DANCERS

Most of them trying to flash smiles into the play of
colored lights.

> ROCKY'S VOICE
> Now show 'em *you* care, kids. A little sprint for the
> wonderful folks out there.

87. FULL SHOT ON BAND

swinging into "Pop Goes the Weasel."

88. ON DANCERS   FEATURING SAILOR AND SHIRL

forced to pick up the pace.

89. TIGHT ON ROBERT AND GLORIA

dancing. Then, as the tempo of the music slows again,
they sag to a sort of two-step shuffle.

> ROBERT
> (after beat)
> Why California?

> GLORIA
> (shrugs)
> You don't freeze while you're starving. And there's
> the movies.

ROBERT

Oh, are you an actress?

GLORIA

I've done four atmosphere bits since I been here. I'd have done more except I can't get into Central Casting. They got it all sewed up.

ROBERT

Have you met anybody who can help you?

GLORIA

In this business how can you tell who'll help you? One day you're an electrician and the next day you're a producer. The only way I could ever get close to a big shot would be to jump on the running board of his car. Anyway, I don't know whether the men stars can help me as much as the women stars. From what I've seen lately I've been letting the wrong sex try and make me.

ROBERT

Oh . . . !?

GLORIA

You in the movies too?

ROBERT

Sort of. I was a dead French villager in "Fallen Angels."

90. A NEW ANGLE

as Rollo skates INTO SCENE. He pirouettes around them before side-breaking to a stop.

ROLLO
(sotto)

Come on, kids, it's opening night. A little smile for the audience.

Robert starts to smile obediently, but:

161

GLORIA

What audience?

Rollo gives her a sour look, shrugs and skates o.s.

ROBERT
(a gentle reprimand)
He could get you disqualified.

91. CLOSE ON GLORIA

GLORIA

I been disqualified by experts.

92. TWO SHOT   ALICE AND JOEL

Alice dancing with Joel . . . yet, essentially alone.
She seems, even when she is moving, to be as still, as
pale as a carefully positioned manikin. Her expression
appears vaguely distant and aloof. She turns for a
moment toward the bleachers, and peers searchingly
across the rows of spectators. Joel watches her with
detached amusement.

JOEL
You're wasting your time, kiddo.
(when she looks back)
The only thing casting's Von Sternberg's "Raw
Earth." And that's strictly an all-peasant talkie.

ALICE
(very serious)
I could play a peasant.

JOEL
(indicating gown)
Not in that you couldn't.

ALICE

Do you like it?

JOEL

Does it matter?

Not as long as they do.

She turns away from him again to look back toward
the audience through one of the spotlight beams.

93. ROBERT AND GLORIA

He gazes toward Alice. Gloria flicks a sideways glance
toward Alice, then looks up at Robert.

SAILOR'S VOICE

Hey, sweetie, you got yourself another partner, hunh?

Gloria and Robert turn to see:

94. NEW ANGLE TO INCLUDE SAILOR AND SHIRL

Sailor makes a mock appraisal of Robert.

SAILOR

Only he don't look much healthier than the last one.

GLORIA

What're you, a doctor?

SHIRL

He don't mean nothin', honey.

SAILOR

Just tryin' to be helpful.
                    (peers at Robert)
Cod liver oil . . . you oughta take some, maybe.

SHIRL
                    (to Robert)
He's just steaming 'cause you've got twenty years on
'im.
                    (looks at Sailor, lovingly)
Or maybe more like thirty.

SAILOR
(piqued)

That's where you got your wires mixed up, sweetie.
Experience, that's what counts! Keep your eyes open!

And Sailor whirls Shirl around in a swooping ballroom turn and moves in front of the bandstand. CAM-
ERA FOLLOWING.

SAILOR
(winking and signaling to leader)

Give me a little more beat. And try to stay up with me.

He goes into a sort of buck-and-wing . . . not good,
but energetic. The other dancers spread back to give
him room.

95. CLOSE ON MARIO AND JACKIE

watching Sailor.

MARIO

Classy! I bet that killed 'em in Roseland . . . back before the Johnstown Flood.

96. LOW ANGLE ON SAILOR

He gives Mario the Italian thumb.

97. SIDE ANGLE ON BLEACHERS

A small ripple of APPLAUSE starts up for Sailor.
Mrs. Laydon consults her sheet to find out who is in-
sulting whom.

98. LOW ANGLE UP TO ROCKY

He looks toward Sailor, then takes up the mike.

ROCKY

That's the kind of contestants we've got for you,
folks.

(claps)

A hand for our very own Ancient Mariner . . .

(checks list)

. . . Harry Klein! Yowza!

99. FULL SHOT ON SAILOR

taking bows while the band does an "Up-Finish."

ROCKY'S VOICE

You can all see that Harry used to be in the U.S. Navy.

100. CLOSEUP ROCKY

ROCKY

. . . but there's something you can't see. I want to be serious for a moment, folks, if you'll permit me. Harry Klein is one of those brave young men who went sailing off to beat the Kaiser. That's right, a veteran of the Great War . . . and let's hope there'll never be another.

(holds up hand)

Harry was decorated in that War . . . for wounds received in action. But that's not all.

101. TWO SHOT ON SAILOR AND SHIRL

For just a moment Sailor displays surprise . . . but then, immediately he plays along, smiling humbly.

(Shirl, Sailor, Rocky speak together)

SHIRL

You ain't got no wounds anywhere, Harry.

SAILOR

(sotto)

You want a sponsor, don't you?! Shut up and keep lookin' dumb.

ROCKY'S VOICE

I know Harry wouldn't want me to tell you this, but RIGHT NOW . . . at THIS MOMENT, there are thirty-two separate pieces of shrapnel still embedded in Harry's body. And here he is, fighting another kind of war, fighting to win.

102. CLOSEUP ON ROCKY

really playing it now.

ROCKY

Isn't that the kind of grit and never-say-die spirit that's made this the great country it is? Isn't it? You bet it is! And I really mean that sincerely . . . from the bottom of my heart.

103. FULL SHOT   THE AUDIENCE

They respond with a patriotic burst of applause.

104. SAILOR AND SHIRL

She beams . . . he bows. He takes her hand ceremoniously and they begin slowly to dance off.

105. FULL SHOT

to TIGHTEN on Gloria and Robert. They have been looking off at Sailor.

GLORIA

I should've learned to tap-dance.

SOUND of a large WAVE against the pilings below the pier.

ROBERT

Can you feel that?

GLORIA

What?

ROBERT

The ocean.

(indicates floor)

The waves . . . you can feel them right through the floor.

(then)

You know, even when you're a long ways away from the ocean, you can still feel it sometimes.

GLORIA

(looking around at the other couples)

Not where I come from.

ROBERT

Where's that?

GLORIA

Ohh . . . around. Kansas. Texas mostly. Dallas.

ROBERT

That must've been nice.

GLORIA

(swinging back to him)

Nice . . . ?!

ROBERT

Well, I mean, I never been through there, but that's the way it always seemed to me . . . like you could look just about anywhere and see land . . . I mean without anything set down on it.

GLORIA

Yeah! It's great. I'm a real sucker for dirt and cactus. That's how come I left.

106. CECIL AND AGNES

dance by, executing a meant-to-be-fancy twirl. Gloria darts a hard, appraising, sidelong glance at Agnes.

ROBERT

Why *did* you leave?

Gloria looks back at him. A beat, then:

GLORIA

You ever sleep with a Syrian who chews tobacco?

Robert does a puzzled take.

GLORIA

Well, if anybody ever asks you, you can tell 'em there's no future in it.

Robert seems about to protest or change the subject, when Agnes' backside slams into Gloria during another attempted twirl.

GLORIA

Hey! What d'you want, the whole floor?!

CECIL
(as he propels Agnes away)
Terribly sorry.

GLORIA
(looking after Agnes)
The way she's throwing it around, her feet'll last longer than her rear end.
(turns back)
He was a butcher.

ROBERT

Who?

GLORIA

The Syrian. How's that for the bottom of the barrel?

ROBERT

Hey, listen . . . I didn't mean to be personal. I was just . . . I didn't mean to be personal.

GLORIA

Yeah? Then why'd you ask?

168

ROBERT

Well . . . just to make conversation. I figure we're going to be stuck together for a long time, so I thought maybe it'd help the time go . . . if I talked some, I mean.

GLORIA

Don't strain anything for me.

ROBERT
(hurt)

All right.

They continue to dance, but silently now . . . and with a sense of strained distance between them.

107. FOLLOWING JAMES AND RUBY

Minimum of movement. Ruby shifts her weight slightly, and James helps her to reposition herself.

JAMES

Okay?

RUBY
(she smiles)
I hope I don't start lugging on you.

JAMES

You ain't ever lugged yet.

She nods, still smiling, but looks down to her swollen belly. Then back to James.

JAMES

Just keep thinkin' about those seven meals each day.

108. STARTING ON SAILOR AND SHIRL

and MOVING PAST MARIO and JACKIE on through CECIL and AGNES . . . around ALICE and JOEL, CAMERA comes to rest on *ROBERT AND GLORIA.* She realizes she has stepped a little hard on him, but forcing herself to patch it over is something else again. She cheats a couple of looks at him, then gestures off toward the bandstand.

GLORIA

Some band, hunh? They probably pay 'em off in beer and peanuts.

ROBERT

Probably.

They dance another beat in strained silence.

GLORIA
(one more try)
I thought maybe *you* came from Texas.

ROBERT
(distant)

No.

109. CLOSEUP GLORIA

GLORIA

Oh, for crissake, stop sulking!!!

110. CLOSEUP ROBERT

as his face suddenly opens into a wide, warm grin.

ROBERT

I guess that's what I was doing, all right . . . I'm sorry.

GLORIA

Forget it . . . Anyway, you're right, we *are* stuck together.
(beat)
Where *are* you from, anyway?

170

ROBERT

Chicago. That's where I was born. But I lived once for a little while in Arkansas. After my father died.

GLORIA

I didn't like it much . . . Chicago. I tried it once, but all I could get was a job in a five-and-dime sellin' sheet music on commission. So I hitched back to Dallas. Boy, was that ever a mistake. At least in Chicago they got soup kitchens. In Dallas there's nothing. I mean nothing! Finally I figured, what the hell, I might as well be in jail . . . let them take care of me . . . so I swiped somethin' from a store and made sure I got caught.

ROBERT
(surprised at so much)

Jesus . . .

GLORIA

But the cop felt sorry for me and let me go . . . and anyway he didn't press charges . . . the Syrian. That's how I met him, he's the one I shoplifted from.
(beat)
I'll say one thing, I never ate so much in my life. Steak for breakfast.

ROBERT

How'd you stand it?

GLORIA

Steak . . . ? Oh, the Syrian.
(beat, then directly to Robert)
I kept my eyes shut.

111. CLOSE SHOT ON MOUTH OF THE SIREN

as it screeches, signaling the rest period.

112. HIGH ANGLE DOWN

to the DANCERS. They stop abruptly, almost in

171

tableau, then they slump and start toward the rest areas.

ROCKY'S VOICE

Ten minutes! And then they'll be back. And the championship marathon will go on. And on and on . . . and on.

113.-120. INT WOMEN'S REST AREA NIGHT ESTAB-
LISHING SHOTS

A beefy MATRON has pointed those who arrived first to cots. But there aren't enough cots so the late-comers are forced to find spots along the floor. A couple of NURSES (bad ones) pass among the wom-en, handing out towels, liniment, etc. A shower area is at one end of the room, the toilets nearby. There is a straggly line-up for the toilets. AD-LIBBED dia-logue and business.

121. ANGLE ON DOOR TO AREA

as Gloria enters carrying her shoes. She looks across the filled cots to:

122. CLOSE ON ALICE

in front of a mirror, patiently, meticulously roll-ing mascara onto her eyelashes, while SILENTLY MOUTHING WORDS INTO THE MIRROR. She looks up for a moment and catches Gloria's eye.

123. GLORIA

holding the gaze for just a beat and then looking away. She leans against the wall, and slides down it until she is sitting on the floor.

124. ANGLE ON DOOR

as Rocky steps through. He looks around and catches Alice's eye.

ROCKY

You got that Tanyakio bit down, Miss LeBlanc?

ALICE
(nods)
I've memorized all of it, every line.

ROCKY

Swell. Come by my office next break maybe. We'll run through it.

125. CLOSEUP   GLORIA

She laughs . . . a quick, sardonic laugh.

126. CLOSEUP   ROCKY

turns . . . looks challengingly at her for a beat . . . and then EXITS.

127. FULL SHOT   GLORIA

rising. CAMERA follows as she moves toward a vacated cot. Before she reaches it she hesitates a moment and looks down at:

128. GLORIA'S POV   RUBY

lying down, eyes closed, breathing heavily. Her hands pressed against her womb-filled stomach.

129. TIGHT ON GLORIA

For a moment we cannot read her expression.

130. EXTREME CLOSE SHOT OF RUBY'S STOMACH

moving laboriously up and down.

131. TIGHT ON GLORIA

staring with a mixture of horror and fascination. She pulls her sweater tighter.

132. CLOSEUP RUBY

She opens her eyes and sees Gloria looking. She smiles.

133. TIGHT ON GLORIA

as she turns abruptly away but is stopped by:

> RUBY'S VOICE
> You better get off your feet.

CAMERA HOLDS on Gloria's back. A beat—then she turns.

> GLORIA
> When's the baby due?

134. CLOSEUP RUBY

Embarrassed.

> RUBY
> I don't know.

> GLORIA'S VOICE
> What'd the doctor say?

> RUBY
> James and I were . . . we've been . . . you know . . . hitchhiking . . . riding in boxcars.

135. CLOSEUP GLORIA

> GLORIA
> Nature's little miracle. *Christ!*

136. TWO SHOT

to include OTHERS in b.g.

RUBY
(puzzled at her vehemence)
. . . Why . . . ?

GLORIA
(snapping)
What's the sense of having a kid unless you've got
enough dough to take care of it?

RUBY
People don't stop having babies just because they ain't
got no money.

GLORIA
Do you intend to keep it?

RUBY
(smiling)
Ohhhh . . . I couldn't . . . I mean . . . James wants
it . . .

GLORIA
Sure! Why not drop another sucker into this mess.

137.-143. INT   MEN'S REST AREA   NIGHT   ESTABLISHING

Except that there are white-jacketed TRAINERS instead of nurses, it is much the same as the women's
area.

AD LIBS
Hey, ain't there no hair plaster in this place? . . . Boy,
if I win, I'm gonna take me that seven fifty and buy
me a brand spankin' new Hupmobile and . . . How
come they ain't got enough cots? There'll be enough
in a couple of days . . .

144. ANGLE ON ROBERT IN F.G.

edging around cots, looking for a place to sit.

In NEAR B.G. a pimply HAYSEED KID is packing

and then closing his cardboard suitcase. As he turns to leave, the older of the two trainers catches his arm.

OLDER TRAINER

You quittin' already, kid?

HAYSEED KID

This ain't for me. I got sensitive feet. Maybe I'll try flagpole sitting—you guys are crazy.

The trainer lets him go, and shrugs as he watches him move o.s. Robert has moved to the SIDE OF FRAME and now flops down.

145. CLOSE ON ROBERT

seated on a pile of canvas and used towels. His shoes are off and he is rubbing his feet. He looks up to see:

146. MED. ON SAILOR

seated on a cot. He has wadded up some paper towels and is drying the inside of his shoes with them.

147. CLOSE ROBERT

looking around and picking up some paper towels. He begins to imitate Sailor.

148. CLOSEUP SAILOR

seeing Robert imitating him.

SAILOR

First one of these, hunh, kid?

149. MED. ROBERT

He nods.

150. OVER ROBERT TO SAILOR

Activity crisscrossing between them.

SAILOR
(shrugs)
It ain't First Cabin . . . hell, it ain't even steerage. But it's better than nothin'.

ROBERT
Well . . . I figured I wasn't doing anything else real important so . . .

SAILOR
. . . you know what I'd do if I was your age? I'd join up.
(flicks sleeve)
All over again. The Fleet.

ROBERT
I don't think I'd like it. I mean, I'd like to be able to move on if . . .

SAILOR
Bumming? That's all right for a while, but a man's got to belong somewhere, be part of something. I mean, that's human nature. Right?

151. CLOSEUP   ROBERT

ROBERT
I guess I've never thought about it much.

152. CLOSEUP   SAILOR

who starts rubbing the back of his neck.

SAILOR
Yeah, well, wait till you're my age . . . you will.

He looks up at Robert.

SAILOR
It's the muscles up here that count. More, even, than your legs.

177

He begins slowly twisting his neck about, hanging way back, turning to one side, then letting his head loll forward.

153. CLOSEUP ROBERT

beginning to imitate him. As he does, a grid pattern of shadows cast by an overhead light fixture splays across his face.

FLASH FORWARD TO:

154. INT POLICE CAR NIGHT ANGLE THROUGH

a wire grille screen to Robert, alone in back seat of police car. His wrists are handcuffed. He wears a splotched sweat shirt. Boldly lettered across it is JONATHON'S IRON TONIC. His face is grey, pallid, and weary. For a moment we hear nothing. Then as the car jolts forward we HEAR the SIREN . . . softly at first, then swelling in volume, escalating in pitch. It continues over as . . .

155. INT BALLROOM NIGHT EXTREME CLOSEUP
    MARATHON SIREN

undulating piercingly.

156. JOEL AND ALICE

dancing.

JOEL

No. No—I can't . . .

ALICE

You not leave Tanyakio. Please. Tanyakio make tiffin for you. And night-night, when you lonely, Tanyakio will—

JOEL

No, you brown devil! You shan't lure me this time.

178

I'm going back. Back to my wife . . . to my family . . . to the world I belong in.

ALICE

Come back to Tanyakio. The petals of many flowers will fall, but Tanyakio will wait . . . forever . . .

JOEL
(a beat)
Alice . . . this is terrible!

ALICE

It just doesn't suit me, I'll speak to Mr. Gravo.

JOEL

I think you better.

157. SAILOR AND SHIRL

SAILOR
(referring to her gown)
Hey, Hotlips, is that from Paris?

ALICE

No, my mother made it—do you like it?

SAILOR
(realizing she's serious)
Yes . . . yes, it's very nice.

158. ROBERT AND GLORIA

in one corner. They move very slowly. Robert's head is tilted back and he has canted his gaze up toward the windows. We HEAR the WASH of WAVES UNDER THE PIER.

GLORIA

Jackie says after the first hundred hours you start getting used to it.
(notices him)
What're you lookin' at?

179

ROBERT

There's a partly broken window up there someplace.
I was trying to see if it was light out yet.

GLORIA

It's four in the morning!

ROBERT

Yeah . . . well sometimes, down by the beach, it gets
light by four. It's like that in Hawaii. You know . . .
because it's an island.

GLORIA

Sure, I know.

ROBERT

Well . . . so you can see way out over the ocean to
where the light is. You can stand in one spot and
watch the sun come up on one side of the world and
go down on the other side.

GLORIA

How'd you happen to go out there . . . Hawaii?

ROBERT

Well . . . I've never been there, actually. But you can
imagine how it would be.

GLORIA

Yeah! Sure! And you imagine you're Gary Cooper, I
suppose.

ROBERT
(annoyed)

No, that's not what I said. Why're you always trying
to start an argument? All I meant was . . .

A HAND THRUSTS INTO FRAME and grabs
Robert's arm, spinning him around.

159. FULL SHOT   JAMES AND RUBY, GLORIA AND ROBERT

James lets go of Robert's arm, then jabs a warning finger toward Gloria.

> JAMES

You tell that twist to lay off my wife!! She was at it again. Every rest period she keeps diggin' away at Ruby. "Whyn't you get rid of it? . . . whyn't you have it cut out?" She's givin' her the jumps . . . and I ain't havin' Ruby upset by no tramp like her.

> GLORIA

You go to hell, you big ape!

160. ANOTHER ANGLE

James starts toward Gloria, but Robert steps in front of him. (NOTE: When he speaks it is NOT aggressive, NOT pleading, no tough-guy or hero-in-the-movies. Just straightforward.)

> ROBERT

Don't . . .

QUICK CUT TO:

161. GLORIA

Surprised.

162. CLOSEUP   JAMES

> JAMES
> (louder)

Listen, next time I'll do more than holler, so . . .

163. CLOSEUP   RUBY

She holds James' arm.

> RUBY
> (quietly)

Honey . . . please . . .

Hey! Knock it off!

164. FULL SHOT   THE GROUP

To include Rollo braking his skates to a stop in front of them.

ROLLO

You know the rules. No fights on the floor. Whatta you think this is, a joint or something?

RUBY

Come on, Jimmy. Don't bother no more.

Grudgingly James lets himself be led away. Over her shoulder Ruby flashes back an "It'll be all right" look.

ROLLO
(turning back to Gloria)
I'm keepin' an eye on you.

GLORIA

Which one?

165. ROLLO

glares at her. Then nods as if to say, "Okay, if that's the way you want it," and skates off.

166. CLOSE TWO SHOT

as Robert and Gloria begin slowly to dance again.

GLORIA

That was stupid. Didn't you see the arms on that corn pone? He'd have killed you.

ROBERT
(recognizing the truth of it)
Yeah, I guess.

GLORIA
(puzzled)

Then why'd you do it?

167. TIGHT CLOSEUP ROBERT

ROBERT
(very simply)

You're my partner.

168. CAMERA MOVES IN TIGHT ON GLORIA AND HOLDS

For that moment, perhaps in spite of herself, she is genuinely touched.

FLASH FORWARD TO:

169. INT POLICE INTERROGATION ROOM NIGHT ANGLE ON ROBERT

sitting behind a plain table. His face is distorted and blurred by the raw light from a naked bulb that glares INTO CAMERA. He is still wearing the sweat shirt with JONATHON'S IRON TONIC lettered across it. His expression is calm . . . yet intent, as if he is trying very hard to be understood.

ROBERT

No, that's not the way it happened. It wasn't like that. We were very close . . . in a way. I was her friend. I guess maybe I was the only actual friend she had.

170. INT BALLROOM NOON ANGLE ON SIGN

It now reads:

DAY 3
HOURS ELAPSED 0068
COUPLES REMAINING 74
HOW LONG CAN THEY LAST?

183

171. ON CONTESTANTS

grouped around tables eating. As they eat, they continue to rock from side to side.

172. INT   MEN'S REST AREA   AFTERNOON   SAILOR IN F.G.

on a cot. One cot over is James. Sailor starts to twist about on the cot to look toward a wall clock . . . then decides better. He glances toward James.

SAILOR

How long we got left?

Without turning his head, James shifts his eyes to one side to glance toward the clock.

JAMES

Four minutes more.

173. INT   WOMEN'S REST AREA   AFTERNOON   NURSE

passing among the women, handing out wet cloths to those who want them.

174. ANGLE ACROSS ALICE TO LILLIAN AND JACKIE

Alice is using one of the wet cloths to wipe dust from her pumps.

Lillian is doubled up in a sort of foetal position on her cot. She MOANS slightly. Jackie looks at her from the next cot.

JACKIE

What's the matter . . . ?

LILLIAN

Wouldn't you know it—I got the curse comin' on.

Well, don't let them give you any codeine, it'll pass you out.

175. ANGLE FAVORING GLORIA

as she takes a wet cloth from the nurse. She presses the cloth against her eyes, then she holds it above her face and twists it, wringing out drops of water.

The SIREN sounds.

CUT TO:

176. INT BALLROOM NIGHT ON DANCERS

as CAMERA PANS across them. Those who are left are beginning to show clear signs of fatigue. None is actually dancing. The distinction between the pros and the amateurs is now clear. The pros put out a minimum of effort, take alternate turns at dozing. The amateurs just keep plodding along. A number of couples—mostly pros—are now sponsored. They are wearing shirts, blouses, jackets, sweat shirts—each with the name of the company sponsoring them: "KRUPP BAKERIES—Fresh Every Day" . . . "ARNOLD'S DAIRY PRODUCTS—Milk, Cheese, Butter" . . . "GARVER'S BABY FOOD" . . . "ACME LOAN CO.—$10.—$1,000" . . . etc.

177. AUDIENCE

It has grown somewhat, but not really changed in character. Between drinks and hot dogs, they watch with a kind of placid fascination. There are occasional SHOUTS of encouragement . . . and a few of derision. But, for the most part, they are simply waiting.

178. ON GLENN AND PAULA

Not so fresh and well-scrubbed any longer. And no more fancy steps. They move now in a plodding disconsolate manner.

PAULA

I thought it'd be more . . . well, fun.

GLENN
(looks about)
We'll never stand a chance of winning this thing.

PAULA

You want to quit?

GLENN

You want to . . . ?

PAULA

If you do.

GLENN

Okay.

They start off. In b.g. Rollo spots them, swoops about and skates up to them.

ROLLO

Hey, you can't leave the floor . . . or I got to eliminate you.

GLENN

Don't bother.
(takes Paula's hand, smiles)
Come on.

They EXIT SCENE. JIGGS skates INTO SCENE beside Rollo.

JIGGS

I figured them two.

ROLLO

They'll never know what they missed.

179. ON JAMES AND RUBY

clinging to each other. They glance off toward the departing couple, enviously, then turn back to each other.

180. ON ALICE AND JOEL

moving easily. Alice still seems impervious to pain or exhaustion.

181. ON SAILOR AND SHIRL

Sailor seems older, tireder, but he is still holding out better than Shirl, who is starting to sag every few steps.

SHIRL
Why didn't you tell me it was gonna be this tough?

SAILOR
You're keepin' your knees too stiff—it knots up the muscles.

182. ON ROBERT AND GLORIA

leaning on each other as they dance. Robert is staring off. Gloria is looking toward the audience.

GLORIA
She's there again.

Robert twists about to look.

183. POV   MRS. LAYDON

sitting in her regular box. She has her lunch basket and she is wrapped as usual in her stadium blanket. She smiles.

184. BACK TO ROBERT AND GLORIA

Robert acknowledges Mrs. Laydon's smile.

GLORIA

She must live here.

Robert nods.

ROBERT

... you want to sleep some?

GLORIA

No, I'm too tired to sleep.

ROBERT

Sailor told me you got to go a long time, maybe five hundred hours, before you get so you can sleep while you're moving.
(studies her; gently)
You look tired.

GLORIA

No kidding!

ROBERT

Why don't you try sleeping on my shoulder? I won't let you slip. You can trust me.

GLORIA

That's what the last guy said.

ROBERT

What ... ?

GLORIA

Forget it.

They continue to move slowly, dancing after a fashion until:

MRS. LAYDON'S VOICE

Gloria ... !

Gloria turns with a start to look at:

188

185. MRS. LAYDON

She waves them toward her.

186. BACK TO ROBERT AND GLORIA

ROBERT
(as Gloria holds back)
We really ought to be nice to her, Gloria. Rollo told
me—she's trying to get us a sponsor.

GLORIA
Nobody asked her to.

ROBERT
Look—it means four bucks a week, free socks and
clean jackets. Now come on.

GLORIA
(shrugs)
Okay.

CAMERA PANS as they "dance" over to Mrs. Laydon's box. Robert smiles at her; Gloria manages a nod.

MRS. LAYDON
I'm Mrs. Laydon.

ROBERT
Yes, ma'am, I know. One of the floor judges told us
. . . about your trying to get us a sponsor.

MRS. LAYDON
That's because you're my favorite couple.
(points)
You're wearing my number: sixty-seven.
(pretend whisper)
That's the year I was born.

Covertly, she holds out a small sack to them.

MRS. LAYDON

It's some divinity I made for you myself. Take it, it'll give you energy.

ROBERT

We're not supposed to . . .

MRS. LAYDON

They won't notice.

ROBERT

Thank you, then.
> (to Gloria)

That's nice of Mrs. Laydon. Isn't it, Gloria?

Gloria makes a small gesture. Throughout this scene she remains apart from Mrs. Laydon. Suspicious. Careful.

ROBERT

We're not supposed to stay too long in one place, so . . .

MRS. LAYDON

I understand. You go right on. But don't give up. Because you're going to win. I'm sure you are.

187. NEW ANGLE ON ROBERT AND GLORIA

as they move off from Mrs. Laydon.

GLORIA
> (after beat)

Sixty-five.
> (at his look)

I figured it out. That's how old she is. God, I hope I never get to be that old.

188. INT BALLROOM AFTERNOON MOVING WITH ROLLO

CLICKING his hand cricket, he skates around and past dancers to:

189. SAGGING COUPLE

draped against a column. The WOMAN has passed out and hangs limply in the arms of the MAN, who has crooked one arm around the column to keep himself up. He looks wearily at Rollo . . . then loosens his hold on the column and tries to hoist his partner back to her feet. But the effort is too much. He loses his footing. As the couple falls . . .

190. ROLLO

BLOWS his whistle.

191. INT   BALLROOM   EVENING   ON GROUP OF CONTESTANTS

surrounding a food cart . . . continuing to move while they grab for food.

> ROCKY'S VOICE
> Watch 'em eat, folks. It's all part of the show. Seven meals a day. Count 'em—seven.

192. SAILOR

shoveling in food with one hand, while handing on a sandwich to Shirl with the other.

> ROCKY'S VOICE
> Believe me, these kids can actually stoke it away. After four days of continuous dancing these boys and girls may not be well *heeled* . . .

193. ON ALICE

to SHOW her standing aside with her back turned on the cluster of dancers. She eats slowly, precisely, as though she were seated at a table. A smidgen of something from her plate—a few grains of rice or a morsel of bread—falls on her gown. She brushes—

needlessly—at her gown until she is sure there is no stain . . . then she holds the remainder of her dinner over one of the trash cans and drops it in.

ROCKY'S VOICE
. . . but you can bet they're well stuffed.

194. FAVORING GLORIA

eating—but casually, almost apathetically. As she folds a piece of bread around some cheese, her gaze falls on:

195. RUBY

eating frantically, grabbing for more food even as she is wolfing at a sandwich. She stops as she is raising another hunk of bread toward her mouth, when she notices Gloria staring at her. A long beat. Then:

RUBY
(apologetically)
I have to.

GLORIA
Yeah. And how're you going to feed it after you got it?

James steps INTO SCENE between them. He glares at Gloria. She stares back at him unintimidated, then turns away . . . and tosses the rest of her sandwich into one of the garbage cans.

196. INT   BALLROOM   NIGHT   CLOSE ON SIGN

It now reads:

DAY 5
HOURS ELAPSED 0101
COUPLES REMAINING 53
HOW LONG CAN THEY LAST?

JOEL'S VOICE
(attempting English accent)

No! I'm through. Through!

197. ANGLE FROM BANDSTAND ACROSS JOEL AND ALICE TO
AUDIENCE

Silhouetted in the circle of a spotlight. Joel wears a
straw hat. Alice's makeup is extra heavy.

ALICE

Pigeon!

JOEL

Sweet!

ALICE

My poor suspicious husband has just returned from
a business trip. Poor . . . suspicious . . . insecure little
darling.

The piano plays campy *Perils of Pauline* MUSIC. The
audience is mildly amused. Rocky closes his eyes in
pain at the lousy Noel Coward imitation.

JOEL

Do I detect cigar smoke?

ALICE

Cigar smoke?

JOEL

Cheap . . . cigar . . . smoke?!!

ALICE

Heavens! He suspects!

JOEL

I . . . . . am leaving you!

ALICE

For all time?

193

JOEL

Forever!

ALICE

But these glorious years!

JOEL

Sheer hell.

ALICE

Heavens!

JOEL

Adieu!

He backs dramatically out of the spotlight.

ALICE
(watches him leave, then turns to audience smiling)
Filthy little beast! To suspect *me* of being unfaithful.
Well! There are some things one cannot reveal even
to one's husband!

She reaches behind her back and with a grand flourish
produces a lit cigar which she puffs dramatically and
then throws out toward the audience.

198. REVERSE ANGLE ROCKY

bounding onto the bandstand, already cuing the AP-
PLAUSE.

ROCKY
(into mike)
Couple Number 66 in a scene direct from the smash
Broadway hit, "Private Wives" . . . our own Ramon
Navarro and Jean Harlow: Mr. Joel Girard . . . and
Miss Alice LeBlanc.

Behind him, Alice whips off her "sarong" . . . Joel
cinches his tie . . . and they bow.

199. ANGLE ON AUDIENCE

APPLAUSE. The audience is more crowded now. People in better spirits. They begin to throw a small shower of coins.

200. ON FLOOR

as coins land and (under a grim code of honesty and Rollo's watchful eye) some of the other dancers scoop them up.

201. BACK TO ROCKY

> ROCKY
> (to audience)

Thank you. Alice and Joel will be back with us again . . . IF there's no Hollywood talent scouts in the audience tonight.

> (beat)

And now, in keeping with our policy of letting you folks know *everything* that happens in our little family here, I'm pleased to inform you that another sponsor has come forward to back still another pair of our spunky kids.

He points toward the dance floor.

202. ANGLE ON SPOTLIGHT

as it PICKS OUT ROBERT AND GLORIA on the dance floor near the bandstand.

> ROCKY'S VOICE

Couple Number Sixty-seven: Gloria Beatty and Robert Syverton.

203. MRS. LAYDON

enthusiastically CLAPPING.

204. ON ROCKY

ROCKY

Let 'em see the company that's backing you to win, kids.

205. ON ROBERT AND GLORIA

Gloria is wearing a sleeveless pullover and Robert a sweat shirt. On the front of each is lettered: *JONA-THON'S IRON TONIC*. CAMERA HOLDS ON LETTERING.

ROCKY'S VOICE

Congratulations, kids! And who knows, folks, with a sponsor like that, they just may win.

CAMERA PULLS BACK TO SEE the spotlight go OFF them. They are left again in the normal tinseled light of the ballroom.

ROBERT

Maybe he's right . . . Maybe we *can* win.

She gives him a sour look.

GLORIA

Fat chance.

ROBERT

Well . . . a lot of couples've dropped out already. We *could* win.

GLORIA

Yeah . . . ? Take a look around. Some of this bunch've been through ten of these things.

ROBERT

I know . . . But suppose we *did* win. What would you do with it?

GLORIA

With what?

ROBERT

With the money . . . if we win.

GLORIA
(starts to shrug it off, then considers)
Maybe I'll buy some good rat poison.

206. ANGLE TOWARD BANDSTAND

CAMERA PUSHES IN toward the $1,500 sign.

CUT TO:

207. INT   ROCKY'S OFFICE   DAY   ANGLE FAVORING COT

on which Rocky is dozing. The room is very dim. It could be night, except that there is a little seepage of light around the edges of a window drape. We can make out some of the furnishings of the room nevertheless: desk, Atwater-Kent table radio, a portable clothes rack with Rocky's various show outfits hanging from it, leftover things from the previous occupant which have been shoved into one corner.

A beat. No sound within the office, but from outside —distantly—are the sounds of the band, the audience, the waves. Then we HEAR the doorknob turning, and a crack of light from the hall corridor spills into the office and across the cot.

Rocky lurches up from the cot, knocking the quilt aside and slashing at the slab of light with his hand as if he could somehow knock it aside.

ROCKY

What the hell is it?!! Shut it off!!

208. ANGLE TO INCLUDE TURKEY

standing inside the partially open door.

It's two hours. You said to get you up in two hours, Rocky.

He crosses to the window and opens the drape, letting grey light from outside fill the room. Rocky sits up on the side of the cot resting his face in his hands. We see now that he is wearing an undershirt and trousers.

ROCKY

Shake me out a butt, Turkey.

Turkey hands him a cigarette from an open pack on the table next to the radio. Rocky lights it, inhales, pushes himself up from the cot. He looks enigmatically toward the still-open door, through which the NOISE of the crowd is heard.

ROCKY

Listen to 'em, Turkey. Those wonderful, wonderful people. Yowza!
(snarling)
Shut it! Shut the goddamned door!

After Turkey closes the door, Rocky continues to stare at it for an instant. Then he turns, scuffs into his untied shoes, and crosses to a wall sink. He glances at himself in the mirror, considers shaving for a moment, but then settles for talcum powder.

ROCKY

Wonderful! . . . But you got to understand them is all. Now you take my old man, he never got out of the fourth grade. But people—he didn't know his left elbow from his right nut about people.

As he continues, he dresses: putting on a fresh shirt, tie, lacing his shoes, picking out a jacket, etc. Turkey functions more or less as his valet, handing him articles he has pointed to.

You know what he was, Turkey? He was a faith healer. I used to travel the circuit with him. *I* was the one he healed. I was his shill—to get the crowd set up.

(hunches back, "cripples" leg; deepens voice)

Walk! When I lay my hand upon you, you will walk. You will walk! Walk!

He slowly straightens, and begins hesitantly—then confidently, glowingly to walk again. Back to his normal posture, he stops and points toward the clothes rack.

ROCKY

The sodden old bastard, he thought it was *him* they believed in. But it was *me*.

He turns to the mirror again, and starts adjusting his jacket.

CUT TO:

209. INT BALLROOM DUSK DOWN SHOT ON DANCERS

wending off the floor.

ROCKY'S VOICE

Remember, folks, one admission is good for the entire night. So don't leave—there's always more to see at the Marathon.

210. ON MUSICIANS

setting down their instruments and leaving the bandstand.

211. ON ROBERT

ambling into the aisleway back of the bleachers and starting slowly toward the men's rest area.

212. INT   EXIT CORRIDOR   DUSK   CLOSE ON PAIL OF GARBAGE

PULL BACK TO SHOW JANITOR holding the pail with both hands while he wedges a fire-escape door open with his back. As the door opens we SEE that it looks out on the pier and beyond toward the ocean. JANITOR EXITS through the door and it starts to swing shut again—but not all the way. It is held slightly ajar by a door stop.

213. REVERSE ANGLE ON ROBERT

behind the bandstand. He stares a moment toward the slit of light from the outside, hesitates, then starts toward the door, CAMERA LEADING him.

214. ANGLE ON ROBERT AT DOOR

as he opens it just slightly.

215. ROBERT'S POV   THE OCEAN

exploding in a cold, red diffusion where the sun has fallen into the far edge of the water and begun to melt across its crinkled surface. Gulls are flapping upward, as if flushed from cover.

216. BACK ON ROBERT

Stunned. Sucking his breath in. Suddenly the door is yanked open wide in front of him, REVEALING JANITOR, who has come back for another pail. As Robert backs off, Janitor steps inside the closing door.

ROLLO

What you doin' here? It's rest period. You're supposed to be off your feet. You better get back.

ROBERT

I was just looking at the sunset.

200

Go on! Get off your feet.

Robert turns and starts off. Janitor picks up another of the pails and repeats the process of backing out the door.

217. ON ROBERT

moving down the corridor TOWARD CAMERA, but continuing to look back over his shoulder at the door.

ALICE'S VOICE
(whisper)
Here!

218. TO INCLUDE ALICE

standing in an alcove, as Robert turns toward her in surprise.

(NOTE: Alice's tone throughout the following is straightforward, casual, conversational.)

ALICE
You knew about the door too.

ROBERT
No.

ALICE
They open it about this time every day.

ROBERT
I didn't know.

ALICE
It's where I come—to get away from all that.
(indicates ballroom)

ROBERT

That's funny, I almost thought you liked it.

ALICE

God, no! I'm only doing it because I have to.

ROBERT

I guess it's the same with everybody—at least they're feeding us.

ALICE

I don't mean that—
(she holds her hands out slightly)
I mean so I can be seen. Why else do you think I'm wearing something like this?—Have you got a cigarette?

Robert starts searching through his pockets . . .

ROBERT

No. I don't smoke. I'm sorry.

ALICE

It doesn't matter.
(nods at door)
Did you go outside?

ROBERT

No. I was going to, but . . . I didn't.

ALICE

Why not?

ROBERT

I'm not sure you'd understand . . . I mean, I don't exactly understand, myself. But—all of a sudden it was like I was afraid. Like I'd forgotten there was anything out there at all. Like there was just all of us inside here going around day and night, night and day, till you don't know which is which.
(drops voice)

And then when I looked out the door . . . there *wasn't* anyone! No one at all. No one on the pier or out on the beach or . . . And suddenly I had this terrible thought that—

(abrupt laugh)

It's weird.

ALICE
(seriously)
No. I understand what you mean . . . I really do.

SOUND of the exit door being pulled open. Robert draws her back into concealment beside him in the alcove. Alice looks at his hand on her arm. He abruptly pulls his hand away. The shaft of murky light fades from the corridor as the exit door is HEARD closing again.

ALICE
What do you think of "Alice LeBlanc"?

ROBERT
What . . . ?

ALICE
The name, "Alice LeBlanc." It isn't my real name, of course. I chose it for the films. Do you like it?

ROBERT
(considers)
Yes, that's just right.
(looks up as if at a marquee; nods)
Sure, if I saw it on a marquee I'd go in to watch you. I really would.

ALICE
But it wouldn't be *me* you were seeing, would it?
(then smiles)
I mean, *actually*, that's what is so special, so different about the films. It isn't *you* they're looking at. It's only a picture.

203

(giggles)

That's really half why I want to be a star in films, I think—so I can sit in the audience and watch myself. Does that sound terribly vain and silly?

ROBERT

No . . . it's just I never thought of it exactly like that.

ALICE

But you *do* understand—you're in films too.

ROBERT

Well, sort of. I was a dead French villager in "Fallen Angels."

The SIREN screeches from the ballroom o.s., startling them. They leave the alcove guiltily and turn to start out of the corridor. They stop short as they see:

219. JOEL

standing at the head of the corridor staring at them. He looks at Alice, and then stares at Robert and smiles. It is a smile of both contempt and pity.

ALICE
(to Joel)

Shut up! Shut up!

220. INT BALLROOM NIGHT PANNING AUDIENCE

OVER SHOT we HEAR "Toot, Toot, Tootsie, Goodbye" being SUNG off-key and in Hungarian.

221. HIGH ANGLE

As the SONG CONTINUES OVER, CAMERA BOOMS down slowly and moves through the dancers to a dark-haired young man spotlighted in front of the band. As he finishes singing the number to AP-PLAUSE, Rocky bounces INTO SCENE behind him.

ROCKY

How about *that*, folks? Each and every word in Hungarian! The boy from Couple Forty-three, JOHNNY...
> (takes long build-up beat)

O'HOULLIHAN.

222. ANGLE ON DANCE FLOOR

as some of the other contestants pick up the coins thrown onto the floor.

ROCKY'S VOICE

Thank you. And I know Johnny and his lovely partner thank you.

223. BACK ON ROCKY

ROCKY

There'll be more. AND ... soon a very special attraction. Watch for the announcements. But, a gentle hint and a word to the wise: tell your friends and get your tickets early.

CUT TO:

224. INT BALLROOM EARLY MORNING RAKING THE NEARLY EMPTY BLEACHERS

No families—just a few leftover tipplers, insomniacs and one handsome and sardonically bored COUPLE in evening dress.

225. PANNING THE DANCERS

who are just going through the motions. Some of the women have their hair tied in rag curls; two or three couples are reading the *Sunday* color comic sections of the morning newspapers.

226. ON CECIL AND AGNES

She is droopy. He—incongruously—is reading the sports section over her shoulder.

CECIL

Gehrig hit a home run. Four hundred feet.

Agnes gives a slight indifferent nod of her head.

227. SAILOR AND SHIRL

He is reading the comics. When he LAUGHS, she twists her head about to look at him.

SAILOR

The Katzenjammer Kids—they put a motor on the Captain's rocking chair, see, so when he started rock-ing—

(at her bored look)

Forget it.

228. JAMES

reading from a Bible to Ruby.

JAMES

"Take heed that ye do not your alms before men, to be seen of them: otherwise ye have no reward of your Father which is in heaven."

229. INT   PALM GARDEN   ON ROCKY

perched casually on an end stool, drinking black coffee and fiddling with an unlighted cigar. In b.g., a NIGHT BARMAN is cleaning up. He stops to offer Rocky a refill on his coffee. Rocky waves him aside, and continues staring off at:

230. GLORIA

shuffling along with Robert in the ballroom. They are

"dancing" side-to-side, neither of them talking. As she stretches a kink from her neck, she sees:

231. ROCKY

continuing to stare appraisingly at her.

232. ON GLORIA

flatly returning the look.

233. BACK TO ROCKY

As he turns, Rollo, who is standing around the curve of the bar, looks speculatively at him. He nods off in the direction of Gloria. Rocky answers with an enigmatic shrug.

234. INT BALLROOM AFTERNOON CLOSE ON A WHITE LINE

being painted to follow the oval contour of the dance floor. PULL BACK TO SHOW several painters, working at various sections of the floor.

235. SAILOR DRAGGING SHIRL

She dozes fitfully on his shoulder. His look toward the white line on the floor is grim.

SAILOR
(to no one)
Uh . . . oh.

236. ALICE AND JOEL

She is in her stocking feet and carrying her high-heeled pumps. His tie is loosened, his shirt partially undone, and his cuffs rolled back.

ALICE
Whatever is all that for?

JOEL
(watching the painters)
Not for fun. You can bet on that.

237. MARIO AND JACKIE

barely moving.

JACKIE
Christ! Here it comes.

238. RUBY AND JAMES

He supports her. She lifts her head from his shoulder
and looks at him.

RUBY
I can't. I don't think I can.

JAMES
Yes you can. Don't think about it yet.

239. GLORIA AND ROBERT

He has a slight stubble now. She looks completely exhausted. She's also been watching the painters.

GLORIA
(quietly)
That sonofabitch.

Robert is puzzled.

FLASH FORWARD TO:

240. INT POLICE STATION NIGHT ROBERT

being fingerprinted, still wearing his JONATHON'S
IRON TONIC sweat shirt and seeming bewildered
and dazed.

OFFICER'S VOICE
(reverb)
Left thumb.
(beat)
That's it. Step back. In front of the screen.

Robert moves back until he is positioned in front of a portable white screen.

A beat . . . and then the flashbulb of a camera explodes into Robert's face.

CUT TO:

241. INT   WOMEN'S REST AREA   AFTERNOON   FOUR
     NAKED WOMEN

taking ice-cold showers. Their backs are to us, but they jump up and down and gasp as the water splays over them.

242. GLORIA

lying on the floor with her legs propped up, trying to get the blood to run back to her head.

243. RUBY

lying on her cot taking deep, rhythmic breaths.

244. JACKIE MILLER

rubbing baby oil onto the bottoms of her feet.

245. SHIRL

snoring loudly . . . her mouth open.

246. LILLIAN

massaging her calves slowly upwards, over and over.

247. DOLLY WITH THE NURSE

as she moves through the aisle, checking the various girls. She passes:

248. ALICE

standing off by herself. She is wearing sheer silk step-ins and a chiffon bandeau. She is shaking out her gown, brushing it, smoothing it. Now she turns and unlatches her multi-stickered valise.

249. EXTREME CLOSEUP ALICE

as she stares down into the valise with a puzzled, confused expression.

250. ALICE'S POV

Her hands in the valise pawing meticulously at first, then with a growing frenzy . . . among the contents. (NOTE: An evening bag, lace handkerchiefs, a syringe rolled in a towel, a comb and brush set with cheap imitation mother-of-pearl handles, a sachet, a curling iron, and a few loose hairpins.)

251. CLOSE REVERSE ANGLE ON ALICE

She stops searching. For a moment she remains utterly immobile . . . then abruptly she whirls about.

ALICE
(shouting)
Matron!!! . . . Someone! . . . It's gone! MATRON!

252. ON GLORIA

as she starts up at Alice's shrieking. In b.g. a Nurse and some of the other women turn and begin to move toward Alice. Gloria stands up and WE PAN with her and the group as they cluster about and stare with a kind of indifferent, lethargic confusion.

ALICE

It's gone.

(clutching at Nurse)

It's gone!

NURSE

What is it? What's gone?

ALICE

My gown.

The Nurse gestures toward the gown Alice is clutching.

ALICE

No, no! My other gown . . . and the chemicals for my hair . . . and my rouge and mascara and— They're gone! They're all gone! Someone's stolen them out of my valise.

NURSE

No one's stolen anything. You've probably just—

ALICE

No!

(points at the other women)

They did it. One of them stole my things.

She starts to lunge blindly toward the other women, but the Nurse stops her.

(Nurse, Ad Libs, Alice speak together)

NURSE

Stop it! Get back!

AD LIBS

DOUSE HER! . . . Tie her up! . . . You touch me and I'll claw your eyes out!

ALICE

Give it back to me!! GIVE IT BACK TO ME!!

211

The SHRILL BLAST of the SIREN slices through the uproar, startling everyone into momentary silence.

253. ANGLE TO REVEAL ROLLO

pushing and elbowing his way through the cluster of women.

                    ROLLO
What the hell's goin' on here?! You heard the siren. Come on!! Come on!! Finish up and get out there.

The other women, some grudgingly, some indifferently, move off screen. Rollo stares for a moment at Alice, and then turns to go. Alice reaches out around the folds of her gown and clasps his arm.

                    ALICE
Please . . . You must help me.

                    ROLLO
                (to Nurse)
She squirrely?

                    NURSE
I don't think so.

She EXITS. Rollo checks his watch, then starts off.

                    ROLLO
Better shake it up. You only got a coupla seconds left.

Alice tries to cling to him.

                    ALICE
Wait! You have to help me. Please.

                    ROLLO
Later. You just hustle your fanny out there.

Rollo wrenches away from her and strides off. CAM-
ERA PUSHES IN CLOSE on Alice.

> ALICE
> (calling)

Wait!

254. LONG SHOT   ALICE

Alone . . . still holding the folded gown in front of
her.

> ALICE
> (quieter)

Wait . . .

CAMERA PULLS FARTHER AWAY.

> ALICE
> (a whisper)

Wait . . .

255. INT   CORRIDOR FRONTING REST AREAS   EARLY EVE-
NING   FULL SHOT OF CONTESTANTS

grouped about . . . some lying down, some leaning
against the wall, facing Rocky, who stands on a
straight-backed chair.

> ROCKY

The thing to remember, kids, is this is the kind of
stunt that packs 'em in. Listen, we'll even get some of
the Hollywood crowd out there tonight. Now . . .
everybody get one of those uniforms they're passing
out, make sure you tie your numbers.

The attendants move among the crowd handing out
shorts and tank tops. Some of the contestants hold
them up to themselves measuring the sizes. A woman
near the front who wears a jacket with "KRUPP
BAKERIES" lettered on it is stretching the uniform
top to see if it will fit her.

ROCKY

Hey, Krupp Bakeries! Easy on the goods.
                    (to all)
Listen, kids, we're renting these track outfits for one
time and one time only—so any rips, tears or malicious
damage, *you* get charged. Okay . . . ?

256. CLOSEUP   ROCKY

ROCKY

We'll have the nurses and the doctor on hand so nobody has to worry. Now . . . you kids that're pros
already know how it works . . .

CROWD NOISES BEGIN ON SOUNDTRACK.
Then . . . A BRASS SECTION INTRO.

257. CLOSER ON ROCKY

ROCKY

. . . and I'm sure the rest of you've all heard about
it . . .

THE BRASS INTRO and CROWD NOISES begin
to be HEARD LOUDER.

258. EXTREME CLOSEUP   ROCKY

smiling as he SHOUTS above the FULL SOUND
of ORCHESTRA and CROWD.

ROCKY

Well now . . . NOW you're going to see it. Yowza!
THE DERBY!!

A CLASH of CYMBALS as CAMERA PULLS
BACK TO SHOW that Rocky is now wearing his
white tuxedo and that the SCENE IS:

259. INT   BALLROOM   NIGHT   FULL SHOT

The painted white line forms an oval in the center of

the floor, creating the effect of a track. The Doctor and attendants and nurses, as well as trainers and judges, all stand at attention inside the line. The bleachers are very full now and the whole ballroom has a "dressed up" quality.

ROCKY

The supreme test of energy and endurance. Ten solid, wrenching minutes of wrack and ruin! The Derby!

260. THE AUDIENCE

responding. They CLAP, STOMP THEIR FEET, WHISTLE. Some hold up home-lettered signs in support of their favorite couple.

261. ROCKY

holding up his hand for attention.

ROCKY

Good! Because you're in for an exciting extravaganza. *Yowza*. The Derby! And—if I may be permitted to share a little thought with you—there's a lesson for all of us in it, ladies and gents, *contestants*—if you hear me out there . . .
(looks o.s.)
You don't need to be Number One as you amble down Life's Highway. But *don't be last*. Round and round and round they'll go—for ten little minutes. Who'll set the pace? Who'll win the race? *Everybody* . . . excepting the last three couples.

He studies his watch and raises one hand.

ROCKY

And now . . . . here they are!

He slashes a signal with his hand.

262. ON TRUMPETER

215

shrilling out a RACING CALL.

263. ON COLORED BALLOONS

being cut free and floating upward.

264. ON CONTESTANTS

streaming out onto the floor in their track suits.
Lagging at the rear and being urged on by Joel is
Alice.

> ROCKY'S VOICE
> And looky, looky, looky, folks . . . they've got *knees!*

265. RAKING SHOT   CONTESTANTS

as they RUN by CAMERA. Their glaringly naked
arms, legs, knees, elbows seeming to flail out at CAM-
ERA. Their nakedness seems lumpy, swollen, wobbly,
weird. Over, we HEAR the audience LAUGH.

266. SECTION OF AUDIENCE

pointing and LAUGHING. Some wave to their fa-
vorites.

267. ON ROCKY AND CONTESTANTS

Some contestants wave to audience.

> ROCKY
> Everybody here? Okay,
>> (pointing off)
> Take a good look.

268. UP SHOT ON SIGN

It reads:

269. ROCKY

grins, addresses the audience.

ROCKY

Get your hankies ready, folks, because three couples
are about to go bye-bye!

270. CONTESTANTS

as they watch Rocky, hitch uncomfortably at their
scanty clothing. An assistant wheels out a brass starting cannon, hands the lanyard to Rocky.

ROCKY

Floor Judges ready?

271. ROLLO AND JIGGS

wave O.K.

ROCKY'S VOICE

Nurses and House Physician?

272. NURSES AND DOCTOR

wave back self-consciously.

273. FULL SHOT ° FLOOR

as the contestants group behind the broad white start-
finish line at the foot of the stage.

ROCKY
(amplified; echoing)

Audience?

A ROAR from the audience.

ROCKY
(to Band Leader)

Mr. Rhythm?

CYMBAL CRASH. Rocky looks down at the contestants.

274. THE CONTESTANTS

ready, in pairs. The men wear leather belts bandolero fashion; the women grip the belts with one hand.

275. ROCKY

He waves in the direction of the band and they break into a tension arrangement. Then Rocky pulls the lanyard.

276. CLOSE ON BRASS CANNON

as it goes off. CAMERA PANS with the smoke as it belches out, delineated against the dark auditorium, over the heads of the contestants, who begin moving counter-clockwise.

277. ON CONTESTANTS

jostling for position. All of them move in the awkward, jerky heel-and-toe fashion, which is one of the rules of the race. They are allowed to fall and then rise and resume the race . . . if they are back up within a count of ten.

278. ROLLO AND JIGGS

skate continuously in and out of the pack.

279. THE AUDIENCE

responds in direct measure to the pace.

280. THE CLOCK

Like a stadium scoreboard clock, it will tick off the ten-minute race period.

281.-296. VARIOUS ANGLES ON DERBY CONTESTANTS

as they jostle for position, jumble together, elbow their way free again. We should be aware of *pulsing veins, clenched fists, flailing arms, eyes smarting from an ooze of sweat, uniforms staining and blotching— and faces . . . sometimes blurred, sometimes sharply etched in pain.* We should hear MOANS, SHOUTS, GUTTURAL CRIES. Above all, we should sense that after the first few turns, the Derby contestants are no longer aware of the audience. Ultimately, they will pass through the barrier of exhaustion and achieve a kind of hysterical single-mindedness. They will be aware only of the race itself—time, place, sight, sound, pain, hope and despair will all be blurred from their immediate consciousness.

297. ROCKY

will spiel out a color commentary throughout the Derby and call the race.

ROCKY

Hold your hats, folks, here come the leaders and they are actually lapping, yes, they are actually lapping the pack! Floor Judges, keep your eyes on the last three couples! *The last three couples will lose!*

298. ON THREE TRAILING DERBY CONTESTANTS

fighting to keep pace. Jiggs skates backward among them.

ROCKY'S VOICE

How about that, folks? Exciting? Well, I want to tell you! OOOOops! Whoa, Nellie! There's a pileup. There's a pileup in the far corner of the track!

299. ON PILEUP

where a knot of Derby contestants are shoving and elbowing each other in an attempt to get around the curve. We HEAR YELLS, CURSES, SHOUTS from the audience. Other Derby couples swing up behind the pileup, strain to skirt clear of it.

300. CLOSER ON PILEUP

A swirl of legs, arms . . . sweat, grime . . . spectators in the adjacent boxes leaning over the railing, shouting, calling, urging, their faces LOOMING INTO FRAME . . .

301. ON ROBERT AND GLORIA

approaching the pileup, which is now beginning to sort itself out and thus spread across even more of the track.

ROBERT

Hang on! Both hands! Get behind me.

Robert swings sharply, like a halfback cutting back into an open field run, and dodges inside the pileup. The abruptness of his turn, however, threatens to fling Gloria away from him. He reaches back, and grabs onto her.

ROBERT

Okay . . . ?

GLORIA
(nods)

Keep going.

302. JAMES AND RUBY

as Robert and Gloria move up next to them. Robert looks over at James, who grimly returns the look.

Now Robert and Gloria move ahead of them and o.s. Ruby darts a worried glance after them. James notices it, and grins reassuringly at her.

> JAMES
> (breathless)
Don't worry, honey—I'm keeping count.

303. MOVING WITH ROLLO

as he zigzags on his skates, then whirls about to point warningly at Shirl, who is straining—even with Sailor's help—to keep up.

> ROLLO
> (to Sailor)
Come on, Chief—heel and toe, or she's out.

With Sailor guiding her, Shirl forces herself back into the heel-and-toe pattern.

304. ON ROCKY

> ROCKY
The Management cautions that no wagering is permitted. But . . . you can always cheer on your favorite couple. And all these wonderful kids deserve your cheers, folks. Because each one of them is fighting down pain, exhaustion, weariness . . . struggling to keep going . . . battling to win. And isn't that the American Way, folks?

305. ALICE AND JOEL

being passed by two other couples. She is suddenly frightened, starts to pull ahead. Joel shakes his head grimly, won't increase his pace.

> JOEL
> (through clenched teeth)
Mervyn LeRoy is here.

ALICE

Whom?

JOEL

Don't look, you silly bitch!

ALICE
(breathless)

Whomever is Mervyn LeRoy?

JOEL

Only the most brilliant young director at Warner Brothers, that's who.

He indicates general direction of MERVYN LeROY.

306. THE AUDIENCE

The spotlight shines in the general direction of one of the bleachers. There is a stir of twisting heads surrounding a white-suited man who takes one of the seats.

ROCKY'S VOICE

Added to our list of celebrities for the night—Mr. Mervyn LeRoy!

307. CLOSE ON MRS. LAYDON

waving to:

308. ROBERT AND GLORIA

as they heel-and-toe past her box.

ROCKY'S VOICE

What about it, Mr. LeRoy? Almost as much excitement here as in "Little Caesar," right?

309. INSERT ON CLOCK

It shows that just over half the Derby race has gone by.

310. ANGLE ON MAX AND MURIEL

among the Derby contestants. Heaving, panting, they hurry into a turn. The girl swings wide, and throws the boy off stride. He skids, grasping wildly . . . then he falls. The girl manages to retrieve her balance and then leans unsteadily over her partner.

MURIEL

Get up!!

MAX
(trying)

Ohhh!!!

ROCKY'S VOICE

Oh-oh!! Trouble at the turn. That's the boy from Couple Number Seventy-one.

311. CLOSER ON FAT COUPLE

as the girl tries to tug at the boy's slippery arms.

ROCKY'S VOICE

Floor Judge! . . . Get a Floor Judge over there.

312. ROLLO

skating up to the struggling couple . . . SNAPPING his HAND CRICKET as he brakes. Immediately he raises his arm and starts COUNTING—*prizefight referee* style—over the fallen boy.

ROCKY'S VOICE

Remember, folks—ten seconds. *Ten seconds to avoid being disqualified.*

MURIEL

Hurry!

MAX

Help me!

ROLLO

... Six ... seven ...

MURIEL

No!

She tries vainly to pull free, but merely falls heavily on all fours.

MURIEL
(raging)

Damn you! Damn you! Damn you!

ROLLO'S VOICE

... Nine ... TEN!

313. EXTREME CLOSEUP OF ROLLO

as he BLOWS his *WHISTLE.*

314. ANGLE ON CLOCK

It shows two minutes left.

315. ON ROCKY

glancing down from clock.

ROCKY

Less than two minutes left, folks!

He signals toward the band.

316. ON BANDLEADER

upping the beat with his baton. The band begins PLAYING faster.

317. MOVING WITH GLORIA AND ROBERT

Their eyes are glazed now. They stare ahead with a fixed blankness. They breathe in steady, wheezing GASPS.

                    ROBERT

Are we behind?

                    GLORIA

I don't know.

                    ROBERT
              (only hearing it now)
Two minutes . . .? Did he say two minutes?

                    GLORIA

I don't know.

                    ROBERT
                (giggling)
Only two minutes! Only—

318. EXTREME CLOSEUP ON ROBERT

as his face suddenly contorts in pain.

319. WIDER ANGLE TO SHOW ROBERT

pulling up sharply. He hunches over, clutches at his right leg. Gloria takes the weight of his body on hers to keep him from falling.

                    GLORIA

What is it? What's wrong?

                    ROBERT

My leg . . . ! I can't move it!

320. ANGLE TOWARD MRS. LAYDON

She strains forward. In the section of audience behind her, spectators are leaping to their feet, beginning to SHOUT.

ROCKY'S VOICE

Couple Number Sixty-seven are in *trouble*, folks! No fooling! They're in *trouble!* Floor Judge!

321. ROBERT AND GLORIA

as other couples move past them.

GLORIA

Try! Lean on me and try to move!

ROBERT

I can't.

GLORIA

Try ... TRY!

He makes an effort to grit down the pain and hobble forward. Immediately his leg goes out from under him and he falls.

Jiggs skates INTO SCENE, WHISTLE ready, hand raised to start the count.

ROCKY'S VOICE

Oh-oh!! He's down! The boy from Couple Sixty-seven is down.

JIGGS
(starting count)

One ... two ...

322. TIGHT ON ROBERT AND GLORIA

She is kneeling over him now.

GLORIA

Hold on to me! Like this! Hold on to me!

He grips her shoulders and she tries to pull him up ... but he *CRIES OUT in pain* and slips back.

JIGGS' VOICE

... FOUR ... FIVE ...

ROBERT
(sharply)

Go on. I can't! I can't!

GLORIA

Yes, you can!

She digs her fingers into his cramped leg and begins kneading it. He writhes, cries out.

ROBERT

Leave me alone!

JIGGS' VOICE

...six...seven...

GLORIA
(shouting at him)

Bend your knee!!! Stretch your leg out!!

ROBERT
(trying to shove her away, angrily)

Stop it!! Let me alone!!

323. CLOSE ON GLORIA

She hammers on his thigh with both fists...

GLORIA

You can!...You can!...

Suddenly, the knotted muscle in Robert's thigh snaps free. His leg kicks out. Gloria begins struggling to get him back to his feet.

324. TO INCLUDE JIGGS

still counting even as Robert starts to regain his feet.

JIGGS

...eight...nine...

GLORIA

Shut up, goddamn you! Shut up!

325. ROCKY

Milking it to the end.

> ROCKY
> He's up! The boy from Couple Sixty-seven is up!
> But will they make it . . . ? They've lost ground.
>> (glances at clock o.s.)
> Forty seconds left! Can they make it?

326. ROBERT AND GLORIA

He holds her arm, still in pain . . . but moving again.
Gloria is grimly determined.

327. SAILOR AND SHIRL

moving even with Robert and Gloria.

> SAILOR
>> (wheezing)
> Hey, that was the greatest, Gloria! You got real guts.
> I mean it.

> GLORIA
> Save your breath.

> SAILOR
>> (pulling ahead)
> I hope you make it, baby.

328. CLOSE ON MRS. LAYDON

Her knuckles, bent across the railing in front of her,
are white. Her lower lip is sucked in between her
teeth. Unconsciously, she is holding her breath.

329. ROBERT AND GLORIA

struggling the last few yards toward the finish line.
A couple passes them . . . another couple. Gloria
twists her neck to look back at more couples closing
in on them. She turns back, tugs harder at Robert.

330. ANOTHER COUPLE

edges up almost even with Robert and Gloria. She cheats a sideways glance at their straining faces . . . turns back to Robert . . . thrusts the last of her strength into pulling him on . . .

331. ROBERT AND GLORIA

move ahead of the challenging couple . . . lunge on . . . and cross the finish line.

332. ANGLE ON ROCKY AND CANNON

He closes his eyes, yanks the lanyard, the cannon FIRES, MUSIC STOPS, and he points at the finish line:

ROCKY'S VOICE
And there's the finish! Hittum with the spot!

333. DOWN SHOT   THREE LOSING COUPLES

The men are stunned and exhausted: the women are hysterical and angry. Whistles SHRILLING: audience ROARING: rest of the contestants glad to be alive.

SHARP CUT TO:

334. INT   WOMEN'S REST AREA   NIGHT

Dead silence except for breathing . . . and some soft moans. The women lie . . . some sleeping . . . some rocking themselves . . . some staring wide-eyed. They have not removed their track suits. CAMERA HOLDS on them for a beat . . . then we begin to hear softly the sound of COLEY JAMES playing "I COVER THE WATERFRONT."

CUT TO:

335. INT   BALLROOM   AFTERNOON   ANGLE FAVORING
COLEY JAMES

He is playing "Waterfront." Behind him the combo members are filtering in to take their places, just coming on for the night.

COMBO LEADER
(to Coley)

How's it been?

COLEY

Slow.

The accordion player arrives, climbing onto the bandstand. He waves to Coley.

ACCORDION PLAYER

Coley.
(in general)
Man, that traffic on Pico—gets worse every day.

BASS PLAYER

You ought to take Olympic, it's wider.

He pauses as he glances out toward the contestants. Smiles at Coley.

BASS PLAYER
(shakes head)

They're crazy.

CUT TO:

336. INT   BALLROOM   EVENING   ACROSS SIREN TO
DANCERS

individually shuffling their way back onto the floor to resume the grind.

337. GLORIA AND MRS. LAYDON

as Mrs. Laydon calls her from her usual box.

230

MRS. LAYDON
How are you tonight, Gloria?

GLORIA
Okay.

MRS. LAYDON
(studies her)
You're not eating enough, you know. You have to force yourself. I know, if *I* were your mother ...

GLORIA
My mother's dead.

MRS. LAYDON
Oh ...

She smiles sympathetically at Gloria, then offers her some gum. But Gloria shakes her head.

MRS. LAYDON
Take it. You can give it to Robert.

Gloria shrugs and takes the gum.

MRS. LAYDON
You're so lucky ... you and ...

GLORIA
Why do you come here every day, Mrs. Laydon?

MRS. LAYDON
(surprised)
Why ... to watch *you*.

GLORIA
(seriously)
But why?

MRS. LAYDON
(thinks a moment)
Because ... because ... I like you. And then, it's so

important to have someone cheering for you . . .
you're all working so hard.

She leans forward and pats Gloria's arm protectively.

MRS. LAYDON

But it'll all be over soon, and then you and Robert
can go . . .

GLORIA

Mrs. Laydon . . . We're just dancing together. That's
all.

MRS. LAYDON

Oh, I've watched you. I can tell.

Almost pensively, Gloria turns and moves slowly off.

338. INT BALLROOM NIGHT FULL SHOT

through the dancers toward the bandstand where Alice
and Rocky are holding an animated conversation.
Rocky holds his hand clamped over the mike so that
Alice's consternation will not be made public. He
nods and smiles mechanically. We do not hear their
conversation but we know from her gestures that it
is about her stolen dress.

339. ON ROBERT AND GLORIA

as he looks toward Alice.

ROBERT

I wonder why anybody'd steal her dress like that.

GLORIA

She probably left it under one of the bleachers.
(as Robert looks back at her)
Why!—you think I copped it on her?

ROBERT
(getting angry)
No. I didn't say that. I didn't even think it.
(then)
232

You mad at me or something today, Gloria?

GLORIA

Why the hell should I be mad at you? You think
we're married or something?

They continue dancing in stiff silence. Then Robert
reaches into his back pocket and takes out a folded
section of a newspaper. He unfolds it and holds it out
to one side to read.

GLORIA
(after a beat)
Is the world still there?

ROBERT

It's yesterday's paper.

GLORIA

It's all the same.

ROBERT

I guess.
(scans paper)
The President vetoed a relief bill . . . And there was
a fire in Long Beach—in a hotel. But nobody was
killed: "Miraculous Escape Credited to Hero Night-
clerk."
(reading)
"Doctors today were continuing their around-the-
clock battle to save the life of Arnold Escudo, night
duty clerk at the Majestic Hotel, where late last
night—"

GLORIA

What're they saving him for? He's just going to die
anyway.

ROBERT
(a beat)
You wanta read the funnies?

GLORIA

No.

He turns another page, and now finds something that engrosses him.

ROBERT

That'd be nice.
          (holds page out to Gloria)
Look.

340. INSERT OF HALF-PAGE ADVERTISEMENT

It shows an expensively dressed couple leaning over a confetti-strewn ship railing. The copy reads: FOLLOW THE SUN. FIVE WEEK CARIBBEAN CRUISE. ALL INCLUSIVE. $95.

341. BACK TO SCENE

ROBERT

Maybe that's what I'll do. Something like that.

GLORIA

Sure, why don't you?

FLASH FORWARD TO:

342. INT   JAIL CELL   NIGHT

Robert steps INTO FRAME. He still wears the sweat shirt with the sponsor's lettering. He looks around at the new surroundings. The shadows of the bars crisscross his face and body. There is SILENCE for a moment as he stands very still. Then the SHADOWS of the bars begin to move and we HEAR the RASPING SOUND of the metal door being closed. On the CLANG of it closing:

CUT TO:

343. INT   WOMEN'S REST AREA   NIGHT   EXTREME
     CLOSEUP OF SHIRL

as she lurches up from a cot. She is SCREAMING, her hands thrashing wildly, her eyes staring off in terror.

344. WIDER ANGLE TO INCLUDE OTHER WOMEN

turning on their cots, poking their heads in from the shower room to stare at her.

SHIRL

GET THEM OFF ME!! . . . GET THEM AWAY!!

She begins clawing at her skin . . . violently shaking her stringy hair.

345. ALICE

turns from the mirror to stare at the berserk woman.

346. SHIRL

violently thrusts aside one of the other women and runs into Gloria.

347. GLORIA AND SHIRL

Shirl clutches desperately at Gloria's arm.

GLORIA

What is it? . . . What's the matter with you?

SHIRL
(whispering)
They're crawling all over me.
(shouts again)
Please! Please! Get them off me!!

Jackie pushes INTO SCENE. She wrenches Shirl's hand from Gloria.

JACKIE
(shakes her)
You're all right! There's nothin' crawling on you.

235

The Matron rushes INTO SCENE with a vial of smelling salts.

MATRON

Hold her!

Jackie and Gloria pin Shirl's arms while the Matron forces her to inhale the smelling salts. GASPING from the sharp stench of the ammonia, she seems momentarily to subside.

GLORIA

What's wrong with her?

JACKIE

She's squirreling.

348. ANGLE ON ALICE

She has drawn back, away from the other women watching. She stares at the berserk woman with a very private horror.

349. SHIRL

suddenly SCREAMS again, and lurches out explosively, knocking the smelling salts vial away from the Matron and breaking partially loose from Gloria and Jackie.

350. ROCKY AND TURKEY

burst into the rest area. Rocky immediately turns back to Turkey.

ROCKY

Get back out there and tell 'em to turn up the Victrola.

Turkey quickly EXITS.

Shirl begins to YELL and THRASH about again. Gloria grabs up the smelling salts bottle and starts as if to thrust it under the woman's nose. But Rocky immediately knocks the bottle out of Gloria's hand.

ROCKY

No! That won't stop her now.

351. ANGLE FAVORING ROCKY AND SHIRL

He grips her shoulders with gentle, almost compassionate firmness.

ROCKY
(softly; hypnotically)
Listen to me . . . Shirl . . . Shirl . . . Listen to me . . . Listen to me . . .
(as she quiets slightly)
Where are they? Show them to me.

SHIRL

They're crawling on me.

ROCKY

Where? On your arm . . . ?
(pantomimes brushing off bug)
It's gone now. Where else? Your shoulder . . . ?

He continues to play out the pantomime of scraping, brushing, plucking insects off her. Finally:

ROCKY

That's all of them.

SHIRL

They're all gone . . . ?

ROCKY

That's right, they're all gone.
(to Matron)
Better douse her in the shower.

The Matron nods, and then leads the now docile Shirl o.s. toward the showers.

352. ALICE

as she watches the woman being led toward the showers. She averts her gaze, turning abruptly toward the mirror. She stares at herself for a moment, then closes her eyes.

353. GLORIA

looking at Rocky, who stares after the woman and then turns abruptly to start out.

GLORIA

That's quite a technique.

Rocky turns back, starts to smile.

GLORIA

Only I'm surprised you didn't put her out on display. Charge a little extra.

ROCKY
(thinks a beat; then, seriously)
No. It's too real.

He turns and quickly leaves. CAMERA HOLDS ON GLORIA, who watches his EXIT and then turns back towards the other women.

354. GLORIA'S POV   THE OTHER WOMEN

exhausted, sweaty, grimy, rank. Swollen legs, pendulous breasts, straggly hair. They are sprawled about in grotesque shapes.

355. BACK TO GLORIA

She stares a moment longer, then pulls her sweater tightly about her and crosses out of the rest area.

356. INT   CORRIDOR FRONTING REST AREAS   TRUCKING
    WITH GLORIA

as she walks through the dark shadows beneath the

bandstands. She hugs herself and moves slowly. As she passes the open door of Rocky's office CAMERA HOLDS ON ROCKY glancing up. Gloria continues on out of FRAME.

> ROCKY
> (calling softly)

Gloria . . .

357. ON GLORIA'S BACK

as she stops, holds still a beat, then turns and CAMERA PANS HER into the doorway of Rocky's office where she leans slowly against the sill.

358. OVER GLORIA TO ROCKY

> ROCKY

I hope that little episode in there didn't shake you up too much.

> GLORIA
> (simply)

No.

A LONG BEAT, as they continue to look at each other.

359. CLOSE ON ROCKY

> ROCKY

Cigarette . . . ?

360. CLOSE ON GLORIA

> GLORIA
> (quieter)

No.

361. CLOSEUP   ROCKY

362. CLOSEUP   GLORIA

GLORIA
(beat; then very softly)

No.

She turns slowly and walks away. CAMERA HOLDS
on ROCKY.

CUT TO:

363. INT BALLROOM NIGHT FULL ON DANCERS

trudging under the lights.

364. AUDIENCE

Larger now, and with a sprinkling of well-dressed
"slummers."

365. ANGLE TOWARD ROCKY

looking toward a section of the audience to which
Turkey is nodding. He gestures to the bandleader to
play softer.

ROCKY
(into mike)

Ladies and gentlemen . . . if I may . . . I've just been
informed that we have a very, verrrry special guest
with us tonight.
(pointing o.s.)
That dancing darling of the silver screen, MISS RUBY
KEELER.

366. ANGLE ON SECTION OF STANDS   LONG SHOT OF GROUP

in evening dress being led down an aisleway, as a
spotlight flickers over them.

ROCKY'S VOICE

Won't you wave to all the folks, Miss Keeler? They're
all your fans.

A CLOCHE-HATTED WOMAN in the group

waves . . . and several spectators start pushing forward
to get autographs.

367. BACK ON ROCKY

ROCKY
Thank you, Miss Keeler. Thank you.

368. ALICE AND JOEL

She has drawn in on herself and stands back of Joel,
as though to shrink from view.

ALICE
(in whisper)
Are they looking this way?

JOEL
I can't see. There're people around them.

ALICE
Let's go to the other side.

JOEL
Why . . . ?

ALICE
You don't think I want them to see me looking like
this, do you?

JOEL
Don't be an idiot—they can't help seeing you.

369. ANGLE FAVORING ALICE

She considers this seriously. Then:

ALICE
I know . . . but I want to go to the other side.

370. INT   WOMEN'S REST AREA   DAY

SILENCE. All the women are asleep; there is no
movement except at the far end of the room. There
Alice stands over a sink dabbing at her dress. CAM-

ERA MOVES SLOWLY CLOSER and AROUND and we see tears streaming down her face. She makes no sound. A beat and the SIREN sounds.

371. INT   MEN'S REST AREA   DAY

The men rise, groggy, stupefied . . . they shake themselves awake. Robert is still sound asleep. Sailor notices and stops to shake his shoulder.

> SAILOR
>
> Come on, kid . . . break's over.

Robert barely stirs.

> SAILOR
> (calling)
>
> Trainer!

Sailor looks reluctantly back at Robert and then EXITS. CAMERA FOLLOWS as Trainer comes to stand over Robert.

> TRAINER
>
> Hey, Frank! We got a dead one!

Frank steps into scene and watches Trainer bend over and begin rhythmically slapping Robert's face. Still no response.

> TRAINER
>
> Give me the ammonia!

Frank hands him a large bottle of household ammonia. He pours some onto a towel . . . then presses the towel into Robert's face.

372. CLOSE ON ROBERT

coughing, hacking, waving with his hand to knock the towel away. He lurches up, literally jerking back into consciousness. Trainer grips Robert's shoulders and stares close into his face.

TRAINER

You know where you are . . . ?

ROBERT

What . . . ?

FRANK

Better give 'im another dose.

Trainer starts to pour more into the towel. At the smell of it, Robert starts to pull back. Frank restrains him, while Trainer shoves the ammonia-drenched towel at him again.

GLORIA'S VOICE

NO!!

373. ANGLE TO REVEAL GLORIA

standing just inside the open doorway.

GLORIA

Leave him alone!!

She crosses to Robert, edging Trainer aside.

GLORIA

You all right?

ROBERT

Yeah, I'm . . .
                    (nods with effort)
Yeah.

She helps him unsteadily to his feet and starts to walk him out, but after a couple of steps he almost buckles.

GLORIA

You sure you can make it?

TRAINER

He's okay now.

GLORIA

I asked *him*, not you!

243

ROBERT
(to Gloria)

I'm all right. Really.

He smiles. She studies him a moment, then turns and starts helping him off again.

CUT TO:

374. INT   BALLROOM   NOON   HIGH ANGLE ON FOOD
        CARTS

being wheeled off the floor. They are littered with the remains of half-finished sandwiches, apple cores, broken stalks of celery, torn pieces of bread, etc.

CUT TO:

375. INT   BALLROOM   EARLY AFTERNOON   DANCERS
        SOLOING

They move separately, indifferent to the scattered spectators and to each other. Some of the women are darning, sewing, knitting, plucking their eyebrows . . . etc. Some of the men are clipping their hair . . . reading pulp magazines, rolling and storing Bull Durham cigarettes . . . etc.

376. MARIO

has a chair draped over his neck and is using the flat surface of the seat as a desk on which to scribble out a letter.

377. GLORIA

off to herself in a corner, cupping a cigarette.

378. SHIRL

bleary-eyed and worn. She seems always on the verge of tipping over and falling.

379. SAILOR

watching her worriedly, using body English to tip her back on center each time she sways too far.

380. ON ALICE

in an open area at one side of the bandstand, alone and circling slowly. Her gown is more soiled, stained and rumpled. The black is more evident at the roots of her hair. Her face is chalky. She is gazing fixedly toward . . .

381. ROBERT

alone at one side of the floor, swaying within the triangular boundaries of a shaft of sunlight through a broken window near the rafters. His head is tilted back into the sunlight. His eyes are closed.

382. ON ALICE

continuing to stare.

383. ON ROCKY

sipping from his paper cup—staring at:

384. GLORIA

who returns his stare openly.

385. ON ALICE

She still stares fixedly at:

386. ROBERT

still in the sunlight. But now slowly . . . slowly the focus of sunlight begins to lift and narrow. He rises on tiptoe, stretching toward the light . . . until finally it is gone completely.

CUT TO:

387. INT   EXIT CORRIDOR   LATE AFTERNOON   ANGLE
TOWARD EXIT DOOR

slowly swinging shut. Light from the outside momentarily falls across several buckets of trash, slop and
garbage set inside the corridor. Something in one of
the buckets flashes and glitters until the light is gone.

388. REVERSE ANGLE TO SHOW ROBERT AT END OF COR-
RIDOR

looking toward the buckets. He hesitates a moment,
then crosses to them.

389. ON ROBERT'S HAND

reaching out to pry loose a piece of sequined cloth.

MATCH CUT TO:

390. INT ROCKY'S OFFICE   LATE AFTERNOON   CLOSE ON
ROCKY'S HAND

as he tosses the piece of sequined cloth onto the top
of his desk. CAMERA PULLS BACK to SHOW
that Robert is confronting him from the other side of
the desk.

ROCKY
Yeah . . . it looks kind of like her dress.

ROBERT
It is. You can see just looking at it.

ROCKY
(nodding)
Yeah.

Robert stares at him expectantly.

ROCKY
Well, even if it is her dress, it's ruined now. There's
nothing I can do.

246

ROBERT

But aren't you going to try to find out? Somebody stole it and ripped it all up.

Rocky offers a gesture of mild agreement.

ROBERT

Maybe you ought to call everyone together and try to find out who did it.

ROCKY

It wasn't one of the kids.

ROBERT
(puzzled)

How do you know?

ROCKY
(a long beat; then flatly:)

Because . . . I took it.

Robert is stunned. He looks at the piece of torn cloth on the desk and then back to Rocky.

ROBERT

But . . . why? Why??

ROCKY
(sincerely)

For the good of the show. That's what we're all interested in, isn't it? . . . the show.

ROBERT

It's a contest. Isn't that what it's supposed to be?? Isn't that what you advertised—a contest?!

Rocky smiles charitably, and points out towards the audience.

ROCKY

Not for them. For you, maybe. But not for them. You think they're laying out two-bits a throw just to watch you poke your head up into the sunlight? Or

Alice look like she just stepped out of a beauty parlor? *They don't care whether you win!* OR James and Ruby, or Mario and Jackie, or the Man-in-the-Moon and Little Miss Muffet. They want to see a little misery out there so they can feel a little better maybe. They're entitled to that.

ROBERT

But . . . but . . . look!
                    (indicates himself)
We're all like this now. Dirty and swollen feet and no sleep. Isn't that enough without making it seem worse?

ROCKY

Sure, as long as they believe it. But how could they with Alice looking like she was on her way to a ball at Buckingham Palace? She was breaking the spell. Now she looks like she's supposed to—so now they can believe in her. Simple enough?

It's all too much for Robert. He merely stares at Rocky trying to assimilate what he's just heard.

ROCKY
                    (quietly)
You better go sack out while you got some break time left.

Robert nods numbly and EXITS. CAMERA HOLDS on Rocky as he flicks the piece of dress into the wastebasket.

391. INT   OUTSIDE ROCKY'S OFFICE   DAY   ROBERT

standing uncertainly. Then he looks off and sees:

392. ALICE

standing alone amid latticed shadows back of the bandstand. They look at each other for a moment. Then Robert crosses to her.

Take me outside . . .

ROBERT
(sympathetically)
We can't . . .

ALICE
Then somewhere . . . ! Please!
(looks about desperately)
In there.

393. ANGLE TO INCLUDE STORAGE ROOM

as Robert looks across the empty corridorway toward
it. (It is actually the cloak room, now being used for
storage.) The upper half of the entrance to the room
is curtained off by soiled red velvet drapes. The bottom half consists of a hat check counter.

A section of the counter is hinged so that it can be
lifted up to provide a passage into the room.

When Robert hesitates, Alice clutches his arm and
draws him across the corridor to the entrance to the
storage room. She raises the hinged section of the
counter and twists her body through the ancient velvet drapes. Still holding onto Robert's arm, she tugs
him after her into the room—leaving the hinged
counter section propped open.

394. INT   STORAGE ROOM   ROBERT AND ALICE

It is a small, sequestered world of discarded fantasy:
haphazard coils of tinsel . . . streamers . . . stalks of
balloons . . . theatre and movie posters . . . advertising
signs—all of it, and the room itself, lighted only by
dust-clotted skylight. Pressed against the skylight and
the room are a few puckered, half-deflated colored
balloons. Some of the posters and signs are torn,
smudged, crumpled. Some are set sideways, some
canted across other posters and signs, so that we see

only bits and pieces of the world they promise: Pepsodent bliss . . . freedom from B.O. . . . Gable's smile . . . Harlow's wink . . . Crawford's legs . . . a Pond's Beauty Bride throwing a bouquet . . . another romance saved from dandruff by Halo . . . and yet another from halitosis by Listerine . . .

Alice picks her way through the clutter to one corner where strips of bunting have been draped over unused clothes pegs. Hesitantly, Robert follows her.

395. CLOSER ANGLE ON ROBERT AND ALICE

For an instant, Alice stares intently at him—as if she might be trying to memorize each of his features. Then she reaches out to him . . . gently at first, hesitantly—but then demandingly, desperately, pressing him back toward a canted poster of Fay Wray promising beauty, love and Lux.

ALICE

Robert?

He stares back at her uncertainly, silently.

ALICE

Robert . . . ? Talk to me. Tell me something.

She contorts her body to slip free of one of the straps of her gown.

ALICE

The other strap! Pull it down.
　　　(as he tries mechanically to loosen the strap)
Talk to me. Please.

ROBERT

What . . . ? What about?

ALICE

Just talk to me. Tell me about yourself. Tell me what you did when you were a child.
　　　(twisting)

250

The hook—undo it! Tell me where you were born.

ROBERT

(numbly fumbling at hook on gown)

Chicago ... I was born in Chicago.

ALICE

Chicago. I've never been there. The zipper! At the side! What was your family like? What did your father do?

ROBERT

He died. He was a pharmacist. But he died. It's caught! He got flu in the epidemic and he died. I think it's caught in the dress. What should I do?

ALICE

Pull at it! Harder!

He does. It slides free. Alice writhes loose of the gown, shedding it as if it were an outer skin.

ALICE

Did you have brothers and sisters?

ROBERT

No ... No. Should we ... I mean, what if—

ALICE

I had a brother. But he was much older. He died at the Somme. I hardly remember him. Hold me, Robert. Close. Please. You'd never guess his name.

ROBERT

Who ... ?

ALICE

My dead brother. Try to guess. Try! Try!!

ROBERT

George ... ? Albert ... ?

ALICE

No.

251

396. ANGLE FAVORING ROBERT

He freezes suddenly as he HEARS the SOUND OF FOOTSTEPS approaching along the corridorway o.s.

397. ROLLO IN CORRIDOR

dragging a box of decorations, programs, unsorted trash and old signs toward the storeroom. He starts to push the box through the narrow check counter passage—but it won't quite fit.

398. BACK ON ROBERT

drawing Alice back further into the blind corner.

> ROLLO'S VOICE
>
> Hey! Give me a hand with this.

399. JANITOR IN CORRIDOR

setting down his broom and crossing to help Rollo with the box. Together they lift it up onto the check counter.

> ROLLO
>
> Get the curtain.

The Janitor pulls back the velvet drape.

400. ON ROBERT AND ALICE

as light from the opened drape splatters past them.

401. ON ROLLO

tipping up the box and dumping the contents over the counter into the storeroom.

402. ANGLE PAST ROBERT AND ALICE

as the shower of rolled posters, decorations, programs, etc., tumbles into the room. A torn program flutters against her. She cringes back against Robert, and whimpers *faintly*.

403. ON ROLLO

cocking his head for an instant, as if he might have heard something. He dismisses it. He pulls the drapes closed and moves off.

404. FAVORING ALICE

standing rigidly apart from Robert now, her eyes closed.

The SIREN BLARES out from inside the ballroom.

> ROBERT'S VOICE
> (softly)

Alice . . . ?

> ALICE

Shhh . . . !!!

She steps slowly into her dress, brushing it off meticulously. Then she starts out.

405. INT   BALLROOM   LATE AFTERNOON   CONTESTANTS

are slowly moving back onto the dance floor to take up their next stint. In b.g. Coley James seats himself at the piano and starts NOODLING.

406. ON GLORIA

searching for Robert.

407. JOEL

looking about casually for Alice. He notices Gloria, smiles at her.

> JOEL

Shall we dance?

Go to hell.

Joel shrugs elegantly, crosses back toward the corridor behind the bandstand. As he does, he sees:

408. ALICE

slipping out of the alcove entrance to the storeroom. She glances about for an instant, as if to make doubly certain that everyone has moved through the corridor and back to the dance floor. As she does, she notices Joel. She stares at him for a moment, her expression calm, self-possessed, almost blank—then she crosses into his arms.

409. TO INCLUDE GLORIA

moving into the corridor and watching Alice cross from the storeroom entrance toward Joel. Joel and Alice move o.s. to the dance floor.

410. GLORIA

stares a moment longer toward Alice, then turns and starts in the direction from which she had come. CAMERA FOLLOWS her as she moves into the isolated area behind the bandstand.

411. ON ROBERT

emerging from the draped storeroom entrance.

412. CLOSE ON GLORIA

staring at him—not immediately in anger, but rather in surprise, shock . . . and pain, then a kind of granite resignation.

> GLORIA
> (flat)

Perfect.

413. CLOSE ON ROBERT

helplessly looking toward her.

414. INT   BALLROOM   LATE AFTERNOON   ON COLEY
    JAMES

ROCKY'S VOICE

And now our own Russ Columbo—Coley James.
(claps)

Coley begins "Easy Come, Easy Go."

415. AUDIENCE

scattered. A few APPLAUD halfheartedly. Most go
right on eating, drinking, talking, gazing hypnotically
at the contestants.

416. ON DANCERS

trudging along.

417. ON ROBERT AND GLORIA

There is a strained silence between them. Robert steals
several quick glances at her, but she pointedly refuses
to respond to him.

418. MRS. LAYDON

looking toward Robert and Gloria with slightly confused concern.

419. BACK ON ROBERT AND GLORIA

He seems on the verge of saying something to her,
but then gives up.

DISSOLVE THRU TO:

420. ANOTHER ANGLE   ROBERT AND GLORIA

The BAND NUMBER has changed, but they have not altered their own tempo. Gloria's mouth is grim, set. Robert is pained, frustrated.

DISSOLVE THRU TO:

421. ANOTHER ANGLE ON ROBERT AND GLORIA

Still the painful, strained silence between them. Again the MUSICAL NUMBER is different.

DISSOLVE THRU TO:

422. ANOTHER ANGLE ON ROBERT AND GLORIA

The silence between them now is like a third partner. Robert has given up even his tentative attempts to force himself to break through it. Gloria's attitude and expression are unchanged.

The SIREN wails, and they stop in mid-step, sagging in simple relief until the SIREN STOPS BLOWING. Then Gloria turns abruptly and starts to move off.

> ROBERT
> (calling softly)

Wait . . .

423. ANGLE FAVORING GLORIA

as she stops and turns slowly about to look at him.

> ROBERT
> (after a beat)

I'm sorry.

Gloria continues to stare at him a moment longer, then she turns again and moves o.s. CAMERA HOLDS on Robert staring after her.

424. INT   ROCKY'S OFFICE   NIGHT

Rocky is lying on the couch. A paper is tented over

his face. The table radio is on, crackling a Commercial Jingle of the period. There is one small low light burning.

425. ANGLE ON DOOR

as Gloria steps through. She waits till Rocky looks up from the newspaper. Then she nudges the door. It swings closed but does not latch.

426. ON ROCKY

as he lets the newspaper slide off to the floor. Then he starts to rise slowly off the couch.

427. ON GLORIA

as she sees him move.

> GLORIA
> (viciously)

Don't touch me!!

428. ON ROCKY

startled, but lying back slowly . . . staring up at her . . . waiting.

429. ON GLORIA

slowly, precisely unbuttoning her blouse.

430. ON ROCKY

continuing to stare at her as we HEAR a RUSTLE of clothing dropped to the floor. Her shadow falls across him. He slowly stretches out one foot and TAPS it against the office door, forcing it shut with a SHARP CLICK. On the CLICK, Gloria drops swiftly to her knees and reaches her hand towards the RADIO.

> ANNOUNCER'S VOICE

This is fifty-thousand-watt, clear-channel KFI.
> (GONG)

And now KFI's nightly weather reporter.

As Gloria's fingers fumble for the knob to turn it off, Rocky's wristwatch-clad hand intrudes. Struggles with hers . . . and slowly brings it back.

                    ANNOUNCER'S VOICE
                       (continuing)
Temperatures in Pomona, Oxnard, Azusa and eastern sections of the San Gabriel Valley generally will approach freezing after midnight. Smudge pots are recommended in . . .

                                              CUT TO:

431. INT BALLROOM NIGHT ROBERT

standing alone near the bandstand. Other dancers coming out of the rest areas. His expression changes as he sees

432. GLORIA

seeming to move toward him. He crosses to her, but she turns aside to Joel, who is standing idly in near b.g. She holds herself out to him in an invitation to dance.

                         GLORIA
I changed my mind.

Joel is mildly surprised. He considers a moment . . . then smiles thinly and shrugs.

                          JOEL
Why not?

Robert is confused, bewildered, stunned—he looks after her. Gloria stares back at him, then nods off.

                         GLORIA
Your partner's waiting for you.

433. ROBERT'S POV   ALICE

coming onto the floor.

FLASH FORWARD TO:

434. INT   PRISON VISITOR'S ROOM   DAY   ROBERT

Dressed in standard prison denims. He sits behind a plain table. In a plate-glass divider in front of him we see the vague reflection of a man listening.

ROBERT

... she was leaning against the railing. She was completely relaxed—completely comfortable. I didn't have a perfect view ... but I could see enough of her face and lips to see that she was smiling ... almost like she was happy ... for the first time.

CUT TO:

435. INT   BALLROOM   NIGHT   ANGLE ON ROCKY

He stands at the mike—one hand holding his stopwatch.

ROCKY

... four ... three ... two ... ONE THOUSAND HOURS!!!

The BAND does CELEBRATION NUMBER. CROWD CHEERS and APPLAUDS. Confetti streams down from the rafters onto:

436. THE DANCERS

overlapped by spotlights. They are fewer now, and much wearier. Eyes are red-rimmed and heavy-lidded, faces puffy, legs and feet swollen.

ROCKY'S VOICE

Yowza!!! One thousand hours of continuous dancing! Forty-one days of grueling, grinding, gravity-defying

259

gyrations! And there they still are. Twenty-one courageous couples still dancing. And how long before one of them, and just one, will survive to win the mammoth, monster marathon prize . . . ? Another thousand hours? . . . Another *two* thousand hours? HOW LONG CAN THEY LAST?

437. ON ROCKY

ROCKY

HOW ABOUT IT, KIDS . . . ? Let's show the folks out there that you're all a long, long way from giving up yet.

(looks toward Bandleader)

The Bandleader cues the musicians into "Pop Goes the Weasel."

438. PANNING THE DANCERS

as they pick up the pace—but not much . . . and only for a moment.

439. MRS. LAYDON

in her regular box. She watches quietly for a moment, then she leans forward.

MRS. LAYDON
(calling)

Gloria . . .

440. ON JOEL AND GLORIA

MRS. LAYDON'S VOICE

Gloria . . .

It is obvious that Gloria has heard her, but she merely stiffens slightly.

JOEL

Who's that?

GLORIA

No one.

441. ANGLE FAVORING ROBERT

looking off toward Gloria. Alice studies him coolly.

ALICE

Why don't you go back to her?

Robert starts, looks back sheepishly at Alice, and then shrugs.

ROBERT

I couldn't. She thinks you and I . . .

ALICE
(decisively)

That . . . never . . . happened.

CUT TO:

442. INT   CORRIDOR OUTSIDE REST AREA   NIGHT   ROCKY

watching the contestants drag themselves toward the respective rest areas. He nods pleasantly to several as they pass by.

ROCKY
(calling softly)

Gloria . . . !

443. ANGLE TO INCLUDE GLORIA

turning near the women's area to look back at Rocky. He crosses to her.

GLORIA

Yeah . . . ?

ROCKY

Haven't seen much of you lately.

GLORIA

Have you looked?

ROCKY

I've looked.

GLORIA

Good.

She turns and EXITS into the women's rest area.

444. INT BALLROOM DAY ANGLE ON FOOD CART

surrounded by contestants. They are eating slowly
and as if by rote rather than desire.

445. ANGLE FAVORING ROBERT

Chewing slowly at a carrot stick, he sidles around the
circle of other dancers to move up behind Gloria.

ROBERT

Gloria.

She turns to look at him over her shoulder. He digs
into his pocket and brings out a small bottle.

ROBERT

They're vitamin pills, Mrs. Laydon gave them to me
for you.

She takes the pills. He smiles at her.

ROBERT

How are you? I mean, you all right?

GLORIA

Sure I'm all right.

She offers nothing more. Finally, he smiles again.

ROBERT

I'm glad.

446. INT BALLROOM NIGHT PANNING DANCERS

as they plod endlessly on. Mario is sleeping draped

262

over Jackie's back, his wrists locked across her chest. Cecil is teetering over onto Dusty. Shirl is lugging badly, and Sailor has to hitch her up with almost every step.

> SHIRL

I'm sorry . . .

> SAILOR

You're gonna make it.

As they pass OUT OF FRAME, CAMERA MOVES IN on

447. JOEL AND GLORIA

moving slowly, silently. After an extended beat:

> JOEL

You want to talk?

> GLORIA

No.

Again a beat.

> JOEL

You want to sleep?

> GLORIA

No.

> JOEL

Want to move to the other side, up by the band?

> GLORIA

No.

> JOEL

Well, what the hell do you want?

> GLORIA

How about a couple of yachts and a Pierce Arrow?

JOEL

Did anyone ever tell you that—

GLORIA

Yeah, they told me.

Long beat.

JOEL

How about switching back—maybe that's what you want to do?

GLORIA

What difference would it make?

JOEL

I thought the point was that you wanted to be with me.

GLORIA

Did you?

He meets her stare for a minute, then shrugs and looks away.

448. INT   BALLROOM   AFTERNOON   FULL SHOT ON DANCE FLOOR

It's the solo period. It takes all the reserve energy most of them still have just to stay erect. CAMERA HOLDS on Gloria.

MRS. LAYDON'S VOICE

Gloria . . .

She opens her eyes, but she does not turn.

449. ANGLE ON MRS. LAYDON

MRS. LAYDON

Gloria . . .

450. ON GLORIA

264

A beat . . . then she turns about to look toward Mrs. Laydon. Another beat . . . then she forces herself to move slowly toward Mrs. Laydon's box.

451. MED. SHOT   MRS. LAYDON AND GLORIA

Mrs. Laydon smiles warmly at her.

MRS. LAYDON

Do you want to tell me what happened? Do you want to talk about it?

GLORIA

No.

Gloria turns and moves off. CAMERA HOLDS on Mrs. Laydon looking after her.

452. CLOSE ON ROBERT

watching Gloria "dance" away.

453. MOVING WITH JIGGS

as he skates around the corner of the bandstand to

454. ALICE

in the shadows at the edge of the floor.

JIGGS

Hey, come on! Get out in the center. That's what they're paying for—so they can see you.

ALICE

No.

(beat)

No.

Jiggs hesitates a moment, then gives up and moves off.

455. INT   BALLROOM   NIGHT   ANGLE ON SECTION OF
AUDIENCE

twisting about to look toward

456. AN EXPENSIVELY DRESSED COUPLE

signing autographs as they move down an aisleway.

457. ON ROCKY

at mike.

> ROCKY
> It's celebrity time again, folks. A welcome for Miss Madge Evans and that rising young star, Mr. Ross Alexander. Yowza!

458. AUDIENCE

continuing to peer while CLAPPING.

> ROCKY'S VOICE
> But every night is celebrity night at the Mammoth Marathon.

459. ON JOEL AND GLORIA

Joel is craning about to look, but Gloria is not.

> GLORIA
> I'm getting sick of all these introductions.

> JOEL
> It'd be different, though, if you were the one being introduced.

Either she ignores or does not pick up the sharp note of sarcasm in Joel's tone, and her response is uncharacteristically subdued and mild.

> GLORIA
> Yeah . . . I used to think that.

Joel cranes about and seems to peer searchingly across another part of the audience, while Gloria continues

staring toward the celebrity couple, who are still signing autographs. Then, after a beat:

GLORIA

She looks like her, kind of.

JOEL

Who . . . ?

GLORIA

Like my aunt.

JOEL

Oh . . .

He turns his attention back to searching another part
of the audience.

(Joel and Gloria speak together)

JOEL

You seen a sort of a short fellow anywhere?
Kind of balding in front . . . horn-rim glasses,
and pits like from acne. He *said* he was going
to come. He's an assistant director, and he's
supposed to go on a ten-day western at Monogram. He said maybe he could get me something in it . . . Maybe he was just stringing
me—the crum.

GLORIA

God, she was a bitch! I mean if there was a
prize for bitches, she'd have won hands down.
Christ, you should've heard her scream: "You
get that mangy mutt out of here! You ain't
bringing no animals into *my* boarding house."
And I never brought him back there anyway.
He just followed me is all. I wouldn't have
kept him—except she started screaming.

Joel trails off and looks back at Gloria. He puzzles at
her, as if trying vaguely to pick up the threads of
her story.

GLORIA

I said I'd tell her husband she was screwing one of

the boarders. She probably was, too. Only he was sick inside with something.

JOEL

Her husband . . . ?

GLORIA

No.

JOEL

Oh . . . the boarder.

GLORIA

No, for Chris'sake—the dog. And it kept gettin' worse, so he'd shake all the time and dirty himself all over and whine and cry all night. The stupid damn thing, it'd just keep whimpering and howling, and it wouldn't shut up. I mean, what the hell's God doing sitting around up there? What the hell good is He, if He can't even keep one lousy, sick dog from crying and waking up all her goddamned boarders?
      (shrugs; then, after a beat, smiles)
So, you know what I did? After everybody was in bed, I carried it down to the parlor—the dog. I fixed it a place on her best mohair sofa. Then I sneaked into the kitchen, and . . .

She trails off. Her faintly lingering smile vanishes completely. She shrugs.

GLORIA

What the hell . . . Forget it.

For an instant, Joel continues to stare at her with blank, weary incomprehension . . . then he turns his attention again to searching through the faces in the audience.

460. INT WOMEN'S REST AREA DAY ALICE

staring into a mirror . . . immobile . . . silent.

461. A NURSE

She moves among the cots, checking the women, all of whom are sleeping—except for Gloria. She sits on

268

the upper edge of her cot, her feet tucked up under her skirt and her head resting against the wall. She is smoking a cigarette.

NURSE

You should be sleeping.

GLORIA

I'd only wake up.

NURSE

You need anything? Something for your feet??

GLORIA

A saw, maybe.

NURSE

I mean anything the doctor can give you. Something to make you feel better.

GLORIA

What's he got?

NURSE
(shrugs)

Some aspirin.

GLORIA

That's what I figured.

She turns her head again toward the wall. The SIREN sounds.

462. CORRIDOR FRONTING REST AREAS

Contestants stagger listlessly back toward the dance floor. Robert crosses along the corridor to where Gloria is standing alone.

463. MED. SHOT   ROBERT AND GLORIA

Silence for a moment, then Robert smiles at her and nods. She doesn't smile back.

269

GLORIA

Yeah . . . ?

ROBERT

Nothing. I just . . . Nothing.

He nods again and moves o.s. CAMERA HOLDS on Gloria, as she continues to stand alone looking at the passing line of other dancers.

464. GLORIA'S POV OTHER DANCERS

as the last of them move out of the corridor.

465. BACK ON GLORIA

She frowns slightly.

466. ROLLO

comes out of the men's rest area. He seems preoccupied and annoyed. Gloria catches his arm.

GLORIA

You seen Joel?

ROLLO
(jerking thumb towards men's room)
Yeah, I seen him all right. That's a real sweetheart you picked this time around. Just like that—and now I'm the one's got to tell Rocky.

467. GLORIA

moves rapidly towards the men's rest area.

468. INT MEN'S REST AREA JOEL

packing the last of his things into his club-style bag. He has shaved, slicked his hair back, changed his ascot. Gloria comes INTO SCENE and pushes past a Trainer to confront him.

270

                    JOEL
              (smile and a wave)
Cheers.

                    GLORIA
Don't give me any of that song-and-dance crap!
What's going on?

                    JOEL
Exactly what appears to be going on. I have shaved.
I have changed. And I am now packing.

                    GLORIA
For what!

                    JOEL
I have a job. Not much of a job, but a job. Ten days
in a Monogram Epic to be entitled—

He clasps his bag, hoists it and starts to turn. Gloria
grabs his arm.

                    GLORIA
You bastard! You're not running out on me!

                    JOEL
No . . . ?
              (pries her hand away)
Just stand there and watch, kiddo.

He turns and EXITS.

469. CLOSE ON GLORIA

staring after him. CAMERA SLOWLY MOVES IN.
MUSIC and CROWD NOISES filter up slowly from
b.g.

                 ROCKY'S VOICE
Will she make it . . . ?

                                        CUT TO:

470. INT BALLROOM NIGHT CLOSE ON SIGN

It reads:

       HOW LONG CAN THEY LAST?

ROCKY'S VOICE

After over eleven hundred hours of incredible endurance, there she is—alone, but still fighting, still trusting, still hoping: GLORIA BEATTY.

CAMERA PANS TO show Rocky.

471. MED. LONG SHOT GLORIA

A spotlight tracks her on the dance floor. She is very much alone, and we sense something more than simply physical isolation. Her eyes flicker over the other couples, as if gauging each woman in turn. And they, like wary prey, have instinctively drawn away from her.

ROCKY'S VOICE

Seventeen hours—that's all she has left. Will she find a new partner before those hours slip away? Will fortune reward her pluck and spirit?

472. VERY CLOSE ON GLORIA

ROCKY'S VOICE

Will she make it . . . ?

                                        CUT TO:

473. INT WOMEN'S REST AREA EARLY MORNING
       GLORIA

pacing at the rear of the room, her sweater strung around her shoulders. She is the only one on her feet. She is keyed-up . . . hypertense . . . broodingly kinetic.

474. JACKIE

looks up at her.

> JACKIE
>
> I'm sorry.

> GLORIA
>
> Sure.

> JACKIE
>
> I mean it.

Gloria moves on past Shirl.

> SHIRL
>
> Gee, honey, I guess that's just the breaks is all.

> GLORIA
>
> Yeah.

She continues on.

475. RUBY

She meets Gloria's look straight on—but with understanding rather than defiance.

> RUBY
>
> I'm not going to quit, Gloria. I'm not going to give up.

Gloria stares flatly at her a moment longer, then moves on and continues out of the rest area into:

476. INT   CORRIDOR FRONTING REST AREAS   GLORIA

alone. She leans against the wall. She digs into her sweater pocket for a cigarette, and finds that the pack is empty. She wads up the empty pack, tosses it on the floor, and starts pacing again.

477. INT   ROCKY'S OFFICE   ROCKY AND TURKEY

Rocky sits behind the desk, counting the night's take.

On the desk top is a steel cash box, and beside it a snub-nosed .38 revolver.

ROCKY
How're the tabs?

TURKEY
(indicating receipts)
About the same—food's down, cleaning's up.

Rocky nods and turns back to the box on his desk. He is about to lock it with a key, when he REACTS to a shaft of light slicing into the office.

478. ANGLE TO REVEAL GLORIA

staring at him from the partially open doorway.

479. WIDER ANGLE

Rocky and Gloria stare at each other as if each is waiting for the other to speak first. Finally:

ROCKY
Yeah ... ?

GLORIA
What happens if I don't get a partner?

ROCKY
You still got eleven, almost twelve hours left.

GLORIA
I can count. What happens?

ROCKY
You know the rules.

GLORIA
You could change them.

Rocky slowly shakes his head.

The crowd's got to have something they believe in.
If they ever quit believing, they'd quit coming.
(shrugs)
Anything else . . . But not that.

Gloria stares at him a moment longer, then turns and
EXITS back into the corridor. The SIREN sounds.

480. INT   MEN'S REST AREA

All the men have left . . . except for Sailor, who is
still asleep. The First Trainer—and behind him the
Second Trainer—come into scene. The First Trainer
bends over Sailor, slaps his face lightly, shakes his
shoulders. There is no response.

FIRST TRAINER

Dead one.

He unbuttons Sailor's pants. The second Trainer then
pulls Sailor's pants off, leaving him in undershorts
and undershirt. One takes Sailor's legs, and the other
catches him under the shoulders. They hoist him up,
carry him over to the ice-water tank . . . and dump
him in.

481. CLOSE ON SAILOR

splashing up out of the freezing water, eyes wide
open and staring wildly.

SAILOR

JESSSSSSUS!!!!!

CUT TO:

482. INT   BALLROOM   NIGHT   DOWN ANGLE ON ROLLO

counting over Shirl, who is collapsed in a limp, half-
conscious exhaustion on the floor. Sailor huddles over
her. Most of the other remaining contestants surround
them in a ragged circle.

... three ... four ...

SAILOR

Don't! Give 'er a chance! She'll get up.
(tugging at her)
Shirl! Come on, Shirl!

483. WIDER ANGLE TO REVEAL GLORIA

standing alone and back from the scene.

ROCKY'S VOICE

She's trying! She's trying! But can she make it back
up?

484. CLOSE DOWN SHOT ON SHIRL

She lies still huddled like a wounded thing that has
finally been run to ground. Her eyes are glazed and
thick-lidded, as she stares up toward Sailor and Rollo.
Her lips move—but no words form ... no sound
emerges.

(Sailor and Rollo speak together)

SAILOR'S VOICE

... Try, Shirl ... Try!

ROLLO'S VOICE

... Eight ... Nine ...

485. NEW ANGLE ON SCENE

Shirl tries to cling feebly to Sailor's hands as Rollo's
extended finger SLASHES INTO FRAME.

ROLLO

... TEN!!

ANGLE WIDENS as the Doctor and one of the
nurses push through and start helping Shirl up.

486. ROCKY

signals the band, which segues into "TILL WE
MEET AGAIN."

MISS SHIRLEY CLAYTON. We're gonna miss you, Shirl. Isn't that right, folks?

487. THE AUDIENCE

claps—respectfully.

488. ON SHIRL

On her feet now, though still unsteady, and being helped off by the Doctor and Nurse. Tears have welled up in her puffy eyes. She stops . . . turns to look at the audience, and waves feebly.

489. ON ROCKY

waving back to Shirl.

> ROCKY
>
> So long, Shirl. But don't despair. Every heart in this room is with you. And that's what really counts.
> (turns solemnly to audience)
> It's hard on all of us, after we've lived all of these hours and days and weeks together, to see one of these wonderful, courageous kids fall out, but . . . life still goes on . . .
> (cues band)
> AND SO DOES THE MARATHON!!

The band breaks into "I FOUND A MILLION DOLLAR BABY."

490. FULL SHOT   DANCE FLOOR

The remaining couples move back together . . . leaving Sailor and Gloria each standing alone. They look across the floor toward each other.

491. ANGLE FAVORING SAILOR AND GLORIA

as they move toward each other.

492. TIGHT TWO SHOT   SAILOR AND GLORIA

Sailor smiles wanly at her.

SAILOR

I guess it's you'n me now, Gloria.

She puts one arm around his back.

GLORIA
(softly)

Yeah.

OVER SCENE we HEAR a SINGLE TRUMPET screeching out the RACING CALL.

493. REVERSE ANGLE . EXTREME CLOSEUP OF SAILOR AND GLORIA

heads bobbing, faces sweat-streaked and strained. As they MOVE INTO CAMERA and then BLUR PAST, we see SCENE is:

494. INT BALLROOM NIGHT FULL SHOT DERBY

(NOTE: The contestants wear their normal clothes, *not* track suits.) Racing around the white oval line on the dance floor are the remaining couples—among them: MARIO and JACKIE, JAMES AND RUBY, ROBERT AND ALICE, DUSTY AND CECIL, ARTHUR AND JEAN, TOMMY AND LILLIAN, SAILOR AND GLORIA . . . AND FOUR OTHER MISCELLANEOUS COUPLES.

There is no precision left to their movements now. They stagger, stumble and cling to each other. Though each of them seems to exert the last fiber of energy, they are all moving slowly. In fact, they seem to race in a kind of painful, wrenching slow motion.

ROCKY'S VOICE

Three minutes left! . . . Three minutes of harrowing, heartbreaking hustle . . .

495. PANNING THE AUDIENCE

The bleachers are *filled to capacity*, and the spectators are more visually involved in this slow, pain-wracked race than in the earlier derby.

496. FULL SHOT DERBY

The couples blindly plodding ahead . . . hanging on to their partners.

ROCKY'S VOICE

Yowza!! . . . Almost 1500 hours of continuous dancing—and yet they're still out there, each one of them fighting . . . struggling to stay in the race.

497. ON ROCKY

at the microphone.

ROCKY

But the last three contestants will *lose*. The last three *will be eliminated!*

498. MOVING WITH SAILOR AND GLORIA

Sailor is straining, puffing, wheezing. Gloria is slightly ahead of him. She grips his bandolier belt, and half pulls him along.

GLORIA
(through clenched teeth)
We can make it.

SAILOR

Maybe—but we sure ain't going to win.

GLORIA

Just so we don't lose. I'm sick of losing.

499. MOVING WITH JAMES AND RUBY

He has one arm cinched tightly about her waist, and she has looped her hand through the front of his bandolier belt. She leans on him for support and moves in rhythm with his steps, letting him take the brunt of her weight. Even so, the exertion shows in her face. He questions her with a look. She nods, and manages a thin smile.

500. ANGLE ON ROCKY

looking down from the clock.

ROCKY

Two minutes! . . . Two minutes left! And remember, folks—if one falls out, both are disqualified. They must cross the finish line together. That's the rule.
(looks)
Oh-oh! Looks like there could be a spill at the turn!

501. ANGLE ON ALICE AND ROBERT

At one turn of the track, Alice's heel has turned under. Robert is trying to keep her from falling, but she slips from his grasp and drops to the floor. Robert bends over Alice, and cicles his hand around her waist—tugging at her. As he is struggling to get her back to her feet, JIGGS SKATES INTO SCENE.

ROBERT
(to Jiggs)
She's getting up! You don't have to count, she's getting up!

JIGGS

Okay, okay.

502. ANGLE TO INCLUDE SAILOR AND GLORIA

swinging around the turn just in front of Robert and Alice.

GLORIA
Get out of the way!!

She shoulders past Robert, while struggling to keep Sailor moving straight ahead.

503. MOVING ON WITH SAILOR AND GLORIA

280

Sailor is puffing harder now, gasping at each breath. His eyes are glassy, his face is grey and drained of color. His breath catches—seems almost to stop. And then, as he desperately sucks in a gulp of air again, he utters A GRUNT OF PAIN.

GLORIA

What's wrong?!

SAILOR

My chest.

ROCKY'S VOICE

One minute! . . . One final furious minute left!!

GLORIA

You hear that, Sailor? You hear that? One minute! That's all we got left. All we got to do is get to the finish line now. Lean on me! That's right. Listen, Chief. Listen. We're gonna make it. I'll . . . count! 59 . . . 58 . . . 57 . . . 56. Show me where it hurts. Your chest? Is that where it hurts?

With her arm circled about him she presses against the side of his chest.

GLORIA

40 . . . 39 . . . 38 . . .
(squeezing his side)
That help? That feel better now?

Sailor is incapable of answering, but he tries to nod.

ROCKY'S VOICE

It looks like our seafaring man and our little hardluck lady are in deep trouble! . . . They're slowing down! . . . They're falling back!

504. CLOSE ON MRS. LAYDON

straining forward, her fingers laced together.

505. ON ROCKY

pointing the crowd's attention to Gloria and Sailor.

ROCKY

There's another couple moving past them! . . . Can they make it? . . . Can they make it? . . .

506. ON GLORIA AND SAILOR

She is keeping him up by sheer will now, forcing him to move with her one step at a time.

GLORIA

The finish line is just up ahead. Can you see it?—Just a little ways now. 28 . . . 27 . . . 26 . . . Listen, you salty old bastard, you can make it. Where's the fight? Just a little more, that's all. For God's sake, just hang on a little more! Just . . . 17 . . . 16 . . . 15 . . . 14 . . .

Sailor—wheezing, rasping desperately for each breath now—starts to slip. Immediately Gloria hunches her body under him, and draws one of his arms across one of her shoulders. Now she clutches his entwined wrists in front of her. She carries all of his weight now, letting him half stumble along behind her.

GLORIA

12 . . . 11 . . . Damn it. Damn it, don't stop now.

507. ANGLE FAVORING SAILOR

Suddenly his whole body wrenches in a shuddering spasm of pain. His eyes roll under. His legs sag. His body goes limp across Gloria's back.

508. ANGLE FAVORING GLORIA

She is aware of the paroxysm that has quivered through Sailor's flesh into her own. She desperately twists her head about to stare into his blank, sightless face. But if she *does* see that he is passed beyond consciousness, she refuses to recognize that fact.

282

(whispering: almost crooning)

We're gonna make it, Sailor. 8 ... 7 ... We're gonna make it now.

She looks ahead again towards the finish line.

509. ANGLE TO INCLUDE ROBERT AND ALICE

as they move past Sailor and Gloria. Robert twists to stare back at Gloria ... and he goes on staring back at her—even though he continues hynotically moving on toward the finish line with Alice.

510. AUDIENCE

Violently excited.

511. INTERCUT THE CLOCK

showing only seconds to go.

512. INTERCUT DOCTOR

waiting near the finish line, his bag gripped in one hand. Near him are some of the Trainers and Nurses.

513. BACK ON SAILOR AND GLORIA

She continues on with him—one step ... another ... another ...

GLORIA
(whispering)

We're almost there now.
(shouting at Sailor)

WALK! WALK!! WALK, GOD DAMN IT!
(whisper again)

Just a little ... Just a little ...

514. ANGLE ON ROBERT

staggering across the finish line with Alice—then stopping and looking toward Gloria.

515. ANGLE ON ROCKY

His hand is poised in the air.

ROCKY

4 . . . 3 . . . 2 . . . ONE!

He signals with a drop of his hand.

516. CLOSE ON CANNON

going off.

517. ANGLE FAVORING GLORIA

Staggering to a stop across the finish line, laughing, trembling, half sobbing all at once, Gloria squiggles around under Sailor's locked arms so that she can look at him.

518. EXTREME CLOSEUP OF SAILOR

His head lolling, his eyes open and staring. He *looks* dead. We can't be sure that he isn't.

519. CLOSE ON GLORIA

For an instant she stares in shock at the death mask that is now Sailor's face—then she seems to reject what she sees.

GLORIA

We made it! We made it, you old fishbait.
(smiles)
You hear?
(starts shaking him)
You hear me?! You hear me?—we made it.
(shakes harder; SHOUTS)
WE MADE IT!!!

520. ON SAILOR

slipping from Gloria . . . sagging forward, collapsing —but slowly, because his fall is cushioned first by

284

Gloria and then by Robert. On his knees, at the end of his plunge, his hands flop out against Alice and seem to entangle themselves in the skirt of her dress.

521. ALICE

yanks at her dress, finally rips it free. Holding rigidly to herself, she begins to back away.

522. GLORIA

staring down incredulously at Sailor, then bending over him.

GLORIA

Sailor? . . . Sailor? . . .

523. FULL ON SCENE

Several of the contestants and marathon personnel have edged around Sailor's body. Rollo fights for a vantage point on the periphery.

524. THE AUDIENCE

strains to see, unable to make out yet exactly what has happened. They buzz and whisper among themselves.

525. ON DOCTOR

pushing his way through the other contestants to reach Sailor, but Gloria flares out at him—trying to push him away.

GLORIA

Leave him alone!! He's all right!

The Doctor gestures to the Nurse, who pulls Gloria away.

GLORIA
(softly; not resisting the Nurse)

He's getting up. Why don't they leave him alone?

The Doctor quickly checks Sailor, then fumbles a

hypodermic and a sterile bottle out of his bag. He starts to plunge the hypodermic needle into the bottle . . . misses the first try . . . then succeeds.

526. ON ROCKY

waving a reassuring hand to the audience.

> ROCKY

Looks like our Ancient Mariner may have taken a little spill. But nothing to worry about. The House Physician's with him. Just routine.
>> (clamps hand over mike; to Turkey)
Find out what the hell's going on.
>> (back to mike)
How about a little hand for our Sailorman? Let's show him we appreciate the kind of determination he showed us out there.

He starts the clapping.

527. CLOSE ANGLE ON DOCTOR AND SAILOR

as the Doctor injects the hypo of adrenalin into Sailor. A beat . . . then Sailor's body moves slightly.

528. ON ROCKY AND TURKEY

Rocky is leaning over the stand toward Turkey.

> ROCKY

Tell 'em to get him out of here. The back way.

As Turkey moves off, Rocky turns back to the mike. He smiles.

> ROCKY

I've just had a message from our House Physician— a little touch of heat prostration. Nothing in the least serious. I understand that Harry, crusty old salt that he is, wants to stay on in the Marathon. But . . . the Doc says No. And when it comes to something like this, the Doctor's word is law.

529. GLORIA WATCHING THE TRAINERS

lifting the still unconscious, now blanket-covered Sailor on a stretcher and starting to move off with him through the parting onlookers.

ROCKY'S VOICE

So long, Sailor . . . but we know you'll be back to see us and to cheer the other kids on.

The band starts PLAYING "TILL WE MEET AGAIN."

530. ROBERT

staring at Sailor as he edges along behind the stretcher.

531. MOVING WITH STRETCHER

until it rounds a shadowed corner at the rear of the ballroom and passes.

532. ALICE

standing completely alone, drawn in upon herself. As she watches Sailor move past, she begins wiping compulsively at the portion of her skirt where Sailor's hands had momentarily caught. CAMERA MOVES IN on her. Suddenly she stops. She stares down at her hands, at her dress. For a long instant, she remains rigid, silent, stock-still . . . then abruptly she turns and begins running o.s., as the SIREN begins to SOUND.

533. ANGLE ON ROBERT AND GLORIA

standing silently, as the SIREN CONTINUES OVER SCENE. Some of the other contestants push past them toward the rest areas. After a moment, they turn and start off with the others toward the rest areas.

534. INT WOMEN'S SHOWER STALL NIGHT CLOSE ON ALICE'S HAND turning on a shower faucet. CAMERA PULLS BACK TO HOLD for a beat on her face, then CONTINUES BACK to see that she is FULLY CLOTHED. Her lips move as if in a remembered litany, and the harsh stream of water drenches over her hair, splatters off her upturned face and soaks her faded gown. She takes the soap and methodically and slowly begins to wash her face, her arms . . . her gown.

535. REVERSE ANGLE

as several of the women begin to come in to use the toilet or wash. One by one they stop . . . stand still . . . stare as a hush comes over the entire women's rest area. The Matron starts forward to turn off the shower but Alice's hand darts forward and covers it. Alice looks as though she could be dangerous as she stares in defiance at the Matron, who turns on her heel and exits.

536. BACK TO THE WOMEN

Ruby averts her eyes. The rest stare silently.

537. ON ALICE

continuing to wash. Carefully . . . thoroughly. The dress begins to come apart slowly and pieces of it fall to the floor of the shower stall.

538. ANGLE TO REVEAL ROCKY

ENTERING the shower area with the Matron. He pushes his way through the women, moving them aside until he sees Alice—alone, cowering in the stream of water, clinging to shreds and pieces of her gown.

> ROCKY
> (to women, quietly)

Go on.

> (when they edge back, but too

slowly, he SHOUTS)
Go on, I said! Get the hell out of here!

The Matron and the other women scatter off, EX-ITING SCENE.

539. MED. SHOT   ROCKY AND ALICE

He stands just inside the stall. For a long moment, he looks at her . . . then he holds his hands out to her. She is silent. Her eyes flicker warily.

> ROCKY
> (gently)
You can come out now. No one's going to hurt you. Don't you want to come out now? You might catch cold in there. You don't want to do that, do you? . . . Please.

He takes a step toward her. She tenses, draws back. He stops.

> ROCKY
I only want to help you. I want to turn off the water. That's all. You see?
> (extends hand)
I'm just going to turn the handle, that's all.

Slowly . . . steadily he moves his hand toward the faucet handle. She watches . . . watches—then thrusts out her own hand and clamps it over the faucet handle before he can reach it. He draws back.

> ROCKY
That's all right. I won't turn it off, if you don't want.

He edges closer to her. His clothes now are soaked and dripping. Water splatters across his arms and back. As they look at each other the stream of water becomes for them both a barrier and something they share.

Finally:

ROCKY

Tell me. Whatever it is, you can tell me.

ALICE
(after a beat)

He touched me.

ROCKY

Who . . . ?

ALICE

He touched me.

540. ANGLE TO INCLUDE MATRON

edging around the corner of the shower stall to peer toward Alice. Behind her is a small cluster of the others.

ROCKY
(turns; glares)

Get the hell away!!

They quickly move back o.s.

541. ROCKY AND ALICE

as he turns back to her.

ALICE

Is he dead?

ROCKY

Sailor? You mean Sailor? No, you got my personal word, he's going to be fine.

She nods slowly as if trying to understand. Rocky touches her hand . . . waits . . . then his hand gently moves to her arm, enfolds it. He starts slowly to draw her to him, and she seems on the point of surrender . . . when the SIREN BEGINS BLARING.

542. ANGLE FAVORING ALICE

SCREAMING—though the sound of her voice is

completely smothered by the SIREN. She clings to Rocky's arm—unaware that with his free hand he has reached across her and turned off the shower. The SIREN STOPS. For just an instant, ALICE'S SCREAMS are heard, echoing in the narrow stall. Then she stops abruptly. Her mouth is still open. She stares closely into Rocky's face. Then:

                    ALICE
Someone was screaming.

                    ROCKY
That was you, Alice.

                    ALICE
Alice . . . ? . . . Alice . . . ? That's not my name. Don't call me that.

                    ROCKY
Sure . . .
          (starting to lead her out)
What do you want me to call you? What's your real name?

She stops . . . peers at him as he is wrapping a dirty blanket around her shoulders.

543. CLOSE ON ALICE

                    ALICE
          (a long beat)
I don't know.

544. INT   CORRIDOR, FRONTING REST AREAS   ROBERT AND
     GLORIA

standing near each other. They are alone in the corridor, but they are staring off in the direction of FOOTSTEPS at:

545. ALICE

A tiny figure huddled in the dirty blanket, being led off by Rocky . . .

546. BACK ON ROBERT AND GLORIA

They continue to look off. Silence—except for the diminishing ECHO OF FOOTSTEPS . . . then the SOUND of a door opening and swinging shut.

Then silence again.

547. INT BALLROOM NIGHT VERY CLOSE ON ROCKY

at the mike.

ROCKY
Boy meets girl . . . boy loses girl . . . boy . . . gets girl. Yowza! That's the story of our Sweetheart Couple:
(points off)

548. ANGLE ON ROBERT AND GLORIA

as spotlights sweep in on them.

ROCKY'S VOICE
Gloria Beatty and Robert Syverton!!!!

549. CLOSE ON MRS. LAYDON

beaming.

ROCKY'S VOICE
Now, I'm no Hollywood scenario writer, but I can guess what the end of this little story should be.

550. ANGLE FAVORING GLORIA

looking past Robert's shoulder and *away* from the bandstand.

ROCKY'S VOICE
Right, Robert? . . . Right, Gloria? . . .

GLORIA

Wrong.

FLASH FORWARD TO:

551. INT COURTROOM DAY ROBERT

sitting in the witness chair. He wears a double-breasted blue serge suit. His hair is neatly combed and he has shaved closely.

ROBERT

No, sir, I *do* remember. I remember everything about it—almost every word. I was the only one. There wasn't anyone else she could turn to . . . I couldn't have just left her there alone like that. I *had* to help her.

552. INT BALLROOM NIGHT CLOSE ON ROCKY

A sustained DRUM ROLL behind him. The spotlight on his face.

ROCKY

The Doctor's decision is:
(a long beat)
Lillian Cramer stays in the Marathon!!!
(leads applause)

553. ANGLE ON DANCE FLOOR LILLIAN AND TOMMY

surrounded by the Doctor and Trainers. The Trainers hold cold compresses against Lillian's forehead.

ROCKY'S VOICE

The Doctor assures me that Lillian just has a slight sinus headache . . .

554. ANGLE FAVORING GLORIA AND ROBERT

They are looking casually toward Lillian.

GLORIA

Headache!!!! . . . For all that quack knows, it could be a brain tumor.

ROBERT

No. I mean, I don't think so.

She turns a puzzled glance towards him.

ROBERT

I'm not sure exactly, but I think maybe it's different with a brain tumor. Different symptoms.

GLORIA

Yeah . . . ? How do you know?

ROBERT

I saw it in a movie. With Anita Louise and Richard Cromwell. That's what she died of, Anita Louise—a brain tumor, but it was different. Everything just got dim for her one day, and finally she couldn't see at all. She couldn't even see Richard Cromwell when she kissed him goodbye.

GLORIA

Yeah, and then she just died?

ROBERT

Kind of. She just drifted off listening to their favorite song, and then she was dead.

GLORIA
                    (mulling it over)
No pain or anything . . .
                              (shrugs)
But they probably lied.

555. INT   MEN'S REST AREA   EARLY MORNING   ON
        ROBERT

sitting on an upended box. His head is resting in the bowl of a sink. The cold-water tap is turned on full, and the water splatters across the side of his face. His eyes are closed. He is asleep. The SIREN sounds over scene.

A beat . . . and then the younger TRAINER COMES

INTO SCENE—poking his head around the corner of the shower area.

> YOUNG TRAINER

Hey, sixty-seven! Come on. The period's over.

Robert shows no sign of responding. He crosses to the sink. He shakes Robert, then turns off the water and raises Robert's head. Robert opens his eyes now and peers blearily at the Trainer.

> YOUNG TRAINER

You all right now?
> (slaps him)

You all right?

556. CLOSE ON ROBERT

He nods . . . then, slowly, a wide, blissful, and rather silly grin spreads across his face.

> ROBERT

I'm fine. I'm just fine.

557. INT BALLROOM EARLY MORNING ON ROBERT AND GLORIA

Robert talks rapidly and excitedly. He seems euphoric and giddy. Gloria is puzzling at him with weary detachment.

> ROBERT

I'll remember! Wait a minute, wait a minute. I'll remember it! . . . Lennie! That was his name.
> (giggles)

Leonard Cormack. He was kind of a fat kid—and short. He's the one I went with—Lennie Cormack.

> GLORIA

Yeah . . . ?

> ROBERT

It was after summer, maybe like October . . . But

you know how it is there in Chicago, the way it gets so hot sometimes, so it feels like the sky is burning right through your clothes. And everything sticks to you, and you can hardly breathe. So what happened, we got halfway to school, and all of a sudden we heard a whistle from one of the coal barges on the lake.

(imitating: loudly)

Hhuweeeee!!! Hhuweeeee!! Hhuuweeee!!!!

(lowers tone)

Like that, and right then both of us decided to ditch school, and we turned around and lit off for the lake.

558. ANGLE TO INCLUDE ROLLO

skating quickly up to them.

ROLLO

(semi-whisper)

Hey, hey! What's all the shouting about?

He peers closely at Robert, then looks aside confidentially to Gloria.

ROLLO

What's wrong with him?—he starting to squirrel?

Gloria gives an indifferent half shrug in answer . . . and Rollo looks again toward Robert.

ROLLO

You okay, kid?

ROBERT

I'm fine.

(silly grin)

I'm absolutely fine.

ROLLO

Yeah? . . . You know who I am?

ROBERT

Sure. You are the Head Floor Judge. You are Rollo Peters. And this is—

296

ROLLO

Yeah, okay, but keep it down, huh?
(to Gloria)
I think you'd better watch him.
(EXITS SCENE)

Robert looks after Rollo for a moment. When he turns back, all of his giddiness seems to have evaporated. His expression is crestfallen and hurt.

ROBERT

I guess he doesn't want me to talk any more.

GLORIA

He's nobody, he can't tell you what to do.

ROBERT

I guess I should be quiet.

559. ANGLE FAVORING ROBERT

For a long moment he is sober, solemn, silent. Then again the wide, silly grin—and then soft, happy laughter.

ROBERT

It felt so . . . so *good*, I mean coming out of the lake with water still in drops all over your body, and then falling down in the sand . . . and rolling over and just looking up at the sky. It felt so good . . . But then a truant officer saw us and we ran . . . But—
(puzzles)
What did I say his name was?

GLORIA

Who? Oh—I don't know. Lennie.

ROBERT

That's it! Leonard Cormack. He was kind of a fat kid and short.

GLORIA

You said.

(accelerating)

So he couldn't run as fast as me. And finally he fell down. But I kept running and running and running. I didn't stop until I was way, way away from the lake. But I didn't have any money, so I snitched a ride in the back of an ice wagon. And you know what the guy did? He let me ride right up front with him. He even let me hold the reins. And when we stopped he let me feed sugar to his horse. He licked my hand for more sugar, the horse. And I remember I said to him, just like he could understand, "I don't have any more." And he looked at me and looked at me just as if I could . . .

He breaks off abruptly—and his euphoric mood slips almost tangibly away, as he becomes lost in another and different memory.

ROBERT
(quietly)

But I couldn't do anything. It was just lying there in the grass where it fell. And it couldn't move at all— except for its head just a little. It could only raise its head just a little bit and it kept looking up at me and looking up at me, as if there was something I could do. But there wasn't anything.

560. EXTREME CLOSEUP   ROBERT

A long beat.

ROBERT

There wasn't anything I could do at all.

561. INT   BALLROOM   EARLY EVENING   PANNING
      DANCERS

as they plod endlessly on. Arthur is sleeping draped over Jean's back, his wrists locked across her chest. Cecil is teetering over onto Dusty, but each time he sways against her she gives him a shoulder and props him back up. Tommy and Lillian stagger sideways. They slide a step . . . drag their feet together.

562. JAMES AND RUBY

swaying together, each with his arms around the other's neck. After a moment, James reacts slightly and pulls back to smile down at Ruby.

> JAMES
>
> I felt it. I sure enough did. I felt it kick me a good one.

> RUBY
> (reassuring)
>
> That's just normal.

> JAMES
>
> I ain't sayin' different. We used to have an old vet. Drunk half the time and shook something fierce with the palsy—but he knew whelpin'. If they don't fight some to get out, they ain't worth keepin', that's what he'd say.

> RUBY
> (smiles)
>
> Well . . . he *is* fightin'.

CAMERA MOVES PAST them to FOLLOW:

563. ROBERT AND GLORIA

Gloria is sleeping on Robert's shoulder, her face pressed lightly against his shirt. He moves slowly with her, exerting himself at every step to keep her from slipping. He glances down at her partially upturned face.

564. VERY CLOSE ON GLORIA

Sleeping, her expression is relaxed, soft—almost vulnerable. Perhaps she is dreaming. More likely, she is simply existing for this moment in a kind of numb, unconscious peace. One stray lock of hair has fallen across her forehead, and it somehow makes her seem even that much younger.

565. FAVORING ROBERT

Very lightly he blows at the lock of hair across Gloria's forehead. She stirs slightly, and—*very* softly, almost inaudibly—cries out.

> ROBERT
> (whisper)

Gloria . . . ?

Still sleeping she turns her face slowly across his chest until she is resting on the other cheek . . . and then she drifts back into some deeper retreat from memory.

566. WIDER ANGLE   FAVORING ROBERT

As he continues slowly plodding across the floor with Gloria, he stares off idly, wearily toward the bandstand . . . the rafters . . . the windows . . . the audience . . . until:

567. REACTION   ROBERT

peering off intently . . . squinting slightly as if to make certain of what he sees.

> ROBERT
> (essentially to himself)

She's not there.

568. TWO SHOT   ROBERT AND GLORIA

Gloria has dimly heard him, and looks fuzzily at him now.

> GLORIA

What?

> ROBERT

Mrs. Laydon—she's not there.

569. GLORIA'S POV   MRS. LAYDON'S SEAT

Empty.

570. BACK TO GLORIA

She continues to stare off for a moment, then:

> GLORIA
> (flat, simple)
>
> She's dead.

FLASH FORWARD TO:

571. INT   COURTROOM   DAY   ROBERT

Still dressed in his blue serge suit (though with a different shirt and tie), he stands—seeming somewhat awkward and uncertain—beside the defense table.

> JUDGE'S VOICE
>
> Does the prisoner wish to make a statement to the court before sentence is passed?

A long, strained pause as Robert seems to be thinking desperately of what more he can say. Finally he looks up and shakes his head.

> ROBERT
>
> No . . . No sir.

572. INT   BALLROOM   EVENING   TRUCKING FAST WITH JIGGS

as he skates past and around dancers.

> JACKIE'S VOICE
> (howling)
>
> He's killing me!!! He's killing me! Stop 'im! Somebody stop 'im!!

573. TO INCLUDE MARIO AND JACKIE

He is shouting muttered threats and curses while alternately hitting and choking her. (NOTE: Given his weary, half-conscious state, his blows are utterly ineffectual.) Jackie is on her knees, shielding her face with one arm, while hammering and clawing at Mario's legs with the other. Jiggs is joined by Rollo from the other side, and together they struggle to part Mario and Jackie.

(Mario, Rollo, Jackie speak together)

MARIO

It was my turn to sleep, not hers!

ROLLO

Shut up! . . . Both of you.

JACKIE

Get 'im away from me! Get 'im away!

574. THE AUDIENCE

drinking it all in.

ROCKY'S VOICE

She's down! The girl from Couple Thirty-four is down.

575. THE DANCERS

some of them sleeping, the others only vaguely and disinterestedly aware of the fight.

ROCKY'S VOICE

The Floor Judges will rule. They have final jurisdiction.

576. ON JIGGS IN F.G.

BLOWING his whistle. Just behind him, Jackie—all the fight out of her now—has collapsed. Mario stands over her. Tears are rolling down his cheeks. All his anger has evaporated. The Doctor and Nurses are crowding INTO SCENE.

(Mario, Jackie, Doctor speak together)

MARIO

I'm sorry.

JACKIE

It doesn't matter any more.

DOCTOR

Let me through.

ROLLO
(to Mario)
· Watch out! Let the Doc take care of her.

MARIO

No! I'll take care of her.
(helping her up)
Come on, Jackie.

ROLLO

You go with her, you're out too.

MARIO

It don't matter.

Not letting the Doctor or Nurses near Jackie, Mario starts hobblingly leading her off the floor. From o.s. the band begins "*Till We Meet Again*."

577. ON ROCKY

ROCKY

You've seen a little slice of life, folks. A moment of intense drama—right here on the Marathon floor. You've seen love and loyalty overcome pain and despair.

578. ON ROBERT AND GLORIA

watching Mario and Jackie leave the floor.

ROCKY'S VOICE

Goodbye, Mario . . . Goodbye, Jackie. I don't know what's waiting for you beyond these doors . . .

GLORIA

I do.

ROCKY'S VOICE

. . . But I wish it to be peace and plenty, hope and happiness.

579. ANGLE FAVORING GLORIA

GLORIA

Nothing—that's what's waiting.

FLASH FORWARD TO:

580. INT   PRISON   DAY   DOWN ANGLE ON ROBERT

as he climbs up narrow scaffold steps. He wears a white collarless shirt. His hands are tied behind his back. Behind him we hear other footsteps . . . and a chaplain's voice droning the Lord's Prayer in semi-whisper.

581. INT   ROCKY'S OFFICE   NIGHT   ON DOOR

It opens abruptly to reveal:

582. ROBERT AND GLORIA

Behind them in the corridor is Rollo, who has escorted them to the door. CAMERA PULLS BACK to include Rocky.

ROCKY

Come on in, kids. Come on.

When they stagger wearily into the office, Rocky waves Rollo off and then closes the door again.

ROCKY

Sit down, kids, just rest—like usual.

After Robert and Gloria collapse on the sofa. Rocky sits down behind his desk—the top of which is covered with his ledgers, account books, receipts, etc.

ROCKY
(after a beat)

I had a little notion, kids. Something could help the
show, and benefit all of us. —And it in particular could
benefit you two. And at the same time give the crowd
something to get worked up about.

GLORIA

Whatta you going to do—lock us up in cages and let
them throw peanuts to us?

ROCKY

All kidding aside.

GLORIA

Who's kidding?

ROCKY
(ignoring this)

The thing I want, is I want you two kids to get married. Right here. Right on the dance floor—a public
wedding. I mean—you get divorced right after the
show . . . if you want. It's just for the effect. What
do you say to that, Robert?

ROBERT

Well, I don't know . . . I guess if—

GLORIA

He says No.

ROCKY

Does she do all the talking for you, Robert?

GLORIA

That's right.

ROCKY
(considers; then to Robert)

Maybe it would be better if just her and me discussed
it. Okay, Robert?

ROBERT

Sure, I guess.

Rocky crosses to the door and opens it for Robert.

ROCKY

Coupla minutes, that's all.
         (holding Robert in door)
But the idea is okay with you, Robert—that's what
you said, right?

ROBERT

No, sir, I didn't say that exactly. All I said was . . .

ROCKY

Same thing.

583. ANOTHER ANGLE

as Rocky closes the door behind Robert, then turns
back to face Gloria. For an instant, he seems on the
verge of moving close to her. Gloria is aware of his
shift in attitude. She studies him sardonically. He
skirts around her back to his desk.

ROCKY

What's the problem? You afraid of gettin' married . . . ?

GLORIA
         (furious)
You're not happy until you've screwed up everything,
are you?

She bolts for the door.

ROCKY
         (catching her arm)
What the hell are you so . . .

GLORIA
         (whirling on him)
I'm not marrying anybody!!

ROCKY

Take it easy. There's something in it for you, you know. Some new clothes. Maybe a bridal gown. And plenty of free gifts—toasters, waffle irons, silverware, that kind of stuff.

GLORIA

What am I supposed to do with crap like that?

ROCKY

Sell it . . . hock it.
(flaring)
Look, for Chris'sakes, I'm trying to help you a little. I mean, maybe you clear a hundred, even two hundred bucks. That's something, isn't it? But suit yourself. You want to come out of this whole thing with just the pennies those people throw, that's up to you.

GLORIA

Yeah, and what if just maybe we win?

ROCKY

Big deal. Okay, you win.

GLORIA

What are you talking about? I never saw 750 bucks in my life.

ROCKY

Don't be naive. Nobody's getting a full 750 bucks. What the hell you think I'm running here—a charity?
(points to desk)
I got bills stacked up. Every day. This Marathon don't run itself, you know. Not with what you kids are costing me. It's all right there.

584. ANGLE FAVORING GLORIA

She shuffles among the papers on his desk, sees her name on one, then pulls it out.

GLORIA

What the hell is this?

307

ROCKY

It's the tabs on you and Robert.

585. ANGLE ON GLORIA

as she runs a finger down one of two ledger columns on the paper, until she reaches the subtotal. Finally she looks up at Rocky with a shocked, numbed expression.

ROCKY
(flaring)

What the hell do you think it cost me for those track suits?—and new shoes—all the extra meals?—your laundry bills—newspapers, magazines?—I mean, it all adds up—

(a beat; then more quietly)

Naturally, you don't win you don't pay. I'm not out to cheat nobody.

Gloria begins laughing—very softly at first . . .

586. ANGLE TO REVEAL ROBERT

as he pushes open the office door. He stands framed in the open doorway watching.

GLORIA
(quietly)

It's all for nothing!

She starts laughing again—the SIREN WAILS. When the siren stops, the room is still. Rocky stares at her in confused uncertainty. Gloria, for a moment, is absolutely silent . . . absolutely rigid . . . Then abruptly she turns and moves past Robert, in the doorway. He hesitates, then follows her into:

587. INT CORRIDOR FRONTING REST AREAS CONTESTANTS

slowly dragging themselves back toward the floor. Gloria watches them numbly.

588. ANGLE BEHIND GLORIA

308

as she looks after the last of the contestants.

GLORIA
(whispering)
You idiots. You stupid, silly idiots.

589. MED. SHOT   ROBERT AND GLORIA

alone now in the shadowed corridor. From the dance floor o.s. we hear—in perspective—the music, the dancers, the crowd, and later the drone of Rocky's voice.

A long moment, then Gloria turns and starts into the women's rest area.

590. ON ROBERT

staring uncertainly after her for a beat, then following her. He stops in the doorway to:

591. INT   WOMEN'S REST AREA   NIGHT   GLORIA

The room is empty, shadowed, silent. It is littered with sweaty, stained clothing. Dirty towels are strewn about the cots, the floor, the basins. For a moment, Gloria stands absolutely still in the center of the room, as if suddenly uncertain of why she is there or what she meant to do. Then, abruptly, she turns and crosses toward the lockers. She knocks some suitcases aside until she finds her own cheap cardboard case. She sets it on a bench, and flips the top open. Inside the case are a few of her meager possessions: rollers, rouge, stockings, walking pumps. Hanging on the locker front are some dresses and coats, and strewn over a rope line strung between the lockers are bras, slips, silk stockings, etc. She shoves through the dresses, knocking and flinging the others aside, until she finds hers. She pulls it down and without bothering to fold it, tosses it into her open case. Then she turns to the things draped over the rope line, and as ruthlessly as before she brushes aside the other women's things to pick out her own. She grabs a frayed bra, a pair of step-ins, and a slip with one strap fastened by a safety pin. She wads them together and drops them into the case. She then sorts brusquely through a line of dangling stockings—some mesh, some cotton lisle, some silk—until she finds *one* of hers.

GLORIA
(frowning; annoyed)
Where the hell's the other one?!

592. TO INCLUDE ROBERT

He has crossed into the room, and now moves to stand behind her. He watches as she starts pawing among the stockings hanging over the line. She interrupts her search to glare at him.

GLORIA
Well, what the hell're you just standing there for?! Help me.

He starts probing among the stockings with her, then stops and turns a confused glance toward her.

ROBERT
What's it look like exactly?

GLORIA
(holding up other stocking)
Like this. What the hell you think it'd look like, a necktie?

Robert nods, and turns back to the search.

GLORIA
I'll tell you one thing, I'm not leaving this goddamned

stink hole without it. That's the last pair I got, and I cut out streetcars for a month to buy them.

Robert holds up one stocking by the toe, looping it out from the rope line for her to see.

> GLORIA

No, for Chris'sakes—it's *silk*.

They continue rummaging, pawing, sorting . . . until:

> ROBERT
> (holds out stocking)

I found it!
> (happily)

Look! Here it is.
> (then suddenly doubtful)

Isn't it . . . ?

Gloria peers critically at the stocking, then nods.

> GLORIA

Yeah, that's it.

Robert smiles with relief—and starts to pull the stocking off the line. But as he does, it catches. The top snags, and a run cascades down the length of the stocking.

593. ANGLE FAVORING ROBERT

holding the ruined stocking.

> ROBERT

Oh, Jesus, I'm sorry. I just—I'm sorry.

594. ANGLE FAVORING GLORIA

A beat, as she stares at the torn stocking still dangling limply in his hand. Then she reaches out and takes

311

it from him. She stands quietly looking at the ruined stocking, until slowly, *soundlessly*, she begins crying.

ROBERT
(after a moment of awkward uncertainty)
Don't ...
(reaches out tentatively)
Maybe you can fix it or something. Sew it up sort of ... Gloria? ... Let me see it. Maybe—

He reaches out as if to take the torn stocking, but she snatches it away from him.

ROBERT
(fumbles change from pocket)
Look, I still got ...
(counts)
... seventy-six cents left. Maybe I can—

GLORIA
Oh, shut up!
(then)
It's not the goddamned stocking anyway ...
(then)
What the hell difference does it make? Forget it.

A beat. She looks at the torn, wadded silk stocking in her hand ... uncrumples it ... carefully, precisely, folds it.

GLORIA
Maybe you're right. Maybe I can get it sewed up somewhere.

A beat. Then she just shakes her head and drops the folded stocking into a trash box.

595. EXT BALLROOM NIGHT ANGLE ON DOOR

opening to reveal Robert and Gloria. Behind them we

312

see the Marathon. The band is playing, the contestants are still trudging around the dance floor. Gloria is wearing her coat and carrying her cardboard case. Robert is still wearing his JONATHON'S IRON TONIC sweat shirt. They let the door close behind them and then cross out onto the pier.

596. EXT PIER ROBERT AND GLORIA

They wait until an elderly woman with a homemade fishing pole passes in front of them, then they cross to the railing. Beyond a pool of light under a lamp post is a NECKING COUPLE. The couple glance toward Robert and Gloria and then pull back into the darkness and more further down the pier and finally o.s.

597. TWO SHOT ROBERT AND GLORIA

standing over the railing. Robert is looking toward the ocean.

ROBERT

It used to be I loved to look at the ocean. Walk by it. Just sit and listen to it. Now I don't care if I ever see it again.

GLORIA

That . . . or anything else.

Robert turns toward her.

ROBERT

What are you going to do now—try the movies again?

GLORIA

No. I'd never make it. And maybe it wouldn't make no difference even if I did. Maybe it's just the whole damn world's like one big Central Casting—and they got it all rigged before you ever show up.

ROBERT

I know what you mean. I know just what you mean.

GLORIA

Yeah . . . ? Do you?

ROBERT

What *are* you going to do?

GLORIA

I'm going to get off this merry-go-round. I'm through with the whole stinking thing.

ROBERT

What thing?

GLORIA

Life—and don't give me no sunshine lectures. Okay?

ROBERT

I wasn't going to.

GLORIA
(then)
What are you looking at me that way for?

ROBERT

I'm not. It's so dark I'm just trying to see you, that's all.

GLORIA

Well, keep looking and stick around for the end.

598. ANGLE FAVORING GLORIA

She fumbles in her purse for a moment and then draws out a snub-nosed .38 revolver. Gloria closes her eyes and raises the pistol *slightly* . . . She wraps both hands about the handle of the pistol. Robert watches her

314

quietly—not saying anything . . . not moving to stop her.

A long beat of silence . . . and then Gloria opens her eyes and lowers the pistol. She turns slowly and looks into Robert's eyes.

                              GLORIA
Help me.

                              ROBERT
How?

                              GLORIA
You do it.

                              ROBERT
Shoot you . . . ?

                              GLORIA
Please. I . . .
          (thrusting the pistol on him)
Do it. Please, Robert. Please, please.

Robert looks down at the pistol now resting in his hand. A long beat . . . then slowly he closes his hand about the pistol.

                              ROBERT
All right.
                    (long beat)
Tell me when.

                              GLORIA
                    (beat)
I'm ready.

                              ROBERT
                    (beat)
Where?

GLORIA
(beat)

Right here. In the side of my head.

She turns her face slightly away from him and looks off.

ROBERT

Now?

GLORIA

Now.

Robert raises the barrel of the gun toward her temple.

599. EXTREME CLOSEUP   REVOLVER

FIRING.

600. EXTREME CLOSEUP   GLORIA

as the bullet thuds into her temple. Her eyes are still open. She still seems to be staring off.

601. ANGLE ON ROBERT

watching Gloria fall.

602. REVERSE ANGLE TO REVEAL ROLLO

standing in front of the closed door to the ballroom. We *HEAR* the *SOUNDS* of a MOTOR IDLING . . . doors OPENING, CLOSING, OPENING . . . RADIO STATIC . . . FOOTSTEPS . . . WHISPERED AD LIBS—jumbled, faint, overlapped, only barely audible: "What happened? . . . There was a shot . . . He killed her . . . Dispatch CQ, 420 answered, one DOA . . . Why'd he do it? . . ." Rollo continues smoking a cigarette as he looks at:

being lifted into the back of an ambulance. Nearby a hushed, disparate group of onlookers watch. A white-jacketed INTERN follows the blanket-covered body into the ambulance and closes the doors from the inside. The ambulance gears O.S. revealing:

604. ROBERT

handcuffed . . . standing near the open back door of a police car. Two COPS stand next to him as he looks off after the ambulance carrying Gloria's body away.

> 1ST COP
>
> Why'd you do it, kid?

> ROBERT
>
> She asked me to.

> 1ST COP
>
> You hear that, Ben?

> 2ND COP
>
> Ain't he an obliging bastard, though.

> 1ST COP
>
> Is that the only reason you got, kid?

A long pause, as CAMERA MOVES into an

605. EXTREME CLOSEUP   ROBERT

> ROBERT
>
> They shoot horses, don't they?

606. ANGLE BEHIND ROBERT TOWARD ROLLO

as the Cop shoves Robert into the back seat of the police car and slams the door after him. The Cop gets into the front seat of the car. The motor turns over. The car's SIREN begins its escalating whine.

As the police car starts up and OUT OF FRAME, CAMERA BEGINS MOVING SLOWLY IN TO-WARD ROLLO. The MARATHON SIREN begins its screech, drowning out the siren on the police car. Rollo tosses away his cigarette, turns and opens the door to the ballroom.

We hear the band starting to play again and we see dancers in the MED. B.G. moving out onto the floor. A vendor, a nurse and two or three spectators cluster behind Rollo trying to peer past him.

AD LIBS
Something happen? . . . What was it?

ROLLO
Nothing. It's all over.

ROCKY'S VOICE
Yowza! Here they are again, these wonderful, won-derful kids . . .

CAMERA FOLLOWS Rollo inside the ballroom and PASSES him as he is closing the door.

ROCKY'S VOICE
. . . still struggling, still hoping . . .

607. BOOM SHOT

as CAMERA SLOWLY RISES over the floor, the dancers, the bandstand.

ROCKY'S VOICE
(diminishing)
. . . while the clock of Fate ticks away. While the Dance of Destiny continues.

(fainter)

While the Marathon goes on and on and on and on.

**CAMERA CONTINUES RISING — HIGHER,
HIGHER.**

ROCKY'S VOICE
(faint, distant—even though he is shouting)

How long can they last?!

CAMERA HOLDS a beat longer as beneath us the
last few couples continue dancing on and on and on.

FADE OUT

*   *   *

The explosive #1 bestseller of the year!

ELIA KAZAN
the arrange- ment

— is about Eddie Anderson, a tough-minded, dynamic ad executive and a brilliant writer, married to Florence and obsessed by the much younger Gwen . . .

— is the devastating story of Eddie crashing out of his arrangement.

"It is a great book. When you touch it you touch a man." Henry Miller

IT HAS ALREADY STUNNED NEARLY THREE MILLION READERS. IT JUST MIGHT JOLT YOU OUT OF _YOUR_ ARRANGEMENT!

W116 $1.25